FLAMINGO

Other novels by Bob Reiss:

Summer Fires
The Casco Deception
Divine Assassin
Saltmaker

FLAMINGO

A Novel by
Bob Reiss

St. Martin's Press New York

This novel is a work of fiction. All of the events, characters, names, and places depicted in this novel are entirely fictitious or are used fictitiously. No representation that any statement made in this novel is true or that any incident depicted in this novel actually occurred is intended or should be inferred by the reader.

Editor: Jared Kieling
Designer: Karin Batten

Library of Congress Cataloging-in-Publication Data

Reiss, Bob.
    Flamingo / Bob Reiss.
        p.   cm.
    ISBN 0-312-03693-0
    I. Title.
    PS3568.E517F55   1990   89-27070
    813'.54—dc20   CIP

First Edition
10 9 8 7 6 5 4 3 2 1

For the good times on the *Sea Dog*

ACKNOWLEDGMENTS

▼▼▼▼▼▼▼▼▼▼▼▼▼▼▼▼▼▼▼▼▼▼▼▼▼▼▼▼▼▼▼▼▼▼▼

A very special thanks to Doug Douglas, Ann Hood, Vicki Impallomini, the Key West Police (who bear no resemblance to the police in this book), Jared Kieling, Don Kincaid, Jim Mayer, Don Munga de la Playa, George Murphy, Esther Newberg, Ruth Ravenel, the Smith Family Singers, and the U.S. Coast Guard at Key West, Florida.

FLAMINGO

ONE

Too many places where Raleigh went, murders happened. They weren't his fault.

That's all over now, he thought.

Raleigh walked down the gangplank toward the two-story houseboat with the stained-glass flamingo on the front door. An old man was coming out, an academic type with a dirty T-shirt, a Van Dyke beard, and round tortoiseshell glasses. The man rushed past, toward an old Buick parked on the grass. Raleigh knew it was not the man he had come to see.

Plastic flamingos lined the upper deck. So did blinking Christmas lights, even though it was April. The Buick coughed to life and lurched off the curb on Conch Boulevard. The mangrove swamp across the street was quiet, as were other houseboats docked in a row.

Beyond the colored lights, the Gulf of Mexico was calm and lavender. A breeze brought a humid salt smell across the flats but failed to rustle the palms overhead. Raleigh heard the lazy drone of a shrimper coming home, and saw the dot on the water.

Before he could ring the bell, the door swung open. A blast

1

of steel-drum reggae hit him. He was looking down at a grinning man with a red beard, round green plastic sunglasses, a pink pith helmet, and a flower-print shirt with blue orchids.

The man drew Raleigh into the boat by the wrist. He said, "Raleigh, Raleigh, Raleigh, Raleigh."

"Jay Salinger?" Raleigh shouted over the music. He recognized the famous tune that had played on every jukebox in the country five years ago.

> I moved from the sun
> To Piña Colada Town
> Aye aye aye aye aye
> Found Coconut Paradise for meee

The man danced backward, gyrating his arms like a fast hula dancer. His head bobbed. "No Jay here!" he cried. He stopped in the center of the room, then threw his arms wide. "It's the King of the Coconuts," he sang. "Mr. Good times! Fast boats at midnight! Fast drugs, fast fastness! The King of Gonzo! King of the Keys!"

Raleigh's ears kept pounding after the man turned down the music.

He took off the pith helmet. Red hair flopped over his forehead. "You love it, right? It'll work on the show?" he said.

"No."

The man laughed. "Okay, I'll try something else. And you," he said, jabbing the air at Raleigh, "look like your book jackets." He crossed the purple carpet to lift two hardback books off a glass and bamboo coffee table. The garish lettering on the covers resembled dripping blood, wet from the glossy finish.

THE MAYOR'S MURDERER read the white book. The black, DEATH OF A MIDGET WRESTLER.

"I don't do true crime anymore," Raleigh said.

The sunken living room was cooled by a four-foot-wide rotating ceiling fan. The bamboo couch had indigo blue cushions with salmon and emerald orchid patterns. There were a couple of sea chest coffee tables with open Coors cans on them. Reggae pumped from freestanding stereo speakers against a wall and beneath a bumper sticker reading ANOTHER BORING DAY IN PARADISE. Raleigh saw a poster of Ernest Hemingway beside a marlin hanging on a dock. Hemingway's head tilted right, the left eye narrow and tough, the right slightly wider and vulnerable beneath a lowered cap.

In front of the couch a Japanese video progressed on a TV set into the bookshelves. No sound. A servant with his black hair in a queue groveled before a samurai on a stool, hand on sword hilt. "Lord Hayakawa," the caption read. "Those filthy *ronin* have gunpowder!"

There were photos of girls all over the place. Near the TV, a blonde in a lavender bikini sprawled on a blanket, eyes closed. Two redheads held hands on the prow of a boat, blue water in the background. A girl with a pageboy haircut sat in a gold sun dress, legs folded beneath her, on a lawn. A slim girl in a one-piece bathing suit smiled coyly from beneath a green visor. She lifted a champagne glass in one hand.

Grinning, the man pumped Raleigh's hand. "You sign autographs, I hope. I'm a fan, a big fan. Write something like, *to my good buddy, Jay*. Make up something good. Want a beer? You're going to be glad you came here when you hear what I have to say." Salinger fell onto the couch, bouncing the pith helmet on his lap. "When I heard you were in Key Rey, I wanted to meet you, but I get caught up in things. You moved here three weeks ago, right?"

"Four."

"Key Rey. Been here eight years. Divorced the wife. Left Pittsburgh. Tell me the truth. Don't you love it? Don't you wonder why you didn't move here before? Isn't this the greatest place in the world?"

"I don't mind being out of New York," Raleigh said.

Raleigh had a flash of what he'd left. He saw the glass room

3

in the middle of the *Daily News* city room. He saw his old editor, Frank, grinning at him as the top of a champagne bottle came out of a drawer. It was deadline time outside Frank's office. Reporters in the city room typed frantically on word processors.

"Congratulations, Raleigh. We're giving you a column."

To Salinger, Raleigh said, "When you phoned you said you had information for me."

"Relax. We're on three-quarter time here." Salinger padded into the galley, returned, and placed an open bottle of Molson's on the glass table. His nose seemed redder than it had before he'd left the room, and he sniffed a couple of times. Beads of sweat ran down the bottle's side. Back on the couch, Salinger unlaced his white canvas shoes. He wriggled sunburned toes on the sea chest. Above his head, beside a brass barometer on a bookshelf built into the wall, Raleigh saw a photograph of an Oriental girl with her shiny hair in a braid that touched the bottom of her black negligee.

Salinger said, "Let's get to know each other a little. We're neighbors, in a little place like this. Believe me, you'll like what I have. A lot of authors move to Key Rey. Carmen Walker, she won the Pulitzer Prize last year, she did. How come you came?"

"I quit my job," Raleigh said.

"To write the book." Salinger laughed. "I heard about you. You couldn't have come to a better place. Key Rey." Salinger pulled off the sunglasses. The crow's-feet around his green eyes looked deeper, like vultures' talons. His skin was a coarser shade than the sun would cause. He finished the beer. Salinger smiled wistfully. "The island even the seventies forgot. No airport. No railroad. Tiny causeway to the Key Bridge. A Spanish outpost for salvage three hundred years ago. Then malaria wiped it out. A hideaway for runaway slaves and smugglers. Then yellow fever wiped it out." He wiped his mouth with the back of his wrist. "Bear with me. I'm setting the stage. Miami got the first boom and Key West the second. Little Key Rey just struggled along. Around the Depression, the first serious settlers came. The shrimpers, the police, we call them coconuts. The locals. In the sixties, the hippies found it, then the gays, then the artists. Now the tourists. Swim. Party. Lots of money to be made."

The phone rang in another room and Raleigh heard the click of an answering machine coming on. Salinger had left the volume up. He sang his message to an old Beach Boys tune. "Ba-ba-ba, ba-ba, leave your name. Ba-ba-ba, ba-ba, leave a BEEEEEP."

Raleigh heard a woman crying. "Pick up the phone, you bastard. It's Nina! Pick it up! I know you're there!"

Salinger's grin dulled, grew soulful. He sat up a bit on the bamboo couch. "My fiancée," he said. "No matter how many times you get married, arguments before the day, every time. We'll work it out."

"Bird Island," Raleigh said. "You said you had something on Bird Island."

"Right." But Salinger went into the galley and returned with more beers. He pulled a Kool from a new pack and lit it with a lighter curved into the shape of a palm tree. He blew a long cloud of smoke. His eyes were watering. Outside, from Conch Boulevard, Raleigh heard the Sharkmobile Tour Train going by, from Old Town. He envisioned each car with its painted fins and gills, each a different shark shape. Hammerhead. Great White. Tiger. The voice of the guide on the loudspeaker carried. "This is houseboat row, the south side of Key Rey, where the Spanish treasure fleet went aground in 15 . . ."

The voice trailed off.

Salinger leaned forward, palms on knees. "Okay, major juicy story." From his breast pocket, he extracted a photograph, reached over and spun it through the air so it landed in Raleigh's lap. It showed a middle-aged white-haired man in a pale blue

5

ing Rey Del Mar, he bribed city commissioners. People got beaten up who tried to stop him. Mob connections. Payoffs. Very big story."

Raleigh finished his beer. The bottle clinked on the glass tabletop. "That's interesting, but I told you. I don't do crime anymore."

On TV, Salinger was kissing the actress on the lips, flapping his arms to show how sexy she was. "No, no," he said. "Quade's behind Bird Island. He's the one who got the government to make it private, and he's the one who's going to land up owning it. Public hearings? That's an act. He wants to build a complex out there, tear up the forest, kill the wildlife. The subsoil's unstable on Key Rey, so he needs a new place. I have proof. We can stop him."

The phone rang again. Raleigh said, "What proof?" as Salinger crossed into the other room. He must have turned the volume down on the answering machine because Raleigh didn't hear the message this time. Salinger came back with another two beers. Raleigh said, "If you have such good information, why give it to me? Why not use it on your show?"

"Hahahahaha! Cable TV?" Salinger drank half the bottle in gulps, went into the galley, and came back with the palm lighter, flicking it on and off without seeming to notice. "Drink up," he said, shaking with laughter, "you need bodily juices in the tropics. You know how much I get paid for that show? Fifty dollars a week! This isn't network, Raleigh, it's the crummy little island show. That's the trade-off for lifestyle here, no dinero. The show," he said with overelaborate sincerity, "is my community service." His grin broadened. "And maybe a little ego. But I'm a bartender at Cap'n Bob's for money. Everybody here has three jobs. Quade's too good to waste on a fifty-dollar show."

Salinger gazed at Raleigh's books on the table. "I always wanted to write a book," he said. "By Raleigh Fixx and Jay Salinger. Or *with* Jay Salinger. Or forget a by-line, we can work

7

"Right, right. We'll have an argument! It'll be hilarious. You'll come on? Good. Think about Quade. I have papers. Tape recordings. You know where to find me."

When Raleigh walked down the gangplank ten minutes later, the sun was going down. It looked huge and red and it turned the water crimson. Five or six other houseboats lined the shore, their paint peeling, more deteriorated than Salinger's. A mustard-colored mutt eyed him suspiciously from the dock on the right. He saw no people. Conch Boulevard was empty. As usual, the blue Mustang had trouble starting, but the engine kicked over. He bumped off the curb and headed west.

He drove along the boulevard, a flat four-lane strip with the sea on one side and the swamp on the other. No houses on the south side of the island. No stores, gas stations, condos. The palms lining the shore waved slightly. Raleigh could see the twenty-foot charter fishing boats coming in from the flats, white wakes dropping away as they grew closer, rods upright like antennas, in holders. He passed Willoughby's South Side Marina, which like everything else on Key Rey was half-dilapidated and half-new. It was a squarish yellow stucco building, more the size of a refreshment stand than a marina, sun bleached on one side, freshly painted on the other, with spanking new Miami cabin cruisers berthed against the rickety pier, beside wooden-hulled boat-homes the welfare bums lived on, and the city commission was trying to evict. A skid row of boats.

Fresh from the taxidermist, a new blue marlin leaped above the hand-painted sign—WE GUARANTEE FUN!

As he cruised, he formed an aerial view of Key Rey in his mind. Four miles long, a half a mile in width. A crown-shaped sand and mangrove key thirty miles north of Key West. The north part of the island was broken into three irregularly shaped bays—the two on either end, flats for charter bone fishing, the central cove dredged for shrimpers who'd come to the island fifty years ago. Caribbean cruise liners were starting to make Key Rey a regular stop.

Within the island, the town formed a rectangular area, six streets running mostly north-south, with names painted white on telephone poles at most corners. . . .

In his mind, Raleigh drifted back to the city room, to his editor pouring champagne. "There's just one tiny difference between the column you asked for and the one we're giving you," Frank had said. "But before we get into that, let me ask you a question. When a guy is good at something, really a pro, does he stop? Or does he milk it?"

"Frank," Raleigh had said warningly.

"I mean," Frank had said, "Could you see Dwight Gooden playing concert piano? George Bush pitching for the Mets? Disasters."

"What's the column, Frank?"

"Just picture this," Frank had said proudly, framing an imaginary column with his hands. "Top of the page, right? Picture of you in the upper corner. Like Breslin. Twice a week, no matter what other news happens, you never get bumped. Because readers love you, Raleigh. They look forward to you. Ask a reader what he'd rather know about, some aid to Ethiopia crap or a Raleigh Fixx piece; hands down, Raleigh. Ready? Are you prepared, you famous, rich guy?" Frank spread the hands again. "Raleigh's Murders," he breathed.

Raleigh had put the champagne glass on Frank's desk. "But I hate writing about murders."

"You hate?" Frank's eyebrows had soared. He was a lean man in a gray three-piece suit. "Charles Manson you hate. But a column that carries a five-thousand-dollar raise? An assistant? Who could hate that?"

"Me."

"Come onnnnnn. That line in the Midget Murder. . . . 'Tiny

Mikey's death sent tidal waves of remorse through Madison Square Garden' . . . was poetry."

Raleigh had dropped the glass in the wastebasket. "Murders are disgusting, Frank. Dead people. Blood. I hate it."

"Here comes the bite, eh?" The editor had rubbed his thumb, index finger, and middle finger together in the universal sign of money. "The raise isn't enough? You want more? Look, you'll get syndication. Talk shows. Movie rights, for Chrissakes. Those unimaginative Hollywood bastards snap up stories like yours. Your ship's in, Raleigh. Celebrate."

"The smell, Frank."

Raleigh had stood looking out at the city room, past his reflection in the glass superimposed over the typing reporters. A man with black curly hair, a cowboy shirt, and boots. A foot taller than Frank.

The editor's hand had fallen on his shoulder. The voice had become sincere, soft. "You have a great talent," Frank had said. "Like, like Mozart had a talent." Frank had nodded at his wisdom. "His talent was music. Yours, well, so it's different. I don't think it's an accident you're always around when murders happen. It's a skill. Unconscious." Inspired by his own eloquence, Frank had paced around his desk, coffee table, hassock, clenching and unclenching an upraised fist, like Hamlet regarding Yorick's skull. "In your brain, you process violent inclinations in our society. You're drawn to places where they erupt. Don't fight it. Besides," Frank had coaxed, "you keep your own hours when you write a column." Frank had leered. "I'd want to stay in bed late if I had a girlfriend like yours."

Raleigh remembered listening to traffic noises on Forty-second Street. The phones had been jangling on Frank's desk. Raleigh had looked down at Frank's half-eaten chicken paste on melba toast, with its dried-out pickle, beside the train schedule to Connecticut, rush-hour departures circled in red.

Raleigh had stepped close. "There's another story I want to

write, Frank. I'm excited about this, it's big. There's this island off Florida. A federal wildlife preserve, except Washington just gave it up for sale. There are birds on the island, Frank. Beautiful birds like you've never seen. Roseate spoonbills. Egrets."

"Birds?"

"It's a major environmental story, a spectacular test case. The government's doing this all over the country, destroying thousands of acres of land."

Frank's eyes had glazed over.

"You want to write about birds."

Frank had fallen into his leather chair behind his desk. Mockery had come into his voice. "What are you, afraid? You were in Vietnam, weren't you? You have scary experiences that make it hard to look at bodies?"

"I was in Vietnam, so what?"

"You were in combat there, weren't you?"

"It was my job. It has nothing to do with this."

"I'm just saying maybe you're a little . . . weak . . . from it. Maybe you have bad dreams." Frank made a bogeyman face. "Gooks chasing you."

"Gee, Frank. I feel so ashamed now that you pointed out the truth. I get chills at night up and down my spine."

Frank's voice had hardened. "I can see we're having a little communication problem." The editor had bitten into the chicken on melba. He'd said, chewing, "Think of the paper like Vietnam. You're the private and I'm the captain. The captain is telling the private what to do. The captain is ordering the private to write a column called 'Raleigh's Murders.' Does the private understand how much free choice is involved here? Nada. Jawohl, Herr Kommandant!"

"The private and the captain."

"He's getting it," Frank had said. "Why don't we enjoy this very good champagne."

Raleigh had stood up. He could still smell the mayonnaise

in the chicken paste and see one of Frank's curly hairs sticking out of it.

Raleigh had said, "The private is going AWOL. I'll send you a copy of the book."

Now, as Raleigh approached the intersection of Conch and Morgan, the only way to reach the town and main waterfront, he saw a crowd gathered beneath one of the island's two traffic lights. BED RACE proclaimed a banner strung overhead. Cheering, laughing spectators in shorts and halter tops jumped up and down for a better view.

As Raleigh watched, two motorcycle policemen in black rumbled into the intersection on Harleys. Beneath their aviator sunglasses and Fu Manchu mustaches, their mouths were serious, downturned. They might have been escorting a governor's motorcade. But behind them followed four running "nuns" in Lite Beer caps and heart-shaped plastic sunglasses, hauling a brass bed on wheels. A mermaid with seaweed hair reclined on the bed, waving. The hairy male calves of the nuns flashed above their running shoes.

The gay bodybuilder's club entry shot into the intersection close behind, the runners in tight-fitting undershirts. A man in a hot-pink bikini bottom pumped a dumbbell on the bed.

With the victorious nuns celebrating and diminishing in the rearview mirror, Raleigh turned north. Morgan Street was narrow, lined on both sides by geiger trees with orange blossoms. The Bahama-style wooden homes were widely spaced, fronted by white picket fences or banyan trees that pushed through the crumbling sidewalks. Artists and shrimpers lived in the older homes. Young professionals moving to the island were renovating larger buildings. Raleigh passed a Spanish colonial mansion with fig and date palms in the courtyard. The famous musician Johnny Coetzee lived in one of these, somewhere in the middle of the island.

Raleigh passed the four-story Federal Customs House, biggest building on Key Rey, where he had spent the last three weeks poring through file cabinets, examining federal documents describing the history of Bird Island and the plan to sell it to private companies, oil or condo interests. Each applicant had filed an outline for keeping their project "environmentally sensitive."

He drove past a Cuban coffeehouse. Men in Caribbean shirts stood around outside, talking and drinking hot sugary coffee from thimble-sized cups.

The houses dropped away as Raleigh approached the main harbor and tourist strip. Restaurants and bars stood side by side, entrances every ten feet. Raleigh caught glimpses of dark cool areas inside, ceiling fans moving above stools that filled at dusk with drinkers. The street was clogged with tourists on rented mopeds. He heard the boom from the four-inch cannon on the schooner that took riders on the daily sunset cruise. Down an alley, on the right, he had a flash of the crowd attending the nightly sunset street shows, watching the Indian contortionist from Brooklyn who tied his legs in knots. The fire-eater from Tulsa, the flaming sword disappearing down his upturned throat. The coconut-head man, who painted faces of Ronald Reagan and Doris Day on coconuts. The trained white poodles who rode bicycles as their Ohio-born owners circled the crowd with French berets extended for donations, crying, "Dogfood! Dogfood!"

The sun melted into the sea like lava. It's shape changed as it sank. It was a dripping ball of fire, welded to the ocean at its base. Then a half-moon, ablaze. A weird oval spaceship shimmering. A last piercing point of light. The sea turned red as the sky went crimson. A flash of vivid green spread outward, for a fraction of a second, along the surface of the Gulf. It subsided.

Raleigh's rented house was a two-story Bahama on Festival Street, overlooking the harbor. A black police car waited in the driveway, red light going round and round.

As Raleigh climbed from the Ford, a second squad car braked to a halt behind him, throwing up sand. Officers jumped out of both cars, guns drawn.

Raleigh said, "Hey, what is this! I'm not the guy!"

The lady cop was short, with narrow shoulders and broad hips. Her oversized hat had slipped down over her forehead. Her gun looked enormous in her fists. "Hands on the car, Bubba. Don't move."

Raleigh said, "My name's not Bubba."

He felt the male cop's hands running along his chest, down his legs and up the inside. "Raleigh Fixx, it's his car, all right," the man said, looking through Raleigh's wallet.

"Okay, Bubba, into the car." The man, who seemed big in a pudgy way, pushed Raleigh's head down so he would not hit it when he got inside. Neighbors were gathering to watch. Looking through the window, Raleigh caught a glimpse of Diane at the window upstairs. He shrugged. They were under way before she could come down. The squad car smelled of fried hamburgers. Catching sight of the chubby cop's face in the rearview mirror, Raleigh decided he was a native-born Key Reyer. He had the kind of high forehead and wide-apart brown eyes Raleigh often saw here. Spanish or Indian blood. Both cops had the jutting asses lots of Key Reyers had.

"You have the right to remain silent," the cop said. He sounded excited, as if he had caught a big criminal. "You have the right to an attorney."

"How about the right to know what's going on?"

The lady cop, who was driving, said, "To the station, Hank, right? Not the scene."

In the backseat, Raleigh spread out. The window could open an inch. There was a nice breeze in his face. He was thinking that many people who moved here never met native-born islanders. It was two separate worlds.

The wire mesh between seats divided the view ahead into little square pieces. Pieces of houses. Pieces of trees. They

15

headed along Drake Street, past a man with a beer belly in a bathing suit, riding a one-speed bike with a grocery bag in the basket.

Raleigh pulled his notebook from his back pocket. "You guys ever go to Bird Island?" he said.

But he had a feeling Bird Island had nothing to do with it. Déjà vu, that was what he felt. The heavy cop was turning to study him with those wide-apart eyes.

Raleigh knew what the cop was going to say next. He knew it. He just knew it.

"Why'd you kill him?" the cop asked.

TWO

"Death by flamingo," said the taller detective, dropping black and white glossy photographs on Raleigh's chair.

"Jesus Christ," Raleigh breathed, looking down. Salinger's body lay faceup, left arm against the torso, right index finger raised as if making a point. He'd been turned into a human pincushion for plastic lawn flamingos. One flamingo appeared to be bending over, inspecting Salinger's hair. The legs were embedded in the shirt with blue orchids. Another was stuck into a thigh, head up, in a listening posture. A third seemed to be preparing for takeoff from its perch in Salinger's arm. A flamingo bent over a pool of blood on the floor.

Raleigh winced. Flamingos.

"Why'd you do it?" said Detective Blaney, twisting his high school class ring.

"You're sick," said Shaw.

"Tell us how it happened," said Blaney.

"You'll feel better," coaxed Shaw. "You'll sleep."

They were in a small room on the second floor of City Hall, also the police station, fire department, ambulance service, and marine patrol. The plastic gray paneling covering the walls

17

reminded Raleigh of Okay Russo's used car lot in Staten Island. The single window was open, tiny, and almost as high as the ceiling. Maybe the builder had run out of materials up there. There was no desk, no decorations. Other than the wooden chairs, the only other furniture was a small white steel table with a single drawer, the kind doctors use for medical implements.

"I told you five times," Raleigh said wearily. "I never met him until today."

The third detective, who was black, sat behind Raleigh and made occasional loud noises, dropping things on the floor to startle him, blowing on his neck. After glimpsing the man once, Raleigh had been ordered not to turn around.

"So you just met him," Blaney repeated skeptically. He looked about twenty-four, with a squarish dull face and tobacco stains under his fingernails. He'd handcuffed Raleigh to the chair three hours ago when the interrogation began, to establish himself as tough.

"Never met him . . ." said the tall, black-haired Shaw, who had immediately removed the handcuffs to show Raleigh he was a friend.

Raleigh yawned. "Am I getting through, finally?"

"Then what's *this?*" Blaney shouted, producing *The Mayor's Murderer* from beneath his seat. He read the inscription out loud. "To my good pal, Jay Salinger."

"I told you. He asked me to write that."

"If he asked you to swim to Cuba, would you do that?"

"This seemed easier." When they'd read him his rights, Raleigh had told the detectives he did not need an attorney. He'd described the old man who'd visited Salinger, and the fiancée's call on the answering machine. He'd told them about Abel Quade.

Blaney nodded to Shaw. "I think we can charge him with mopery."

Raleigh sat up. "What's mopery?"

18

"Did I ask you a question? Joe, did you hear me ask him a question?" In the tiny misshapen window, Raleigh watched a cone-shaped shadow drift across the face of the full moon. A night parasailer over the harbor.

Either the black detective or the air conditioner was blowing air on the back of his neck again. Blaney rotated the ring on his finger when he asked questions. "Which one of those pictures Salinger had was your girlfriend?"

Shaw lecherously jerked his hips back and forth in his chair. "Cute girls," he said, rocking. "Beautiful girls."

"The one wearing the string bikini? The Chinese girl in the negligee?"

"They were all my girlfriends," Raleigh said. "Every one of them. Will you just call New York?"

He hated the undersized wooden chair, the kind he had taken tests in, in high school. Names were carved through the varnish on the arm. KEVIN. MAE. Someone had gouged out PHILOSOPHY.

He heard a thwap behind him. Probably the phone book dropping, to unnerve him. Raleigh said, without turning, "Getting bored back there?"

From the room on the other side of the wall, he heard a boy yelling. "You guys are gonna be sorry! When my father hears you arrested me, you're in trouble, you're outta here!"

An older voice answered. "*We're* in trouble? We didn't go after the bouncer with a steel pipe."

"My father's Eddie Miller, he's Eddie Miller, you hear?"

There was a pause. Then: "Who the hell is Eddie Miller?"

Raleigh heard the scrape of a chair. He envisioned the kid lunging out of it. There were scuffling sounds. "Don't you talk about my father that way!" the boy yelled.

Shaw looked at Blaney. "He's a big guy," mused the tall detective to the one with the ring.

"Very big."

"Big enough to drag Salinger to the back of the boat."

19

Raleigh sighed. "There is one thing I want to say."

The cops leaned forward.

"What's mopery?" Raleigh said.

"Okay, Bubba." Blaney's patience seemed at an end. He wore a green Hawaiian shirt with green vines across the chest, and a gold coin in a lanyard around his neck. In his rough-skinned hand, the hypodermic seemed to take a long time coming out of the white steel drawer. That was because it was the biggest needle Raleigh had seen in his life. It looked like some sort of horse or elephant hypodermic. It looked like the hypodermic in National Geographic specials, where scientists shot them out of low-flying airplanes with rifles to disable immense carnivores.

It glinted in the light, six inches long. Red translucent liquid sparkled in the sausage-thick tube. Blaney held up the shot to the light. He gazed at the liquid, which seemed banded with residue on the bottom. Gently, he depressed the plunger, just a fraction, so that a single ruby drop oozed from the needle and fell on the linoleum floor.

Raleigh could tell from the pained lowering of Shaw's eyebrows that he just hated this part of the interrogation. He looked genuinely sorry.

"This won't hurt—hardly at all," Blaney said, grinning.

"Some people have chemical reactions to the shot," Shaw explained. "But you probably won't."

"Use it, Joe, he'll be okay," Blaney said. "At least we'll get the truth."

"Only one in a thousand, and we get them to the hospital in time," guaranteed Shaw. "Long before they finish choking."

Raleigh peered into the recesses of the hypodermic, like a schoolboy on his first trip to the aquarium, watching the shark. Inside the needle, the light went opaque, then clear.

Raleigh sat back. "Is it cherry Kool-Aid, or strawberry?"

Instantly, Raleigh heard the door open behind him and a

20

voice with authority said, "You boys been at this awhile. Take a break."

Raleigh turned around. The black detective with big forearms was gathering up the phone book off the floor. The three men left and the new one pulled a chair around so that he sat a foot from Raleigh, arms draped over the back of his seat, his head resting sleepily on his forearms. Pearl buttons fastened his shirt pockets. His light brown boots had pointy toes. He didn't say anything. He just gazed at Raleigh.

Raleigh decided he must be the chief of detectives. He seemed about forty, with medium-length blond hair, bleached by the sun and brushed straight back, the strands clumped together. Because of the narrowness of the lower half of his face, his mustache formed an angular inverted V. The most arresting feature was the eyes. Centering lazy blue irises, the pupils seemed to float sideways, diamond-shaped. The throat was slightly puffy. Raleigh guessed the man had a glandular condition. Beneath muscled, thickly haired forearms, Raleigh made out the Marine tattoo. The gold nameplate read, SEZAR.

"Your car'll stay impounded until tomorrow," the detective said with the slow tones of an islander. "I'll drive you home."

Lions Club gum-ball machines lined the halls. The upstairs consisted of narrow passageways in the same gray paneling. Gold stenciled letters on office doors read, CHIEF OF DETECTIVES. CHIEF OF POLICE. CITY MANAGER. Police reports were stuffed into manila folders hanging on the locked doors.

The boy in the other room shouted, "My father's a parole officer in Dade County, that's who!"

They descended a wide circular staircase perfect for debutante coming-out parties. Many voices were coming from downstairs, and bursts of laughter. But before the stairway brought the gathering into sight, Raleigh saw a dirty, barefoot blonde girl trudging up toward them. Her honey-colored sleeveless blouse was smudged. She wore a thin gold anklet with a heart on it. Fixing on Sezar's nameplate, she stopped two steps beneath him. She had an open, stupid face and a small mouth smeared with lipstick. Her lower lip thrust out in fury.

She demanded, "Are you a policeman?"

"I am, honey."

Raleigh guessed her age at twenty. She burst out, "You arrest that man! Make him give me my money!"

"What man?"

She dragged out her vowels, pronouncing money as muh-nay. "He said he'd pay me to have sex with him and I did, and he won't pay!"

Raleigh watched the right edge of Sezar's mustache rise a fraction. The detective stepped down so that he stood even with the girl.

"He was supposed to pay you for sex?"

"Twenty-five dollars!"

Sezar nodded. He glanced at Raleigh and winked, but to the girl he was trying to look serious. The girl squeezed her hip with one hand, waiting for justice.

Sezar laid a hand on her shoulder. "You got a license to sell, don't you?"

The girl's look faltered. Sezar said, "That license that cost a thousand dollars. You have that license, right?"

The girl burst out, "I don't have no thousand dollars! Nobody has a thousand dollars!"

A burst of male laughter came from below, amid the murmur of voices. Sezar told her, "Honey, if you didn't pay that thousand dollars, how am I going to make that man pay you? You see my problem? Why don't you go to another island, and not Key Rey, where you don't have to buy a license. Okay?"

The girl slumped back down the stairs, muttering, leaving dirty marks on the white steps. Following her, Sezar said, "There's no such thing as mopery. We make it up. Some people don't want to cooperate, so you bring out the needle or tell

22

'em about mopery. Of course, a smart man like you would never fall for that."

The stairway opened into the main City Hall foyer. Men and women in leisure suits or flower-print dresses were funneling boisterously into the open doorway of a meeting room, beside another gum-ball machine. Raleigh paused as he glimpsed a shock of white hair. He recognized Abel Quade, arm around a larger hulk of a man in a powder blue jacket and open-necked shirt. The larger man let out a huge laugh, tossing back his head. Quade seemed shorter than he had in Salinger's picture. A policeman closed the door behind them. CITY COMMISSION.

City Hall had the alkaline humid tang of buildings in the tropics.

They took a side exit. Outside, the night had gone April cool, breezeless, brilliant with more stars than Raleigh had ever seen at one time in Manhattan. The blue Mustang sat forlornly in the middle of a row of parking spaces, by a patrol car and a battered old Toyota. Sezar unlocked an olive-colored unmarked Chevrolet with a five-foot antenna on the rear hood. As Raleigh sank into the leather bucket seat, he heard Shaw's voice complain on the police radio, "Edna, that wasn't an emergency. Bill's collie was stuck in the fence."

Exhausted, he sat in silence as they rolled into the Morgan Street strip, crawling between bumper-to-bumper revelers; convertibles with tops down and college girls on the hoods, vans with mountain scenery painted on the sides and doors open and boys with beer kegs inside. The license plates were New York white, Georgia red, Colorado green, Wyoming yellow. The sidewalks were crowded with Ohio businessmen in pink Lacoste shirts, and Boston writers on fishing vacations. Skateboarders. Insurance conventioneers. French girls from cruise ships. Teenage runaways.

Every twenty feet, another open door gave Raleigh a flash of the inside of a nightclub. A bald black drummer in an emerald

23

jacket with sequins pounded sticks and howled. A middle-aged hippie woman in a fringed leather vest played flute beside an upright piano. A punk band leaped in unison, orange spiked haircuts under yellow and blue strobe lights. The rock music blended into jazz blended into tinkling Sinatra from the gay piano bar with the white Steinway on the balcony. Girls in slit dresses sipped daquiris as they hung over the railing, watching the street below.

"I called New York about you," Sezar said. They were drawing past a row of black motorcycles parked in front of a club with a yellow neon CHAINS. Sezar slowed to eye a teenage boy lighting a cigarette or joint in the doorway. He said, "Your editor laughed when I told him we'd taken you in."

"Frank has a great sense of humor."

"He told me about your special history."

Sezar drove with one hand on the wheel, one elbow on the windowsill. "You do a piece on Yankees practice," he said. "A relief pitcher staggers out of the bull pen with a knife in his back. You try a story on meter maids. A pizza parlor owner from Queens goes berserk and strangles three. The last murder we had in Key Rey was two, two and a half years ago. A man killed his lover with a ball-peen hammer. Now you come here. What would you think about you, if you were me?"

Raleigh was transported back to Madison Square Garden, where it had all started. He saw the wrestlers' dressing room down the hall from the Felt Forum. He saw the blue steel lockers and smelled the concrete floor. Raleigh pictured the huge bearded face of Igor Trotsky, the commissar from Siberia. Trotsky was leaning into Raleigh's nose. Trotsky ate a pound of raw garlic for prowess before every match, his press releases said, and bathed biannually so the health department would not deport him. Raleigh's olfactory senses had seemed to verify these claims.

"I keeeeeel Marvin the Marine in Hindu Death Match!" Igor

24

had boasted, shaking his open locker, which held his Oscar de la Renta suit.

"Come on, Trotsky. Stop talking with that phony accent. I know you went to Julliard."

"Pho-neeee? What is pho-neee?" Trotsky's right eyebrow had shot up. "Only one man escape steel cage alive!" he had bellowed.

That was when Raleigh had noticed a three-foot-tall man lurching from the men's room, hands pressed against his stomach. The man had been dressed like a leprechaun, with green felt shoes that curled up at the toes, a green hat with a feather in it, green gloves, green facial makeup, and green plastic tips on the top of his ears. Dublin Luke had been Tiny Mikey's tag-team partner.

"I'm gonna be sick. It's Mikey." Luke had gagged.

Now, in the car, Raleigh snapped back to the present. Sezar turned off Morgan and onto Drake, which was residential, deserted. The sweet smell of geiger blossoms came to them. "I talked to a friend of mine in the New York police about you, too. They didn't even have to look you up in the computer. You're pretty famous up there. She said they'd investigated you a couple of times but came up with nothing. She said you were a natural phenomenon. You a jinx, Raleigh?"

"This isn't the way to my house."

They were cruising between two large banyan trees that blocked out the moonlight. Sezar said, "And then you write these books on the murders and make all kinds of money. How much money can you make on one of those books anyway?"

"My house is on the north side of the island. Festival Street."

"Weeeel, it's hot in the office. I thought we might take a ride."

Through the open window, Raleigh caught a whiff of rot from the swamp. At the end of Drake Street, Sezar turned onto Conch Boulevard, heading east toward Salinger's boat. There were no cars or streetlights. A barefoot man on a bicycle passed in the other direction, pedaling slowly away from houseboat row.

"They liked you up there," Sezar continued. "Said you helped them solve murders. You make lots of money on those books of yours?"

Salinger's boat was coming up on the left, but they didn't slow down. And then it was receding, the Christmas lights blinking merrily, the plastic flamingos still on the top deck. Salinger must have been killed with the extras. Raleigh still saw the man in his mind, dancing around in the sunken living room while reruns of his show played on the video screen. He remembered Salinger spread on the floor in the police pictures. Houseboat row was gone now. White empty beach rolled by on the left. A tiny green blinking light headed south in the sky, flying for Key West, probably.

Sezar said, "Detective Blaney told me you had some idea who might have killed Salinger."

A shooting star arced from the sea over the swamp, and out of sight. Raleigh was alerted. "I don't know who did it. I just said Salinger wanted to show me information he'd uncovered. About a developer. Quade. But I never saw it. Salinger wanted to sell it."

"Quade. Ah, Uncle Abel."

Abruptly, Sezar swung the wheel right. Raleigh hadn't even seen the opening in the swamp, but the road was gone and they were rushing through the mangroves on a pitted dirt embankment. The long, scoop-shaped leaves shone silver in the headlights. The branches scraped the sides of the rocking car. Raleigh caught sight of pools of swamp water below each time the road twisted. Crouched over the carcass of a small animal, caught in the glare, a possum dragged its prey out of the way, blood on its pink snout.

Sezar switched off the radio. The static went silent. He was humming, not any particular tune, just a series of flat, sharp noises.

26

"You hear lots of stories about Uncle Abel," he said. "Raleigh, you know what they call us here, the people who were born here? Coconuts. Because we're dumb and we float on the sea in our shrimp boats and we're brown from the sun. A bunch of stupid inbred locals. All those wealthy stockbrokers and artists from New York fouled their own nests and bought up the rest of the Keys. They like to laugh at the poor, funny coconuts with their houses falling down. But they like to buy our land and build on it. Well, Abel beats them. Someone's going to build those condos whether we like it or not. So why not one of us? Why not Abel?"

The car stopped.

Sezar half-turned in the bucket seat to face Raleigh. Raleigh again grew aware of the powerful muscles rippling in the forearm reaching to the wheel. The ends of the inverted V-shaped mustache were wound into points. Raleigh had a vision of Sezar in front of a bathroom mirror, waxing them.

Raleigh leaned toward Sezar. "Cut the crap," he said. "Let's go home."

Instead, Sezar flicked off the lights and the engine. The night was plunged into black. For a moment, Raleigh lost sight of even the mangroves, and Sezar's soft voice issued from the shadow shape on the seat beside him.

"I have conch on a roll, or grouper. Take your pick."

When Raleigh didn't say anything, Sezar said, "You can spare me twenty minutes, can't you, Raleigh? All that money you made writing about police work? I know it's late. Come on, you didn't have supper. You ever try conch?"

The grouper tasted thick and juicy. The mayonnaise was sweet and the tomato dripped down the sides. Sezar opened two pints of milk and propped them on the front hood, which was warm as they leaned against it. Raleigh rested one boot on the bumper. He kept waiting for people to come out of the mangroves. His eyes had adjusted to the darkness and the leaves were thick here and sometimes seemed to move. The sandy clearing looked luminous. Beer cans and paper wrappers formed shadows on the ground. Sezar had parked in front of a canal. Thirty feet of dark still water separated them from more mangroves on the far side. Raleigh thought he heard a fish jump. He glanced back into the car and saw the moonlight reflecting off Sezar's knobbed nightstick on the backseat, next to the portable police light Sezar would fasten to the roof if he had to go somewhere in a hurry.

Raleigh left half the sandwich on the car and strolled to the edge of the water. A hot salty smell came up to him. "Ever go out to Bird Island?" he asked.

"I wouldn't go near that canal in the dark," Sezar said, chewing. "Alligator. I think you would have liked this conch."

In disgust, Raleigh said, "There aren't any alligators in Key Rey."

"Native-born ones, no. But someone flushed one of those cutesy baby ones down a toilet a few years back, and he lives in there and he's half-blind." Sezar stretched. "Of course, he'll spit your foot back out as soon as he realizes you're not a racoon."

Raleigh noticed a log floating in the water near a heron. At least it looked like a log. He went back to the car.

Sezar crumpled his Saran wrapper and tossed it inside the car. He folded his arms and sank down lower, his left boot heel digging into the sand. He sang, softly, " 'Maybe I love her, maybe I do. . . .' Bird Island," he said. "I went there a lot when I was a kid. Nobody goes out there. What do you want to write a book about Bird Island for, anyway? Who'd read it? 'Ohh, maybe I love . . .' We used to sing that in Galveston, in the brig."

"In the Marines."

"Once in, never out. Married a Texas girl, brought her back here and made her a coconut. It's quiet and beautiful in Key Rey. It's the greatest place in the world." In the moonlight, his smile was a pale slit. "See? I like outsiders."

"You were in the brig."

Sezar had a soft, clean laugh. "I ran the brig. It wasn't a bad job. I liked it. But I blew it." He wiped his fingers on the Saran wrap. "I kicked a prisoner's face in."

Sezar inched toward Raleigh. He was munching hush puppies. He reached for the milk and his throat muscles worked as he drank. "He'd raped a seven-year-old girl, a *seven*-year-old. He said to me, 'Sergeant, when I get out of here I'm going after the first little juiceball I see.'" Sezar shrugged. "I lost it. That temper."

Raleigh grew aware of a droning noise far away, getting louder. From the deep growl, he identified a powerful inboard motor or motors. The sound grew, fast.

In the canal, a shape shot past, prow up, long, needle-nosed. The swamp vibrated from the engines. The boat disappeared around a bend. Raleigh guessed the cigarette boat had been painted black.

He didn't know where Sezar had gotten the flashlight, but the beam switched on suddenly, blinding Raleigh.

From behind the light, Sezar's voice said, curious, appraising, "That's one batch of powder'll never reach New York. My men are up there a half-mile away, waiting."

Raleigh pushed the flashlight away. The beam bounced crazily in the mangroves. "Congratulations. But I don't write stories about crime anymore."

He sensed Sezar's flat, oddly shaped pupils boring into him, watching to see if he was involved. "Someone's losing a lot of money tonight." Raleigh said nothing. Sezar said casually, "Been to Tampa lately?"

"Never. Are we going home now? It's about midnight, I'd say."

"Earlobes, Raleigh. What do you think about earlobes?"

Salinger's earlobes had been hidden by his hair in the photos Raleigh had seen. Raleigh got into the car and shut the door. He talked to Sezar through the window. "Gee, let me think. I wonder about earlobes all the time and it's hard to narrow down the subject, to know where to begin. Look, I'm tired. I like cops. I worked with you guys in New York. If you want to ask me something, ask. I'll answer."

Sezar got in and backed the car up. When they were bouncing on the sandy road again, Raleigh said, "Salinger was a dealer?"

"How do you think he afforded all that expensive furniture? On a bartender's salary?"

A drug hit, Raleigh said to himself. The possum was back on the road ahead. Sezar slowed the Chevy. "What does Tampa have to do with it?" Raleigh asked.

Sezar went back to humming. He had terrible pitch. Raleigh realized he was trying to do a song, but the humming was so bad it was impossible to guess the tune.

Raleigh said, "The Tampa people are moving south. What are they? Colombians? Cubans? They kill rivals in weird ways to scare competitors. They cut off an earlobe as a sign of who they are. They cut off both earlobes. They throw earlobes all over the corpse. They write the word *earlobe* on the victim's chest, in lipstick. How am I doing?"

"Why don't you work for the police department, with such a fine, precise mind?"

"What about Uncle Abel?" Raleigh asked. "What Salinger said about him?"

The humming started again. Ten minutes later, Sezar steered the Chevrolet into Raleigh's driveway and cut the motor. The light was on in the upstairs window. Diane was awake. Sezar got out of the car when Raleigh did, instead of driving off.

"Those conch steaks make you thirsty, with all that salt. I don't suppose I can get a drink of water?"

"If I say no, you come back in the morning with a search warrant, right?"

"Absolutely not. I can wake the judge up in five minutes."

The house belonged to a Manhattan art dealer, a friend

whose furniture on the Upper West Side consisted of cardboard sections glued together in weird curving configurations, only ten thousand dollars apiece, designed to comfortably seat four-hundred-pound dwarves and give anyone else backaches. He'd rented the Key Rey place to Raleigh at cost when he'd heard the subject of the new book. "Birds," the art dealer had lamented, wistful, staring out of his tinted blue floor-to-ceiling picture window on West Fifty-seventh Street, watching a literary agent kissing a client in a sixty-story office window across traffic. The agent's dress had been hiked to her thighs. The art dealer kept a telescope in the corner of his office, near the concrete couch. "I love birds. I don't get to see birds in New York, Raleigh, and I don't count those horrid pigeons." The art dealer had gripped Raleigh's hands at the wrist. "Save the blue herons. Save those exquisite blue herons."

Fortunately, the Key Rey furniture remained functional, comfortable, although the art dealer was threatening to make the house into a gallery, too. The interior walls had been knocked down to create a sunny, circular central room with picture windows and track lighting over the Haitian paintings on the white stucco walls. Raleigh's word processor was set up on a makeshift table, a door laid over two file cabinets beneath a back window looking out over the bay. He could see red and green lights of boats moving on the water.

From upstairs, a woman's voice cried, "Bend over and grab your ankles! Bend over and grab your ankles!"

Raleigh went to the sink and added ice cubes to the water. The detective was standing by the word processor when Raleigh got back, looking up toward the bedroom. Raleigh flicked the machine on. The words *Bird Island* appeared on the amber screen.

Raleigh said, "Uh oh. My plan to murder Salinger, right on the set."

The voice upstairs cried, "Grab a buddy! Sir! Grab a buddy!"

31

Raleigh pulled a sheaf of papers out of a wire basket on the desk. The letterhead read, "Study of Wildlife on Bird Island." He'd picked up the federal documents at the Customs House.

"It's a code," Raleigh whispered. "Drug deliveries."

Then he saw Sezar's eyes widen and he knew Diane had come into the room. She was barefoot in a purple spandex body suit, with her frizzy black hair in place beneath a magenta headband. A sheen of sweat tanned her face. She'd been exercising again. No matter how often Raleigh saw Diane, he always felt as if it were the first time. The air went out of his chest a little and his temples grew warm. She was like some kind of magnificent animal. Sometimes when she was sleeping, he propped on one elbow and watched her. He might fix on a single hair shining or the curves on the outer edges of her closed eyes. He might watch the way her lips seemed to expand and contract when she breathed. It wasn't just the way she looked. He loved her so much sometimes he felt he could explode from it. She was smiling now, stopped in the middle of the room. Raleigh found it hard not to stare at her mouth.

Sezar was standing absolutely still.

Diane said, "I didn't hear you come in. I was practicing for a test." To Sezar, she said, "Stewardess refresher." She shrugged. "Trans Europe." Her voice was low and relaxed. She seemed to be in repose even when she was moving. "Safety," she said.

"No, no, passenger safety is important," Sezar said. He'd turned into a different person in front of Diane. "I mean, I'm a passenger." He added, after a pause, "On planes." He said, staring at Diane, "not to Europe, but my wife's parents live in Galveston. We fly there. On planes. Well, of course, on planes. How else do you fly?"

Diane looked from Sezar to Raleigh. "He didn't do it," she said. "I thought he shot my cousin at first, but it turned out to be the man who sold pencils."

Diane filled half a glass with ice water and said, "Back to

work." After she'd run up the stairs, Raleigh grew aware of the sea breeze coming through the window.

Sezar looked at Raleigh without any expression. "Nobody has a girlfried who looks like that," he said.

Upstairs, the voice cried, "Jump and slide! Jump and slide!"

Raleigh imagined her on her back on the bench upstairs, lifting and lowering the dumbbells. He imagined sweat running down the side of her face. He willed Sezar to leave.

Sezar shifted his weight to the other leg. He was coming out of a trance. Raleigh could tell he was going to hide his embarrassment by getting tough. Sezar growled, "If you have any ideas of writing a book about this, of working on this, forget it. Stay out of it."

"Ah, good news. I'm eliminated as a suspect."

Sezar drank his water all at once. He walked halfway to the door. "Not completely, but mostly. It's better to get easy things out of the way in the beginning. I just let the fellas have a shot at you to see what would come out."

Raleigh flicked off the word processor. "I'd hate to see the way you treat people who you think are guilty, if that was easy," he said.

"That's right," Sezar said. "You would. Stay away from my investigation."

"Don't worry. It's Bird Island I'm interested in. Do you know at one time there were more than a thousand roseate spoonbills on—" Sezar's eyes were glazing over—"that island."

"No questioning suspects. Or bothering my men."

"Sure. No questions."

"Stay away from them."

"Guaranteed. I told you."

"Because if you start asking questions," Sezar continued, as if he had not heard, "I can make trouble for you." He stood there, blinking. "Maybe you think because you were a hotshot in New York you can act the same way here."

Raleigh soothed him as he led him to the door. "I came to

33

Key Rey to get away from that kind of reporting. I'll leave the suspects alone."

After Sezar started his car, Raleigh added, in an undertone, "Except for Uncle Abel, but that's because of Bird Island, not because of the murder."

He shut off the lights and brought a bottle of Madeira upstairs with two glasses. In the bedroom, Diane had opened the picture window so that the bay breeze washed into his face and ruffled the curtains. The bed and walls were powder blue. She'd put roses in a vase on the night table, beside her yellow writing pad. She'd shut the light and lit a long candle. She'd taken off the exercise costume; he could smell the shower smell from the bathroom, humid and scented with her musky perfume. Naked, she lay sideways on one hip, raising and lowering her right leg, slowly. Her waist was tiny and her hips bony, the way he liked them. She'd taken off the headband, so her hair obscured the sides of her face. Her breasts were cup-sized. He saw the muscles of her stomach moving.

"I went down to the station," she said. "He took you out the back way."

Raleigh flipped open his wallet. He held an imaginary detective's shield out to Diane. He was unbuttoning his shirt with two fingers of his other hand.

"You're arousing my prurient interest," he said. "I'm going to have to arrest you, dressed like that."

"Good. It's okay then." Diane rolled over on her back and slid toward him as he sat on the bed. Her hands were on his shoulders, pulling off the shirt. They were cool through the fabric. "By the way, what's the charge?" she said.

Raleigh straddled her. His fingers came down and squeezed the tip of her breasts a little. She was smiling up at him with green eyes.

"Mopery," he said.

THREE

▾ ▾ ▾ ▾ ▾ ▾ ▾ ▾ ▾

"Why couldn't Wheeze have just met you in Key Rey?" Diane shouted over the engine, "instead of Bird Island?"

"He's paranoid, that's why. He doesn't want anyone to know he's passing information. He likes to play spy."

The last sight of Key Rey, the pink towers of Rey Del Mar, had faded into mist twenty minutes before. Raleigh stood at the wheel of a sixteen-foot Piranha speedboat, throttle up, bound southeast into the Gulf at 7 A.M. He'd bought the boat when he moved to Florida.

The sun burned red to gold. They threaded an area called the back country, lush mangrove islands separated by calm green channels marked for depth with sticks. Farther out, the horizon dipped, and treetops seemed at eye level. More distant islands were the color of broccoli. They looked like the stalks had been shaven off. To the south, a lone shrimp trawler spread its nets, white on blue, a dot smudging the boundary of sea and sky. The earth seemed finite and limitless simultaneously. The notion of the planet as a great disk sailors could fall off made sense.

"I never know if Wheeze is going to have something useful for me or just another crazy theory."

They cruised over tarpon shadows in the flats. They cleared the last island and bumped into darker water as, thirty yards to port, a thrashing in the sea subsided. The shark that had caused it moved off. A flying fish rose out of the water, wings flapping, kept pace with the Piranha for five seconds and fell back into the sea.

Diane was propped on one elbow in the prow, near the anchor, smearing sunblock number eight in the hollow of her left shoulder. One foot was thrown casually over the other knee, rocking.

She shouted, "So Elise says 'Meet me by the wine vat.' So Achmed says, 'Which one, red or white?' "

Raleigh had known Diane for six months before she'd confided to him she was writing a play. She called it *De Gaulle's Daughters* and set it in central France in the 1880s. The lead character was an obscure ancestor of the French president, a miserly wine merchant trying to save dowry money on his three daughters.

"Brown, gold. The Moroccan waiter's eyes changed color," she said.

Diane switched to oiling the right shoulder. Her yellow pad lay beside her, nothing on it. Diane composed on subways riding to Kennedy Airport. She wrote soliloquies on 747s, in between wheeling trays of chicken and manicotti down the aisles. At night, she dreamt complete dialogues, which she remembered and wrote down the next day.

Raleigh needed total silence to write.

"Last night, I dreamt Madeline's pearl necklace fell, in a restaurant. A Boston ship magnate picked it up."

Delicately, Raleigh said, "I don't know if people are really interested in De Gaulle, Diane. I mean, some people don't even know who he was. Maybe you should let me read it."

"When I'm finished."

36

"I just wouldn't want to see you disappointed if the play doesn't work out."

"Look," Diane said. "They made a musical about Pippin, didn't they? I'm sure whoever wrote Pippin, all his friends told him it was a bad idea, too." She made her voice deep, nasal and exaggerated. "It'll never work," she said. "Who cares about Charlemagne's son?"

Raleigh knew when to keep quiet. Diane said, "What if Salinger's death had nothing to do with Bird Island?"

"That would make me happy," Raleigh said. "Keep me out of it."

"The girl who called him. You think she did it? Or the old man who was leaving when you arrived?"

"I don't know. The neighbors seem to keep track of visitors to houseboat row. They saw my license plate. They would have seen his if he'd gone back."

"Then they would have seen anybody's."

"Unless they weren't looking then," Raleigh mused.

"Or the killer came on foot."

"Or swam."

"Or the killer *was* the neighbor," Diane said. "If it was my play, I'd make the killer the neighbor."

"This isn't a play," Raleigh said. He thought, *De Gaulle's Daughters* has got to be so bad.

Ahead, a small speedboat detached itself from the horizon and approached. As it grew closer, Raleigh saw round glasses on the driver's face, and a Van Dyke beard. He recognized the man who had left Salinger's boat when Raleigh had arrived yesterday. Professor Pete waved as he passed.

As always, Raleigh felt his mind loosening up on the water. The muscles in his neck eased. A pleasant drowsy feeling suffused him. Three miles from Bird Island, they passed the wreck of a frigate, which had been carried to the reef during a hurricane and deposited so the tips of its iron-ribbed hull jutted above the waterline. Double-crested cormorants stood motionless on each exposed beam, beaks frozen above long skinny necks. With their heat-struck attitudes, they looked like missionaries who had gone dumb and been turned into birds.

The helicopter and marine patrol boat seemed to arrive at the same time, the copter visible and low to the water, probably looking for marijuana bales a few miles off, the boat roaring around the side of the frigate. The birds didn't even move. The patrol boat was a big twenty-two footer, shark gray with a Bimini top to protect its crisply attired lone occupant from the sun. The boat pulled beside them; the officer waved for Raleigh to stop. He was a broad-shouldered man with a scrubbed, shiny look and the deep tan of someone with a naturally dark complexion. Raleigh looked over the pressed gray shirt with black epaulettes, and the matching stripes down the pants. All policemen seemed to wear the same aviator sunglasses above the same tightly pressed mouth.

Raleigh had a sudden thought. Sezar had asked this man to check the boat.

"Fishing today?" the man called over, wary and professional. "Oh. Going to Bird Island." His gold nameplate read, KAZAN-JIAN. His leather holster was unsnapped. The boats rocked slightly and Diane leaned between the gunwales to keep them from knocking. Kazanjian went through the standard opener. "Any guns on board? License? Registration? Is your radio working?" He maintained the distantly cordial attitude, yet Raleigh felt cold eyes on him from beneath the sunglasses. The man hardly looked at Diane. Kazanjian's right hand remained close to the holster but never touched it. "Mind if I poke around?"

Three minutes later, when he was going through the aft luggage compartment, he straightened. For the first time, real emotion came into his voice. "What do you know? Bagpipes!"

"My grandfather's," Raleigh said.

The sunglasses came off. The sun lines around the black eyes crinkled in a grin. "Bagpipes, heck, I haven't heard bagpipes since my dad used to play. He'd go out on the water,

38

too, because the neighbors couldn't stand it. He was in Borneo, in World War Two. A Scottish regiment, but an American bagpiper. They used to march into battle with these. The Scottish were fierce, they never took prisoners." Kazanjian leaned against the boat. "The Japs would run away in terror, through the jungle."

Wistfully, the marine patrolman fingered the cherrywood pipes. "Look, I know I stopped you and you're probably wanting to get going, but I don't suppose . . ." Kazanjian trailed off.

Raleigh hefted the plaid air sack and positioned his fingers on the smooth varnished holes in the wood. He loved the smoky taste of the reed on his tongue. When he started blowing air into the bladder, the startled cormorants on the wreck wheeled into the air, circling.

Raleigh closed his eyes when he played "Amazing Grace."

As the last note of the pipes died out across the water, Kazanjian applauded, put the glasses back on. "You're that writer," he said. "Fixx. Sure. Bird Island, I heard about you. They're all talking about you at City Hall this morning. I was on Salinger's show once. He wanted to know about drug busts. He seemed like a nice guy. Flaky, but okay. Sezar must have grilled you last night."

"We had a nice talk."

Kazanjian laughed. "A nice talk with Sezar. Sure." More somberly, he shook his head. "What a way to die," he said. "First I figured it was robbery. He had a lot of stereo equipment on the boat, and he always wore that old coin around his neck. A valuable coin. But Sezar said it was still on the body."

"Flamingos," Raleigh said. Diane, holding the side of the patrol boat, said, "Ugh."

Kazanjian paused when he got back on his own boat. He wiped the glasses with a tissue, between thumb and forefinger. "I had lots of good times on Bird Island," he said. "I used to go there with my wife." There was silence and then he said, more earnestly, "Mr. Fixx, I'd be in trouble if you let this out,

39

what I'm telling you, but if you're going to be spending time out here alone, you might want a firearm. A .38 or shotgun. You don't need a license in Florida. These are weird waters. Someone dropped bales from a plane last night. A boat like yours, someone might want it." Raleigh had a feeling the man had not reached his main point yet. Kazanjian added, "If you're going up against Abel Quade, which I hear you are, it's just protection, that's all. I'm in the Audubon Society. We're trying to keep him from getting the island, but he usually buys what he wants."

Kazanjian started the engine. He called, "I'm on channel sixteen. Give me a call if you're out here and you have a problem. I've got a short-barreled shotgun. Give me a location and I'll be there."

Diane seemed thoughtful when he left. "Did you notice how sad he looked when he mentioned his wife? I think something bad happened to her."

"You have *De Gaulle's Daughters* on the brain. He seemed fine to me."

Twenty minutes later, Raleigh turned down the throttle and brought the Piranha into a narrow channel splitting Bird Island in two. At high tide, the water rose to two feet, but during low tide it sank to an inch in many places. He dropped anchor several feet offshore in a pool by exposed mangrove roots. Even at low tide, he could get out of the channel from here.

The shore consisted of mangroves alternating with sand strips and stumpy pine forest. Raleigh smelled the humid odor of lush, rotting vegetation. Two great egrets drifted in the air across the channel, wings beating slowly against the blue. The slender cartilage in their wings was visible. The fan-shaped tails trailed skinny legs.

He splashed into the warm water as Diane reached for her diving tank and regulator. The Gulf was soothing against his thigh. The silty bottom oozed into a hole in his sneaker.

"OOOOOOOOOoooooooooo," came the cry from across the channel. Howler monkey. Raleigh noticed a four-inch brown lizard frozen on the upper curve of a root, half-hidden behind salt-encrusted mangrove leaves. The scarlet throat sac expanded in a territorial display. The lizard slithered the rest of the way down to the muck.

"Someday you ought to learn to dive," Diane called as he made his way to the boat. "OOOOOOOOOoooooooooo." The howler monkeys had managed to come ashore in a hurricane two hundred years ago when a Spanish galleon sank. Now they ran rampant on the smaller island, screaming and throwing twigs at visitors. They never crossed the channel, even when the water was an inch deep.

Raleigh waded onto the powderlike strip of beach, where a flock of sanderlings raced after retreating wavelets. He slipped across the saw grass and into the forest. Entering the dappled shadows, he glimpsed a two-foot-high, fully grown Key deer bolting off the dirt path into scrub. Monkey echoes mixed with birdcalls Raleigh had learned to recognize. The hollow rattling garoo of the sandhill cranes. The quick tcheek of the oven-birds. He heard a whiplike sound above the trees. Storks were taking off.

The sun's position told him he was slightly late for his meeting.

The birds were everywhere. Two hairy woodpeckers, robin-sized, pecked at a dead cypress for termites. Their heads moved so fast the crimson slash on their crowns blurred. He noted a turban-shaped blue-heron nest crowning the broken crest of a thirty-foot pine. He broke out of the forest and in a grove surrounded by Jamaican dogwoods, saw an osprey overhead, a black snake wriggling in its hooked beak.

For an instant, Raleigh remembered Abel Quade disappearing into the city council meeting last night. The image of Quade melted into one of Salinger, in the orchid-covered shirt, on his back on the floor.

"Hey man, that is a beautiful sight. That spoonbill is really something. I will never get tired of that."

From the opposite direction, Wheeze advanced into the clearing. The roseate spoonbill was wading slowly in the middle of an algae-clogged pool, swishing its bill, slowly, through the shallow water. "That is a rare fucking bird, man," Wheeze said, voice lower as he rounded the pool so he wouldn't startle the bird. The delicate pink of the spoonbill's legs meshed into an orange splash on its tail, making the bird seem like a big piece of candy.

Wheeze looked like a forty-five-year-old hippie. He had a salt and pepper beard, and thick gray hair that frizzed out of his oval-shaped face to fall in waves below the clerk's bent shoulders. He retained the industrial pallor of the north even after ten years in the tropics. He wore a pressed red pinstriped dress shirt with sleeves rolled up and an ink stain on the pocket, round gold wire-rimmed glasses with paper-thin lenses, khaki climbing shorts, and running shoes with bunion holes.

Raleigh had met him two weeks ago at City Hall, while researching Bird Island. Wheeze had called him up that night. "I want to help," he'd said.

"Okay man, the ecological James Bond spy has brought you key information."

He carried a manila file from which papers protruded.

"Wheeze, you could have come over to the house with this."

Wheeze seated himself on a log by the pool. The sun was hot in the clearing, striking them directly. "Time for a hit," he said. He pulled an atomizer from his breast pocket and inhaled deeply. For an instant, his breath went ragged, but then it returned to normal. When he laughed, he sounded like a wren, a "tsuk, tsuk" sound. "If you think that, you don't know how small a place like Key Rey is. Peyton Place of the sea, man. The cops pulled you in at seven-oh-five last night. One of Salinger's neighbors had described your car. They got you in that closet interrogation room on the second floor, the weird

42

one with the little window. There were three of them with you. Sezar drove you to the swamp and showed you a bust. Then he took you home and went through your computer. And Jay Salinger's dead. Muerte. Finito. Termino. How am I doing? Sezar figures it was Cubans, druggies. They did some nutty ritual to the body, like in Tampa, but only the cops know what it is."

Raleigh just stared. Wheeze leaned back. "All I did was sit at the bar at Cap'n Bob's last night and listen to people talk when they came in. It's the coconut telegraph, man. You think I want Abel Quade finding out I went to your *house*? He's related to half the city council. I am the spy in place, the 007 of the Customs House. Mild-mannered clerk by day, who has access to the Department of Interior computer, man, and finds the secret plans of the enemies of freedom and birdhood everywhere."

Raleigh was continually amazed by the smallness of Key Rey. "What do you have for me?" he said.

"Hey, what's this business attitude? Relax. You know, Raleigh, I get up every morning and I can't decide. Do I take a swim? Dive off the dock? Give Lucy a kiss, lay in the sun? We have a whole school of black-tipped sharks under the dock. You really ought to settle here after you finish the book. This is the greatest place in the world."

OOOOOOOOOOOOoooooooooooo.

"Feast your eyes, man." Wheeze extended the manila folder. Beneath the Department of Interior logo on the top page, Raleigh saw a chart listing national parkland all over the country. In New York. Montana. New Mexico. Minnesota.

Wheeze said, "The upgraded list came in yesterday. They're getting rid of everything. Cutting costs so they can buy more missiles, man, to blow up everyone no matter what their race, creed, or color. They're selling some land to bidders. They're leasing it away for oil. They're giving it away to cities, like here, when the Department chooses it for the program."

A second paper revealed an artist's conception of a waterfront community. Line drawings showed a narrow beach with neat, identical stucco homes in the background, all featuring patios and picture windows. Girls in bikinis lounged on the sand. Cabin cruisers were docked at a pier on the right, and smiling couples sipped drinks on lounge chairs on deck. One woman with a poodle on a leash was being helped onto the dock by a handsome younger man in a jacket and tie.

Raleigh said, "What's this?"

"What do you mean, what's this? Don't you recognize it? Look around, man. You're in it."

Raleigh stared at the page. "This is Bird Island?"

Wheeze grinned. "Luxury condos, man. No more birds. No more monkeys. Little golf carts and old fat men. You could get this stuff under the Freedom of Information Act, and it would only take you eight years if you knew where to look in the first place. But the deft fingers of our secret agent purloined the evidence. Am I great or am I great?"

"How much of the island would it cover?"

"I don't think he plans to pave over the channel yet. What I want to know is how come Bird Island made the list. Quade tried the same thing five years ago. We stopped him."

Startled, the spoonbill took off, a blur of orange.

Wheeze touched the front of Raleigh's shirt. "That was the easy part," he said. "Now the dangerous. Remember that group that stopped Abel before? Ike White, he edits the Key Rey *Sunfish*. He was big in it. He had a motorcycle accident on the way to a meeting. Hit and run. Nan Grant. She was with Greenpeace. She stopped going to the meetings. Then she stopped going out of her house. She got really freaked out, Raleigh. They did something to her."

Raleigh leaned back on his palms. "Salinger said he had something on Quade."

Wheeze's right eyebrow went up. "Maybe he did, man. Maybe he did. If Quade was going to pay people off, it could

44

happen in a few places. El Presidente in Washington tells the Department of Interior to dump land. Quade pay off the commander in chief? Give me a break. But wait a minute, *who* in the Department of Interior *chooses* Bird Island. The Great Wheeze pulls the answer out of a hat."

With a flourish, Wheeze produced another paper. He read out loud. "In accordance with presidential directive thirty-two O seven of the Public Lands Act, which directs the Department of Interior to identify and recommend federal lands for privatization, blah blah blah," Wheeze said. "Signed, Mark Politowsky." Wheeze grinned and held the paper up, away from Raleigh. "So where do they file this public information? Want to guess? Was it under Bird Island? Nooooo. Department of Interior? Lands Act? Uh uh. 'Studies. Mangroves.' They filed it, all right. But no one ever would have found it."

Raleigh scanned the paper, which carried an Atlanta Office letterhead.

"You wouldn't happen to know if Politowsky ever came to Key Rey," Raleigh said.

"Of course he came. It was in the *Sunfish*. He had to see the place, didn't he?" Wheeze cleaned his glasses. The forest filled with the flutelike whistle Raleigh recognized as coming from an oriole. He caught sight of the orange sheen of the bird high in a willow.

Wheeze shuddered. "What a way to die. Little steel legs all over. No disrespect to the dead, but with Salinger, though, anything he tells you is a little bit true and the rest turns out to be Salinger. Poor guy would have been better off staying in jail."

"Salinger was in jail?"

"Before he came here. Why? What story did he tell you about how he came? The ex-Peace Corps story? The ex-wife in New Hampshire? Yeah, he had one in New Hampshire, and one in Pittsburgh. He was a rampant penis, man." Wheeze stood up and looked both ways. "And now I must sneak back

45

to my double-O-seven speedboat for agents of ecology. You have the documents, and my enemies must not see me, man. The message is in my shoe. Watch out for the ejector seat. This message will self-destruct when I leave."

"Our secret," Raleigh said.

Diane had changed out of her diving gear back at the boat, and brought the cooler to the beach. The inside was stuffed with treats she had brought back from Europe. There was Taittinger's champagne from France and cheese from Geneva. There were chocolates from Belgium. Scones and marmalade from England.

"I swam through a whole school of tarpon," Diane said. "Shooting stars."

They ate in silence. The channel had drained to low tide. Hot streaming water mussed the inch-high turtle grass and carved millions of back-to-back silver-dollar-sized indentations to cup water and throw back the sun. Raleigh figured Abel Quade would dredge the channel; otherwise, it would be impossible to get the cabin cruisers to the docks.

The heat seemed to emanate from everything visible, the pale blue of the sky, the baking sand, the fetid mangroves and twisting dried-out pines. After a while, it even felt like it was coming from inside him, oozing from his head, from his joints. The salt was on his lips. The coldness of the champagne stung the inside of his mouth. Diane lay with the concave curve of her belly a sun scoop.

Raleigh said, "This is what I wanted." The champagne glasses tilted toward each other in the sand, fizzing. Raleigh's eyes were closed but he felt the sun on them anyway. He said, "Right about now the tenth car alarm is probably going off on Third Avenue."

"The subway's stalled on the way to Kennedy again. The air-conditioning is off."

"That skinny guy from the building association is leaving messages on our answering machine. Put bars on the windows."

Raleigh dabbed marmalade an inch above her belly button. With the tip of his tongue, he licked it off.

"Remember the first time we came here?" she said, twining her fingers in his hair.

"I rented a boat. This was the only island you could go to that nobody owned."

"I never would have thought we'd take a vacation together when I saw you at the Yuk Yuk Club," Diane said.

Raleigh thought back. Eleven months after coming to the *News*, he'd been assigned to write up the Yuk Yuk Club. The hot new club featuring aspiring comedians who would try new acts. Agents and talent scouts frequented the place. Two or three comedy stars had started their careers at the Yuk Yuk Club. All over Manhattan, waiters and hatcheck girls and Nedick's hot dog salesmen and law students who would rather be in show business honed routines for late-night appearances on the Upper East Side.

"Take a break from crime. What could happen at the Yuk Yuk Club?" Frank had said.

Raleigh remembered a small underground room crammed with round tables. Red track lights had gleamed off the floor-to-ceiling photographs of comedy stars who had played the club.

He'd sat bored and yawning through the mime nun from Boston and the Queens car salesman who imitated Ronald Reagan singing "At the Zoo." Then all he did was go to the bathroom. People go to the bathroom all the time without serious consequences. But when Raleigh came back, tables were overturned, police were advancing on him from three sides, and a girl in a tight strapless dress was screaming, "He did it!"

As the officers pinned him, Raleigh thought he had never

47

seen anyone so beautiful. He kept staring while a voice recited his legal rights to the wail of sirens outside. Her lips were full and perfect, mouthing the word *murderer*. He could tell her long fingers would feel hot on his chest. Her body could stretch beside his forever. He barely felt the handcuffs. . . .

"I miss Gina," Diane said.

Her cousin Gina, an NYU medical student, had been scheduled to take the stage in twenty minutes. In a fit of nervousness, she'd gone to the ladies room at the same time Raleigh had disappeared. By the time Frank arrived at the station house with the *Daily News* lawyer, Raleigh was out of the cell, conversing with detectives about *The Midget Murders*. Police on the scene had found the open window in the ladies' room. They'd dusted the .22 found in the alley for prints, and found plenty, but not Raleigh's. They'd verified Raleigh's presence in the other bathroom at the time of the murder, from the Yale junior who had been throwing up Tequila Sunrises while he was there.

"You're a jinx," the desk sergeant at Midtown North had said as Raleigh left the precinct. "Call up if you're ever coming to my neighborhood, so I can evacuate."

Now Diane said, "I wouldn't go out with you after that."

He rubbed her shoulder. He hadn't blamed her. Even though he was innocent, his voice had brought on bad associations. But Raleigh hadn't been able to forget her. He'd been felled by the Turkish sledgehammer. It was as if when he'd seen Diane, a bald fat Mamluk had crushed a club over his head. He'd found out she was a stewardess, diver, graduate of the playwriting program at NYU. He wrote *Diane* in his reporter's notebook during interviews and crossed it out. He hadn't mooned around like this since Doreen Vanucci in PS 92. He found himself on her street or outside her health club at convenient moments. He asked her out to dinner, lunch, snacks, movies. To Broadway plays. To museums. On hikes. He had roses delivered as her flights landed in Cairo. Egyptians in suits

stood meeting passengers and holding signs that read, DAR-
LING'S PITCHING TUESDAY NIGHT. I HAVE BOX SEATS.

Each night, he dreamt of Diane pointing at him, screaming,
"He killed Gina." Each morning, he awoke helpless before his
love.

"They weren't even good pencils, either," Diane said now.
"The points broke."

Despite his best efforts, Diane had taken up with a Manhattan neurosurgeon named Kokowski. "I'm going to marry
him," she'd announced to Raleigh. "Leave me alone." Raleigh
had decided she was weakening. He had thrown himself into
the Gina investigation, stopping at pay phones to ask Diane
out. "Kokowski lives by *saving* lives, not by sensationalizing
murders," Diane had said. He loved her voice. From Gina's
fellow med students, he'd learned that Gina's comedy routines
had made fun of her boyfriends. A girl with a crush on Raleigh
had told him something she'd not shared with police. Gina
made tapes of her acts and gave them to the friend to critique.
"I have a ski vacation planned," the woman had told Raleigh,
"and I don't want to call it off because the police make me stay
around here." The woman had invited Raleigh to her apartment,
played the tapes, and touched his knee a lot. But Raleigh was
a one-woman man, even when his love was unrequited. What
had excited him most about the evening were Gina's jokes
about a pencil salesman who was married, who was psychotic,
and who dreamt of being a neurosurgeon. Her description of
the man matched the photograph Diane had showed Raleigh
of Kokowski.

Diane's foot rocked back and forth over her knee now. She
poured the last bit of champagne evenly. She reached over
and rubbed his shoulders. She nuzzled her face against his arm.
"You were cute on TV," she said.

The climax of the story had made the six o'clock news on
channels nine, five, seven, and two. He'd checked every medical

association, hospital, and insurance company and found no Kokowski. He'd staked out Diane's apartment until Kokowski emerged alone after a date. He'd followed the man home to a tract house in Teaneck, where he lived with his wife and three children. Kokowski turned out to be Raoul Miller, who peddled pencils to school boards in New York, Connecticut, and New Jersey. He had started dating Diane in the hope she had Gina's comedy tapes. He'd gone crazy with rage when Gina stopped dating him, and the idea of people laughing at him in a night-club had driven him over the edge. But even when he'd learned Diane didn't have the tapes, he'd been unable to stop seeing her. He'd fallen in love with her. But Diane had begun to guess he wasn't a doctor, had grown suspicious over his questions about Gina.

On the night Miller bought a single one-way airplane ticket to Brazil, Raleigh knew Diane was in trouble. He'd reached the cable car that went from Second Avenue to Roosevelt Island just as it was taking off with Diane and Kokowski-Miller inside. It was 2 A.M. He'd hammered on the token vendor's booth, but the man had buried his head in *Iacocca*. He'd leaped onto the moving cable and, as he'd guessed, the operator had shut down the whole thing.

Hand over hand, Raleigh had worked his way over Second Avenue toward the Queensboro Bridge. Horns had started honking below, and sirens blared in the distance. He'd done this sort of thing in Vietnam, traversing rivers. He could see Kokowski-Miller through the glass, banging at him to stay away. And when Diane had tackled Miller, Raleigh knew he'd guessed right. The man had planned to kill her on the island.

As she fought, Raleigh had forced his way into the car through the trapdoor on top. The attendant was on the floor, wounded. Miller was coming at him with a knife. The whole thing had been captured for love-struck New York by Channel Seven's mobile-unit helicopter.

Diane's hand traveled up his thigh now. Soon there wasn't

50

any leg left, she was up so high. "When you see a man hanging over the East River for you," she said, "how can you not go out with him after that?"

They started kissing on the sand, and then they rolled into the channel. The tide was running out fast, rushing over their bodies. There was a hot, sexy flats odor, a randy swamp smell of mangroves, salt, mud, sea animals. The earth was sweating and they rutted in it. The tide filled the moving spaces betwen their bodies. The sea was in his mouth with her tongue. He glimpsed the bottom of her tangerine-colored bikini in the turtle grass, string trailing in the inch-high water. Monkeys were screaming on the small island. He felt the sand abrasions on his knees.

Sometimes when he had sex with her, he lost vision.

They lay back, breathing. Sensation returned to the areas they had ignored. He felt the silt washing its way into the cracks of his body, and the sting of the sun on his forehead and lips. Lust floating off the civilized continent. A baby crab wandered into his heel and kept bumping against it.

As he lay there, a low breeze stirred the mangroves and he watched it lift a paper out of the boat. The paper floated over the channel and he retrieved it from the water beside him. The line drawing of Bird Island was still visible on the soaked paper. It was a nighttime scene. The men wore dinner jackets and the women high heels. They were disappearing into a club where the marquee read MUSIC. They all seemed to be having a fabulous time.

When Raleigh reached home four hours later, the phone was ringing. Frank had never bothered to say hello even in New York. When he wanted something, he cooed as if talking to a four-year-old. "Is this my great writer? Is this my Pulitzer Prize-winner? I know you're going to take this offer, Raleigh. Ten. Thousand. Dollars. More. Plus you stay in Key Rey. Just start the column with this flamingo thing, eh? Eh?"

51

Diane blew him a kiss, disappearing up the stairs.

"Frank, why don't you ever listen?"

There was a big sigh. "You should have been an agent, you know that? Some kind of movie agent, one of those sharks with padded shoulders and sunglasses. Fifteen thousand. Last offer, Raleigh. Play coy on this and it starts going down. You need money even in paradise. Remember Ray Knight and the Mets? He wanted a million and he had to move to Baltimore."

"Frank," Raleigh said, gazing out the picture window at the blue water, at a windsurfer on the harbor. "It's sunny here. We just got back from the island. You want me to spell it?" Raleigh started spelling. "N—"

"We'll talk," Frank said, and hung up. The phone rang.

"Frank," Raleigh said wearily.

But it wasn't Frank. It was a man with a muffled voice. Something between a hiss and a whisper. "Get involved and you're going to regret it," the voice said.

"Get involved in what?" Raleigh said.

"What happened to Salinger is none of your business," the voice said. "Stay out of it."

"Believe me, I just told my editor. I'm here writing a book about Bird Island."

"Because if you start on Salinger, we're going to cut your balls off, Raleigh. We're going to take you out in the boat." The voice hissed at him, dragging out the *S*'s.

Raleigh opened the refrigerator. Rats. No orange juice. "I'm telling you," he said patiently. "Bird Island. *Bird Island.*"

"And that cunt," the voice continued smoothly. "Her, too. Not just you, Raleigh. Work her over, know what I mean? Do it to her, know what I mean? Poke around. Cut around. You don't want that to happen to her, do you, Raleigh?"

Raleigh sat down at the table. He looked up at the ceiling. He could hear Diane padding around upstairs.

On the harbor, the windsurfer fell over and started climbing back on his board.

52

"Wait a minute, you're threatening Diane?"

"You heard me, Bubba."

Raleigh felt a big depression coming on.

"Why'd you have to say that?" he said.

"Bye, Bubba," the voice said.

Raleigh looked at the buzzing receiver. He hung up slowly. Upstairs, Diane was putting clothes into her stewardess suitcase. She was humming something. It was "Going Down the Road" he heard as he came into the bedroom.

"How long's the trip this time?" he asked.

"Three days. Madrid and Dubrovnik. I miss you already, Tonto."

Raleigh stretched on the bed. "Why don't you trade with Cynthia. Make it longer. Call me if you can."

"Got another lover?"

Raleigh smiled. "Five other lovers. Twelve."

She pressed a pair of tennis shorts on top of her yellow evening dress. "Who just called, Raleigh?" He said, "Nobody. I need to work." Diane sat beside him and looked at him a bit. Then she said. "I'll see what I can do."

Raleigh went downstairs again. He ran the water in the kitchen faucet until it was icy cold. When he filled the glass, he sat in his easy chair by the makeshift desk. He turned on the computer and watched the words *Bird Island* come on the screen. He flipped the Off switch and the light went out. He half-turned so he could see the phone, quiet, pink.

"Now why'd you go and make me mad?" he said.

FOUR

The diving instructor's T-shirt read, DRINKING DIVING DIDDLING. She said, "Professor Pete had a house, but he had to sell it. He couldn't pay his crew, so he let them go."

She bounced up and down on her toes as she spoke, stretching. She was a tall, lean girl with honey-colored hair and a lavender bikini. Raleigh's eyes followed the line of her finger across the sandy parking lot and past the ramshackle Raw Bar to the shrimp-boat pier with gray pelicans on the pilings. The morning breeze carried no coolness. The lone sixty-foot trawler at the dock had no nets, just two odd-looking elbow-shaped pipes in back, four feet wide at the openings, suspended from a winch. Raleigh had never seen anything like them.

"He lives on the boat. Those pipes are called mailboxes," the girl said as her morning class shuffled out of the dive shop at her back, the students looking nervously out to sea. A Cunard liner was steaming into the harbor. A pasty fat man in billowy print trunks and a T-shirt showing a devil lying on a beach said, "This sure is different from Detroit. We had thirty people in the pool there, swimming into each other. You promise there are no sharks out there?"

Above the devil, the shirt read, I LOST MY SOUL IN KEY REY.

"Be with you in a minute, folks," the instructor said cheerfully. "Head over to the boat. Tommy will fit you with masks and flippers." A Johnny Coetzee tune, "The Island That Time Forgot," pumped from inside the shop. The instructor told Raleigh, "When he's looking for treasure, they lower the mailboxes into the sea. Propellers blow the water through the pipes and make holes in the bottom. Divers swim into the holes to look for whatever the magnetometer picked up, usually old beer cans. Anyway, he can't even afford the divers now. What a wild-goose chase."

A handprinted sign in the shop window declared, SAVE BIRD ISLAND.

Raleigh thanked the girl. She called after him, "You sure you don't want a lesson?"

He held up both palms, backing. "Claustrophobia."

The girl winked, rocking up and down. "I'll show you the delights of the deep," she promised.

Abel Quade was in Tampa, on business, his secretary had said. Raleigh could come to his house at two. Plenty of time to talk to Professor Pete first, and others. He ambled down the pier. Gulls mewed overhead. THE MOTHER LODE was painted on the trawler's high, jutting prow, black words against white peeling paint with its silver trim.

A shiny new speedboat bobbed, tied to the stern of the trawler. Soft blue letters, which looked like powder blown into the air to form words, named the boat DADDY'S GIFT.

Raleigh flashed back to his phone call to Sezar an hour ago.

"Tell me again," the detective had drawled, "exactly what the caller said about Diane?"

"I said it three times. I'll trust your memory."

Raleigh had envisioned Sezar in his office, maybe writing notes or signaling another detective to pick up an extension. Sezar had persisted with his dry, cop distrust, "Why would someone threaten *you*, Raleigh? I thought you weren't going to involve yourself in this. Bird Island, isn't that your big interest? Not drugs? Not Salinger?"

Raleigh had been tying his sneakers, getting his car keys off the bureau for the drive to the docks. Diane had left for her trip an hour earlier. She would drive down to Key West and fly up to Miami to hook up with her airline. Raleigh had said, "That's what I like about you. We think alike. You don't think I got the call. I'm thinking maybe you made it."

Now, on the dock, Raleigh saw a note tacked to the piling in front of the trawler. "I'm in the office," it said. "Come on board."

He used one of the rubber tire bumpers to step up to the narrow deck between railing and pilothouse. He stuck his head in the door. The pilothouse smelled like a combination fish fry and locker room. Mesh bags of potatoes hung from hooks in the ceiling, above the pilot's wheel. There was an empty wooden table in a larger eating area, and a bottle of Myers's rum on it. Two folding chairs were pulled back. He saw the galley to the right, iron skillets hanging from the wall. A shower curtain with a print of leaping dolphins was visible in another room, and a third door was closed.

Raleigh started to cry hello but he heard the sharp sound of a slap, muffled but unmistakable behind the door. The door slid open quickly. A young looking girl ran out, eighteen or nineteen, long hair flying, hand pressed against her cheek. She was sobbing. She did not look at Raleigh as she squeezed past. He heard her bare feet pounding as she fled down the deck.

Then Raleigh's attention was taken up by a skinny giant emerging from the bunk room, ducking to clear the doorway. The man swaggered into the pilothouse. He was zipping up grease-smeared work pants. The last gleam of copper-colored pubic hair disappeared from view. The man was bare-chested, tightly muscled, with wide shoulders for someone so thin. A lewd grin curved the top of his Fu Manchu mustache. The thick straight hair, dirty blond and sunbleached, was parted in the middle. It fell to the shoulders. Raleigh heard the cough of the pleasure boat starting up outside. He found himself level with a pair of metallic black eyes, burnished bright with pleasure. Even at first glance, it was easy to tell this man did not let go of fun easily.

"Rich girl." The man grinned, offering to let Raleigh in on the joke.

"I'm looking for Professor Pete."

The sailor realized Raleigh didn't share his amusement. The mood change rippled over his face, narrowing his eyes and flattening his lips slightly. His teeth needed a shine.

"The fuck are you?" the man said.

Raleigh stepped closer. He'd caught a glimpse of a thin gold bracelet on the girl's upraised wrist. He'd seen the edges of the red welt on her face, sticking out around her hand. "Maybe you want to hit me, too," he said.

There was a pause during which he heard the speedboat leaving. The man's eyes narrowed, puzzled. He was unaccustomed to being challenged. He seemed to realize he and Raleigh were the same size. He scratched his crotch lazily and turned away. "Aaaah," he muttered. "It's too early for this."

Raleigh waited, the adrenaline rushing, even after the man had gone. Then he made his way to the stern of the trawler, alert, wondering where the sailor had gone. When he called the professor's name into the hold, Pete's face thrust itself into the shaft of light angling down the ladder. "There you are! Come down! Don't hit your head!"

Raleigh followed Pete through the trawler's dark engine room, along a steel catwalk between two looming Volvo Penta diesel engines, which rose from pits in the floor to nearly touch the ceiling. Mallets and screwdrivers lay scattered on the catwalk and Raleigh smelled the strong reek of oil. The skinny giant labored in one of the pits, struggling with a wrench, cursing. He didn't look up.

Pete led Raleigh through a narrow hatch and into a large

arrow-shaped room conforming to the bow of the trawler. It blazed with light. The professor beamed up at him, drawing him inside, finally shaking hands. "So glad you could come," he said, sounding like he was hosting a faculty tea. Shrimp had probably once been stored here, but the hold had been turned into an office and library. Bare bulbs hung from wires running diagonally across the ceiling, to illuminate rows of bookshelves along the back wall, on both sides of an old walnut desk that supported a small computer and a larger microfilm machine. There were at least a hundred old books: frayed diving manuals, first-aid paperbacks, leather-bound volumes with Spanish titles in gold leaf. A lumpy shredded couch leaned against one wall, near a safe. One leg was missing, replaced by a cinder block. The refrigerator looked about thirty years old. Raleigh noticed that to save money, the professor used the back sides of hand-outs and letters as typing paper.

"Sit down, get comfortable." Pete beamed, indicated a plush old easy chair in slightly less dilapidated condition, opposite the couch and beneath a series of underwater topographical maps pinned to the walls, aswirl with brown and blue lines and marked with red *X*'s. Raleigh saw a half-eaten baked potato on a paper plate beside the microfilm machine. Pete said, "Beer? Juice?" He thrust a cold four-ounce can of Donald Duck orange juice at Raleigh. The fish fry smell was down here, too. "Stand up! Look at this!" Pete said. "What are you all the way over there for?"

He must have been working with the microfilm before Raleigh arrived. The machine, volcano-shaped, hummed errati-cally when Pete switched it on. The writing filling the screen, magnified stylized script, had to be hundreds of years old. Some of the words were ripped. Raleigh recognized Spanish but could not read it.

Pete leaned forward in his swivel chair, his forehead almost touching the screen as he read excitedly. "Cof-fee. Bah! There was no coffee! Hardtack. Lies! Sit! Relax! Watch out for the spring on that cushion. I'm going to tell you the story of the greatest adventurer, the most fantastic robbery of the seventeenth century, Mr. Gower. . . ."

"My name's n—"

"A genius," Pete whispered. He swiveled away from the machine, which remained on. Its light spread a yellowish halo around his head and shone through the edges of his thick lenses, making his eyes large. "This is a true story." He nodded. "Close your eyes, Mr. Gower. I want to set the scene. I want you to imagine those beautiful waters off of Key Rey, and then I want you to envision them three hundred years ago."

"Excuse me, but—"

"Tut tut, do it!" Professor Pete dropped his voice again. "They were highways for gold, Mr. Gower. More wealth than you could conceive of. The richest fleet in the world. Every year, once a year, it would sail past our little island. Gold. Silver. Jewels. Ivory. Open your eyes, what are you, asleep?"

Raleigh bolted upright. A bag of potatoes swayed above the couch. It must have been there awhile, because vines grew out of it.

Pete was at the map of the Caribbean, poking the Pacific Ocean on the western side of Panama. "The Spanish fleet," he said. "It carried the entire year's budget for the greatest empire on earth. The booty would come from two continents. It would start in Macao. They'd load the galleons with silks and porcelain from China and Japan. Ivory. Spices. They'd sail to the Isthmus, *here*, and unload the cargo onto mules. They'd haul it across the jungle, put it on ships and take it to Havana."

Someone in the engine room yelled, "Ouch, damnit."

Pete's finger moved slowly, to Peru. "The gold and jewels came from the New World. Thirteen thousand Indian slaves mined their silver in Potosí. The Spanish fashioned it into bricks. They minted coins at Mexico City, Santiago, Lima, Bolivia. They plundered the gold of the Incas, buttery gold they smelted into bars the size of Milky Ways. They made

59

chains with it, yards of chains." Pete turned from the map. He looked like a Princeton professor who'd gotten religion. His eyes were glazed. "The gold and silver would arrive at Cartagena, *here*, on ship and mule train. So would emeralds brought out of the mountains. The treasure would be shipped to Havana for a rendezvous with the other fleet. Every year for three hundred years. Hundreds of millions of dollars a year. Gold to finance wars with the Dutch. Gold to run the empire."

He was rummaging in the bookshelves, looking for something. He said, "They lost an eighth of it. One eighth of sixteen billion dollars in all, sank off Florida, Mr. Gower. There's a wreck every quarter mile between Key West and Miami."

Raleigh was captivated. He was barely distracted by the small explosion from the engine room. BOOMbuddabuddabudda-BOOMbudda . . ."

Professor Pete said, "Ah! The book!" He pulled out a fat volume and flipped pages. "They were terrible sailors," he said. "They would lumber north through the Keys, needing land as reference points. They weren't like the Norsemen, good with stars. They'd hit Hatteras and turn right, like a traffic light. I dream about them every night."

"I'm not Mr. Gower," Raleigh said.

"Eh?"

"Gower. You keep calling me that. My name's Fixx."

Professor Pete's hand paused above the book on his lap. "You're not the man from the *Herald*, the Sunday-magazine writer? My goodness. My goodness." Professor Pete jumped up. "Fixx!" he cried. "Bird Island!"

"That's me."

They went through the handshaking again, Pete's enthusiasm undiminished. "That's magnificent what you're doing, fighting Abel Quade. I'm on the committee myself, to save the island. Oh, I know I've been a bad citizen lately, missing meetings, but I've been raising money for my search. Temporary problem,

Mr. Fixx. I'm used to it. You'd think after thirty-two years I'd lose enthusiasm, *but I know she's there!*"

"Your ship."

"The *Nuevo Mundo*," Professor Pete breathed. "She was beautiful. Look at her." He brought the old volume close, put it on Raleigh's lap. Raleigh looked at a color painting of a ship, twin masts unfurled. A Spanish pikeman stood on deck, helmet gleaming. A sailor with a rag around his head peered west from a crow's nest.

"She was a tiny little thing, big as this trawler. The *Nuevo Mundo*," Pete said, chuckling with admiration, with delight. "The final step in the plan. The getaway ship, so to speak. Not a treasure ship, not a big galleon. A little supply boat. A dirty little *nao*, they called it. A scout. It was supposed to be loaded with food but it wasn't." Pete laughed reverentially. Back at the Keys map, he smoothed his palm over the little yellow swordfish above Antigua, over the western tip of Cuba, over Key West. He was trying to sense the wreck. Raleigh had the feeling Pete spent hours touching the map. He noticed some of the lines on it were worn, faded.

Pete cried, "He was a genius! *What do you want!*"

The skinny giant filled the hatch, shoulders touching the sides. Only his face and neck protruded into the office. Grease smeared the right cheek and one tip of the mustache.

Pete snapped, "Did you fix it?"

The giant, so belligerent upstairs, went shy in the professor's presence. He stared at the floor. He would not lift his eyes.

"Jake!" the professor demanded.

The man glanced at Raleigh, muttered, "What's he doing here?"

Pete crossed the five feet between himself and his crewman. He told the sailor, soothingly, "He's not looking for the *Nuevo*. How are we going to get out there if you don't do your work?"

"I fixed it. It was the cooling system."

61

"Then test it. I don't want it breaking down when we get out there again." After the man left with a last sullen glance at Raleigh, Pete shrugged. "My son's afraid someone will find her before we do. My son's the last one with me now, until I raise more money."

Raleigh stared at the door where Jake had disappeared. "He's your *son*?"

"He knows engines. A genius with engines," Pete bragged. "I brought him up here. He's got some rough edges but he's a good kid. He just gets nervous when I talk about the *Nuevo*." Pete gripped the desk. "But I have to talk about it. It's all I think about." He moved to the easy chair, leaned over it, started the caressing ritual with the underwater topographical maps. Raleigh looked over the beige background with blue and brown marks for ridges and valleys. Pete whispered, "It doesn't seem like I've been here thirty-two years. It seems like I've been here one year. One month."

The explosion came from the engine room again. "BOOM-buddabuddabudda. . . ."

Pete fell into the easy chair, next to an old file cabinet. "I was a teacher, at the University of Minnesota. Medieval Spain. It was a nice steady job. Tenure track. Security. I was married, had a little house. I'd been fascinated by Spain since I was a boy. The conquistadors." He clenched his fist. "Everything seemed possible in those days, in those books." He raised his head slightly, looking at a place Raleigh could not see. At that moment, the round glasses made him look younger.

"In the summers, I dragged my wife to Spain. We saw castles. Cervantes's house. Don Quixote, he was my hero. You know why? Because he was old when he started out, a nobody. Not a young strong buck with a sword. An average man, like me. I thought to live that kind of life, you had to be born in another age, but I was wrong. In Seville, I pored over the archives. Old letters. Ship manifests. Reports from the explorers and the rogues." He sat up. "That's how I found the Marquis d'Biza."

62

This time when Pete shoved a book close, Raleigh found himself looking at a Spanish nobleman. A confident-looking brown-haired man with a long nose and a neatly trimmed Van Dyke beard above a lace collar. A gold chain hung around his neck, but whatever it held had not been captured by the artist.

Pete's voice echoed slightly in the metallic room. "A loyal follower of Philip the Fourth, that was the Marquis, a trusted adviser. Philip sent him to Peru to oversee the mines." Pete's brow wrinkled in disgust. "Peru. Malaria. Indians. Heat. Mud. He went because he loved the king. But by leaving Castille, he opened himself up to his enemies. They turned Philip against him. The king stripped the family of its estates. When the news reached the Marquis, he couldn't believe it. Philip would never do such a thing, he thought."

Raleigh stirred uneasily. "He wrote about the robbery in the archives?"

"No, no, no, no, no. You have to piece it together." Pete poked his finger at the painting in the book. "See this man the way I saw him. Meet him as I did, across two hundred and fifty years, reading his intimate letters, letters the family gave up in 1932. Even they didn't understand the significance." Pete began to pace, driven by excitement. The engine noise smoothed a bit. Pete said, "Read the pleas from his family. And his replies, assurances that they must be mistaken. The king would never do what they were accusing. And later, his bitter tirades against his enemies but his certainty that Philip would know the truth when he heard it. Then the realization of betrayal, the cold rage. And finally a strange, *wait . . . here it is!*" Pete gestured Raleigh to the microfilm machine, to the huge looped letters again. He read out loud as he unscrolled the letter. " 'All will be well. I have arranged it.' "

Pete spun around. "What does he mean? It's not like him, bland assurances. He never exaggerated." The two men leaned close, staring at the handwriting. Pete said, "What had he 'arranged'? I'll tell you what. Six days after this letter was dated, the mule train loaded with gold from Peru was ambushed in the mountains. Pirates slaughtered the guards and made off with the entire amount. Ten million dollars!" Pete chuckled. "Did I say pirates? It wasn't pirates. *It was the Marquis!*"

"Only *he* had known the exact route. *He* had arranged for the location of the guards. He stole the fortune and brought it into Cartagena anyway. As supplies! The *Nuevo Mundo* was loaded down with the very gold the Marquis had stolen for his family. It's all in the letters if you know how to read them. This manifest is lies! *He* was in charge of supplying the fleet. *He* arranged for extra supply ships that year. *He* refused to ride on the comfortable galleon and insisted he go on the *Nuevo Mundo*, with his personal guards. No records from the British or French ever make mention of what happened to the stolen gold. No pirate chief ever claimed credit. *He* stole it. He loaded it. And he went to the bottom with it."

Raleigh frowned. "That's not a lot to go on for thirty-two years."

Pete grinned and tapped the side of his head. "Instinct. I studied him. I know him. He could have smelted the mint marks off in Europe and sold the gold on the black market. He never planned for the storm."

The two men faced each other in the arrow-shaped room. The lights were hotter suddenly. Pete was weaving a spell. Raleigh felt a light sheen of sweat on his forehead, and it wasn't only the temperature, it was history.

He said, "People say you're on a wild-goose chase."

"Good! Let them think that. Who wants competition." Pete seemed exhausted by the story but exhilarated. He had gone hoarse. "The storm," he said. "What a hurricane, even for the Caribbean. Two-hundred-mile-an-hour winds. The fleet had delayed leaving for Spain that year. They'd been held up by the Pacific contingent. They were arguing whether to go. Thirty-four ships, pathetic little things. The captain general of the fleet, he would make the choice. Go or wait. But if he waited, there would be no money in Castille. The wars with the Dutch would stop. The armies wouldn't be paid. Merchants would go broke. The king would go begging. The captain general would be responsible. Can't you see him standing on deck of his galleon, looking at the sky? It's warm. Does he suspect a hundred miles south the storm is coming? We'll never know. The fleet sails, the lead galleon, the *Capitana*, armed to repel attack. The *Altimiranta* at the rear, two thousand tons, rows of cannon on deck. The *navios*, Philip's floating fortresses, hundred-gun ships. The little *urcas*, the freighters. The *naos*, or scouts."

"And the *Nuevo Mundo*. And the Marquis d'Biza."

Professor Pete opened the little refrigerator, pulled a plastic water bottle, and drank deeply, his throat working. Pete wiped his mouth with his index finger. "Four days later, the sky gets hazy in the south, the first warning. The sailors' bones start to hurt. They see sharks following the fleet. Soon it's so dark, the lanterns are lit, even during the afternoon. They hear the rain coming. The wind is getting stronger, it's up to eighty miles an hour. It's driving them toward the Florida reefs." Raleigh heard the storm in his head, howling. Pete was inching toward him on the swivel chair, moving it with his feet. "The sailors are on their knees, praying. The first mainmast snaps, the galleons are losing their rudders. The hulls split open when the hurricane drives them onto the reefs and the sea pours in, past the shot and powder and gold in the rear of the ship. I've spent over four million dollars hunting for the *Nuevo Mundo*. I'm going to find it."

Professor Pete struck the map, once.

"It's here," he said.

Raleigh wiped his brow. "Boy, you convinced me. Where do I sign up?"

Pete laughed suddenly and the spell was broken. They were back on the shrimp trawler with bags of potatoes hanging overhead. "You come to one of my sessions sometime," Pete said. "We tape the presentations so when the investigators

65

come around like they always do, I can prove my pitch was legal. The dangers of investing and all that. Every Friday morning at Rey Del Mar. Now," he said, taking another Donald Duck orange juice out of the refrigerator and giving it to Raleigh. "I guess our man from the *Herald* is lost. Your turn. What can I do for you?"

Raleigh needed a few seconds before he could switch subjects. In his mind, he still saw sailors clinging to a beam, tossing in a stormy sea. He'd regularly interviewed friends of murdered people when he'd worked for the *News*, but it never got easier. "I'm sorry about Jay Salinger," he said. "I know you were close."

"Close?" Pete said. He waited, looking puzzled. "Jay Salinger? You're not here because of Bird Island?" Then his face changed, his eyes grew huge. "Now I know where I saw you," he said uneasily. "You were going onto his boat when I was coming out. You're the one the police took in."

Pete's glance flickered toward the door. The engine was still booming. Raleigh had seen this type of look before. You killed him, Professor Pete was thinking. Quickly, Raleigh said, "I'm writing a story about it." That was the lie he had decided on. "Freelancing for a New York paper. To earn a little extra."

"Making money so you can work on Bird Island," Pete said, looking slightly relieved.

"That's right."

"Well, I certainly understand that. Only I wasn't friends with Salinger. He was a sleazy little blackmailer, and a bad one at that."

"But he told me . . ."

Pete said, "There it is. *He told you.*"

"He was blackmailing you?"

"He was trying, but he had no style. Didn't he try with you, too? If he called you to his boat, he had something in mind, believe me, the little spider."

Raleigh looked around at the cheap broken furniture, the

meager fare on the paper plate, the water bottle while Pete saved more expensive juice for guests. "You don't exactly look like a target for blackmail," Raleigh said.

"No, but he tried anyway. I told you raising cash for treasure hunting is tricky. People have to trust you." He laughed. "After all, I've lost all their money for thirty-two years. That can make it difficult to get more. I sell points, Mr. Fixx. A thousand dollars a point. The investment makes you a partner for a year. If I find something during that time, the investors split it with me. If not, I start all over again the next year. That way, I keep a flow of capital coming in to run the boat." He went to the safe. Dialing, he kept talking. "I fly all over Florida to coin fairs. I buttonhole people in bars and invite them to the talks at Rey Del Mar. I'm shameless when it comes to raising capital for my search."

The safe opened. He rummaged inside.

"Four years ago, I had a little find. Not the *Nuevo* but a sister ship. The *Isabella*. Some silver bars. Some coins. Two million dollars' worth. Take a look."

The coin he placed in Raleigh's palm was thin and gold, irregularly shaped and gleaming under the bulbs. Raleigh felt a thrill when he saw the date—1634. In the shield in front, two lions reared, facing each other diagonally in the northwest and southeast corners of a coat of arms. The other two spaces were occupied by castles. A fleur-de-lis design surrounded the shield.

"This is what I show potential investors. You'll notice the coins weren't perfectly round, but the Spanish cared more for weight and the assayer's mark than appearance. Bogota was the only mint in the New World to turn these out. Beautiful coin, isn't it? Feel it. See how it shines."

A clear inscription on the other side read, DEI GRATIA REX HISPANIARVM.

"By the grace of God, King of Spain and the Indies," Pete

said. "It was in a little mahogany chest under two feet of sand." For the first time, the professor's lips pressed together in an expression of disapproval.

Raleigh remembered reading about the find two years ago. He was surprised the man who had located the treasure seemed so poor.

"Everyone laughs at you when you spend your life looking for treasure," Pete said, putting his feet up on the desk. "But the minute you find something, the same people try to take it away. Florida took us to court. So did Spain. The federal government tried to get the treasure for the Smithsonian. I fought them and won. Then my competitors said I never found the coins, I salted the wreck. That means I bought coins and planted them to fool investors. But I proved the find came from the *Isabella*, by the mint marks and date. And my books were in shape, Mr. Fixx. This trawler may be falling apart, and maybe we run on a shoestring, but I can account for every penny I raise. My records have been examined by everyone from the Justice Department to the Florida state police to Swiss accountants for Arab sheiks."

Raleigh said, "What about Salinger? I don't see how he fits."

Pete wrinkled his face in contempt. "Oh, he fits all right. I spent my share of the money from the wreck a long time ago, looking for the *Nuevo*. Salinger knew I needed money. He knew I meet with investors every week. He knew rich businessmen were coming down from Boston this week to hear the talk. He was going to dredge up the controversy from four years ago on his show, ask the old questions. Were my books *really* honest? *Did* I salt the wreck? Just tell the facts, create an impression, interview the investors to make sure they knew about it, drive them away."

"But if you didn't have any money, what did he want from you?"

Pete laughed. "Points, that's what. Permanent points. He figured sooner or later I might find something, and he was ready to wait until I did. He offered to use the show to raise money, to feature regular segments on treasure hunting. He threatened to keep driving away investors if I didn't go along with him."

"And you didn't do it."

Scornfully, Pete said, "I fought the Justice Department in the Supreme Court and won."

"Where were you when Salinger got killed?"

Raleigh asked this softly. Pete had been reaching for the water bottle but he stopped. His right brow went up. "Oh my, am I a suspect? How exciting. But I'm afraid to say I was on my way to Rey Del Mar, to meet two investors. I'll give you the names. I gave them to the police. I got three thousand dollars in pledges, too. Where were you when he was killed?"

"I was, er, alone in my car."

"There's an airtight alibi for you." But Pete was smiling. He glanced down at the paper plate with the half-eaten potato on it. He said, "Baked potatoes and fish, Mr. Fixx. Grouper. Swordfish. Shark's not bad. But the potatoes. I hate potatoes. You can mash them or bake them, whip them or fry them. In the end, they remain potatoes. Now tell me something before you go. What's the news on Bird Island? Have we found a way to stop Abel? Has Wheeze been giving you things you can use?"

"Wheeze?" Raleigh said innocently, through his surprise. "Who's Wheeze?"

"Your instincts are good, but he helps everyone," Pete said. "Sneaking around the island with that bushy beard of his. Whenever there's going to be a visit from the Feds he finds out about it somehow, calls up and tells me. Not that I do anything different." Pete pulled a sheet of paper from a drawer in the desk. It was the same Xerox copy of the proposed condominiums on Bird Island that Wheeze had given Raleigh. Pete said, "He's a lot healthier than he used to be. The longer he stays away from that institution, the better he is."

69

"What institution?" Raleigh said. He added, "Who's this Wheeze, anyway?"

"I think it was called Happy Valley. Or Valley of Peace. A sanitarium. Didn't he tell you? He always gets around to it sooner or later. Five years, Mr. Fixx. He thought he was an alien."

Raleigh said, hopefully, "Someone from another country."

"No, someone from Neptune. Neptune, I think it was. A spy from Neptune."

"Well," Raleigh said, "whoever he is, I'm glad he's better." But Pete had the glazed look on his face again. He was standing gazing at the map of the Keys, as if it were three-dimensional, the real thing, as if it were a long stretch of ocean with islands on it, with clouds. There was a small golden sailfish leaping on the bottom of the map. It was the kind of map fifth graders take from *National Geographic* and hang on bedroom walls. The kind of map children look at each night before they go to sleep.

"I've been searching to the south," he said. "But it's north, north. I had a dream last night. That's how the atom got deciphered, from a dream. I believe in these things. Unconscious thinking."

Pete sat at the microfilm machine. He flicked it on. It hummed.

"North," he said, gazing at the writings as Raleigh said goodbye.

Outside, Raleigh was surprised to be in the twentieth century. The diving boat had gone. A middle-aged man in a seersucker jacket and gray slacks was ambling down the pier. He carried a pocket-sized Sony tape recorder. He peered up at the name of the boat.

"You're Gower, right?" Raleigh said.

The reporter seemed moody and wanting to talk. "This place looks so beautiful. The girls. I wish . . ." He trailed off. Raleigh could smell the city room on him, a big room with no windows

70

and lots of ink, a room filled with people in a rush to find out what other people were doing.

"Imagine," Gower said wistfully. "A real live guy actually making his living finding treasure, not slaving in an office. I'm here for two days. Then back to the grindstone. This place is, it looks like . . ."

Wearily, Raleigh said, "Don't tell me. Let me guess. It's the greatest place in the world."

FIVE

Nan Grant never leaves her house, Wheeze had said. Quade did something terrible to her.

Raleigh stood in front of a small pink Bahama-style home on Drake Street. A banyan pushed up chunks of sidewalk in front of the torn picket fence. Peeling shutters covered all the windows, even on a sunny day. Raleigh pressed his finger against the buzzer a long time.

After a few minutes, he heard footsteps inside the house. A woman's voice cried, close by on the other side of the door, "Go away!"

Raleigh spoke calmly, patiently. "My name is Raleigh Fixx. I'm writing a book about Bird Island."

The voice's pitch rose. "Nan isn't here!"

There was a swing on the porch, with dead leaves on it. "Can I leave a message?"

"She doesn't want messages. I don't know where to reach her."

Out on the street, two boys with coon tails on the back of their bicycles cruised beneath the geiger trees, eyeing Raleigh's Mustang.

Raleigh said, "How about if I leave a message anyway, just in case."

A moan came from the other side of the door. Raleigh wondered how groceries got delivered here. Were they left on the porch?

Raleigh softened his voice. "Listen, I have a girlfriend who's been threatened. I don't want anything to happen to her. I know Abel went after people who tried to stop his condo." Raleigh thought he heard a whimper inside. He said, "I'll phone if you want. You don't have to open the door. What's your number? Or we can talk through the door."

No answer. He said, "I'll push my address and number through the slot. Write me a letter. My name is Fixx."

The mail slot wouldn't open. He tried to slide the paper under the door but the slit was blocked. A girl with towels stuffed under doors, he thought.

He imagined he could hear her heart roaring two inches away.

"I'm leaving my address and phone number on the porch, under the conch shell. If there's a back door, I'll put another one there, under a rock. Write me. Call me."

"I'm not Nan. Nan isn't here! Nan isn't here! Nan isn't here!"

He still had an hour before his appointment with Abel Quade. The managing editor of the Key Rey *Sunfish* was a thin, balding man with a black leather vest and a gold coin around his neck. Raleigh found him in an upstairs office in the two-story shore-side cottage the paper used as headquarters. "Raleigh Fixx, the author?" Ike White said. "I was going to send someone to interview you. But with only two reporters it takes time to get around to things."

With a light flourish, White deposited the story he'd been editing beside his big standard typewriter on his old wooden desk. A poster of the Golden Gate Bridge decorated one wall of the office, near a psychedelic Big Brother and the Holding Company poster from San Francisco's Avalon Ballroom.

"Did you see me last night?" White asked coyly. "At the costume fest?" He glanced at Raleigh's crotch. "I wore a black body suit, a black boa, and hip-high boots." He added breathily, "I looked like some kind of *Nazi*."

"I missed the parade. Sorry."

White looked disappointed. "How can you move here and not go to costume fest? It's the spirit of Key Rey." He smiled again. "Know what I'm going as next year?" White struck a dramatic pose, chin in profile. "Nemo, King of Atlantis."

The editor's good humor faded when Raleigh brought up Bird Island. "Maybe you know I've been looking into Abel Quade, his business practices. I was hoping you wouldn't mind talking about your accident."

White's languid pose stiffened. He shifted his seat closer to the desk, an unconscious protective move. The brightness left his eyes.

"I was on my Honda, on Conch Boulevard. Doing thirty, thirty-five at sunset." Raleigh envisioned the deserted stretch between sea and swamp near Salinger's houseboat. White lost a little color. "I was on my way to the committee meeting, at Nan Grant's. We'd been collecting petitions against Rey Del Mar. A pickup truck swung out of the swamp, in front of me. I remember the bumper sticker. NEVER MIND THE DOG, WATCH OUT FOR THE OWNER." White blew out a long breath. "There were two men inside, giving me the finger, you know, yelling. I couldn't hear what. Then the truck swerved and hit me and I went into the swamp. The bike pinned me. I was in water and I could only breathe through my nose. I'd landed on a broken-off mangrove root, like a stake."

"Sounds painful."

White stood up and limped up and down beside the desk to show what had happened to him. Raleigh noticed a pair of toy handcuffs on the windowsill behind him. White joked,

74

"See Long John Silver at the Playhouse. The sixteenth to the twenty-first."

"Who drove the truck?"

White shrugged, massaged his leg, and sat down in a way that showed the injury still hurt. "There was mud on the plates. The police . . ." He frowned. "Quade pays the police. And you'll never find any of this stuff in the newsclips, either. The publisher's a coconut."

"So how do you know Quade was behind the attack? Maybe it was an accident."

White smiled bitterly. "Well, that's the right question, isn't it? Car accidents. Phone threats. I wasn't the only one who had problems." From outside, Raleigh heard the muffled electric echo of the Sharkmobile Tour going by. "This is our local rag," the announcer was saying. "Maybe you saw our editor, Ike White, win second place at costume fest last night." White was still rubbing his thigh. "Nobody ever found out what happened to Nan Grant. The second the condo went through, all the threats stopped."

White reached for the article he'd been editing when Raleigh had come in. "It's on where to buy funny hats. With wings and cute sayings. I have one that says CAPTAIN NOVOCAINE. Real journalism." Bending over the article, he said, "You don't drive a motorcycle, do you?"

Raleigh asked one last question. "Why'd you stay in Key Rey?"

White looked up as if the inquiry was odd. In White's "in" basket, Raleigh saw an invitation sticking out from beneath a purple envelope. *Ocean Front Bash* were the only visible words.

"It's fun," White said. "It's the greatest. You just have to know its limitations. Stay away from Abel Quade."

It was like walking into a trailer house and finding the Palace of Versailles attached outback. From outside, Abel Quade's home had looked like a small shingle ranch. With a neat tiny lawn. Blooming rosebushes. A late model Chevy pickup in the driveway, construction beams sticking out back.

Inside, Raleigh followed a secretary in a miniskirt, through the longest hallway he'd ever seen, past what had to be the seventh bedroom. Each was so different from the previous room, it might have been in another house. The second living room had featured zebra-stripe wallpaper, ceramic lions on shelves, and velvet images of Zulu warriors meeting the Pope. The third was filled with expensive antique French Renaissance furniture, beneath a crystal chandelier and an oil of Marie Antoinette. Raleigh mentally assigned nicknames. The Shaker room, the Civil War room. There was even a video arcade, a glassed-in area filled with laughing teenagers and electronic games. After he passed, he still heard video gunshot noises, whooping spaceships, bells.

Who decorated this place, Raleigh thought. Sybil?

"Abel's in the garden," the secretary said with a South Florida accent. "He don't like confined spaces." The thick carpet muted her four-inch heels. The rest of the house appeared to be empty, and the secretary finally twitched into the last room, a glassed-in patio dining room with a flagstone floor and a silver rolling bar by a long glass table. She slid the picture window aside. Hot air hit him as he stepped into the walk-in courtyard. The garden was alive with birdcalls—"tchuk tchuk tchuk," "garooooooooo," "wippah wippah." The house was an addition to an old fort or prison, he saw. Forty feet off, through the riot of palms, vines, and flowers, he glimpsed the partially crumpled brick outer walls of Quade's domain, with l-shaped musket slits and round towers at the corners, for defense. The secretary led him toward a second, smaller horseshoe-shaped wall in the center of the garden, which Raleigh guessed enclosed a patio. They passed wild fig trees wrapped in vines, macarangas dripping with moss, riots of moth and crimson orchids, shrimp plants, peach angels, fire gingers, and ten-foot-high ferns.

Garoooooooo.

He didn't see any birds.

What he did see, standing in shadows around the garden, were men. A tall man in tight jeans and a T-shirt reading KISS MY BASS leaned against a wall, watching. A heavier man petted a Persian cat on the brick walkway, not getting out of Raleigh's way. "Beautiful Anna," the man kept saying. "Furry Anna."

Raleigh was reminded of New York City Hall. Guys standing around who looked like they weren't working. Guys paid to hang out with more powerful guys.

The outdoor inner sanctum was a tinier courtyard inside the horseshoe-shaped wall. The shadows grew cool in here. There was a sweet smell from wild fig trees and Senegalese mahoganys. Abel Quade was getting up from a lounge chair flanked by two wooden folding tables, one piled with folders and reports, one supporting two pitchers filled with fruity-looking drink, an ice bucket, glasses. All that was missing was a pool.

Quade's blue eyes twinkled behind steel-rimmed bifocals. A child's homemade pencil holder—an orange juice can wrapped with paper, and fingerpainting—pinned down the folders.

"Mister Fixx," Quade said delightedly, pulling *The Mayor's Murderer* from beneath a manila folder on the table. It was not the voice that had threatened Diane. "Your book kept me from work last night," Quade chastised with a smile. Close up, he looked fit in a compact way. A freshly laundered red and white striped shirt fell loosely over the hip of his cotton slacks. "Would it be too much trouble to write a couple words inside the flap? 'To Abel Quade, my good buddy.' " Raleigh looked up sharply. Salinger had said that. Quade said, "Mrs. Q loves true-crime stories." Crime was pronounced *crahme*.

"Where are the birds?" Raleigh said through the racket, looking around.

"Mrs. Q's scared of 'em. It's a tape."

Quade waved for Raleigh to occupy the other lounge chair.

He said, "Imagine, a mayor paying someone to murder his wife's lover. And the way you discovered it. I just about split my stitches from my appendicitis operation, laughing."

Raleigh had to admit it had been an odd story. One winter, Frank had assigned him to cover a swinging singles weekend at the Crystal Hotel near La Guardia Airport. "I envy you," Frank had said. "I went to one of those for the paper in sixty-eight. Ten thousand singles came. You'd think girls that beautiful could get dates. I barely got out of my room, if you know what I mean. Dream assignment, you devil."

"Nobody goes to swinging singles weekends anymore," Raleigh had protested. "Nobody *is* a swinging single anymore."

"Trust me."

Arriving at the Crystal Hotel on Friday evening, Raleigh had pretended to ignore the sneering of the desk clerk when he asked for the "Swingles Weekend Package."

"Sir, you are going to have a terrific time," smirked the clerk. "Dancing. Fine cuisine. Last time we sponsored this, some marriages resulted."

"How many people checked in so far?" Raleigh had asked.

"Rock 'n' roll, sir," the clerk had continued, bending to write on the check-in form when he felt a chuckle coming on. "We're going to feature a well-known band Saturday night. I can't *promise* this, but it might be the Beach Boys, sir."

"How many?"

"On Sunday," the clerk had said, taking Raleigh's credit card, "a special brunch for members of the group. Free Bloody Marys."

Raleigh had sighed. "Just tell me how many people have checked in so far."

"So far, weeeelllll, it's early, and I just got back from a break."

At 11:30, Raleigh had phoned Frank in Connecticut, interrupting a dinner party for the taxi commissioner. "Let me go home. There are fourteen guys here, that's it. Perverts, Frank. It's worse than the Great Neck school board. Someone's explaining how to expose yourself on the subway and jump off at stops."

"Be patient. I'm missing the cherries jubilee."

"Yeah? *I'm* watching a Tarzan movie in my room. Does that sound like a great weekend to you? The only swinging single in sight is a chimpanzee going from tree to tree."

Frank had soothed him. "When I was there, the best girls didn't show up until Saturday night. You've been monogamous too long. Hang out with the guys."

Midnight had found the guys in the hotel bar, trying to pick up cocktail waitresses with puffballs on their body suits. The Riverdale computer analyst had come up with an idea. "Let's walk through the halls, we'll listen for parties. There's got to be horny girls all over a hotel like this. I read about it in *How to Meet Terrific Girls*. Beautiful stewardesses, from all over the world."

"From Thailand?" asked the shortest member of the group, the Islip, Long Island tax lawyer. "I gave up Forty-second Street for this."

"Thailand . . . Paris . . ."

"Party hardy, men," had cried the second-grade teacher from Brooklyn Heights.

Half an hour later, the group was wandering along the eleventh floor, Raleigh hanging back while the others listened at rooms. Suddenly, 1122 had swung open. "Murder!" the blonde in the orange chiffon nightgown had cried, running into the hall. She'd grabbed Raleigh. "They killed him! Oh God! My husband!"

What she'd meant, it turned out, was that her husband had hired killers to murder her lover. Bleeding on the suite-sized bed, dead from silenced gunshot wounds, the victim was immediately recognizable to Raleigh. It was Nathan Bauman, eccentric Broadway playwright, author of the controversial and futuristic *Rabbis of Mars*, currently drawing big crowds at the

Minskoff Theater, with its depiction of a war between Lubovovitch and Satmar Hasidic spacemen.

By the time Raleigh finished questioning the mayor's wife, he had his prizewinning story of how the mayor of Allio, New Jersey, had slowly turned the town over to the Mafia over the last five years, in exchange for their services.

Quade gestured at the pitchers. "Punch, Mr. Fixx? With or without bourbon?"

The developer poured Raleigh a tall glass. Outside the patio, in the main garden, Raleigh noticed a heavy man in a powder blue leisure suit, and a tall man in print shorts and a Hawaiian shirt, talking. "You like the house?" Quade asked, settling into his seat. "Mrs. Q went to Washington a couple of years ago. She got back, she said, 'Poppa, they got *theme* rooms there. Blue room. Lincoln room.'" Quade held up his hands, which were calloused and powerful-looking. "The missus wants it, I do it. Long as I have building, I'm a happy man."

"It's very unique," Raleigh said.

"Thank you very much. But this," he said, sweeping his arms to encompass the lush, stunning garden outside, "is my pride." He lay back, pointing at trees. "Eugenia. Christmas palm. Silver buttonwood." With the vines and creepers wrapping the trunks, the fort walls resembled a half-buried Cambodian temple in the jungle. "The Spanish built this place three hundred years ago. Pirates. English. Everyone wanted a piece of those treasure fleets. I'll show you around. Look at those ox tongues," Quade said when they were walking, indicating purplish shoots curling out of a planter set into a royal poinciana palm. "They really look like an animal's down there, under the ground, strangling. I hate offices. Give me the outdoors. Look at those gun slits."

Raleigh noticed the tip of a cabin cruiser's antennae poking over the wall. He smelled the fresh sea smell. Private dock.

He said to Quade, pausing by a skinny date palm, "It's funny. The same man who wants to rip up Bird Island, having a garden like this."

Quade pulled a thin cheroot from his breast pocket and lit up with a plain plastic lighter. The smoke balled out, casting a sweet aromatic smell. Two gardeners in overalls crouched over shrubs, tilting red plastic watering cans, and Raleigh heard a pleasant tinkling sound from water dropping from pool to pool in a Japanese rock garden.

"I can call you Raleigh, right?" Quade said. "Where did you live before this? Mind if I ask? Manhattan?"

"That's right."

Puffing, Quade started walking. He was moving across the brick circular walkways, making a straight line toward the outer wall. The man in the leisure suit and the man in the flower shirt always seemed to be nearby when Raleigh looked, and they were usually gazing in another direction, seemingly disinterested. Quade said, "You do a lot of environmental work up there? Spend your Sundays cleaning up Central Park?"

Raleigh didn't say anything. Quade said, "Funny how I knew that." They reached an iron gate, which Quade swung open. The vista opened up, the sea. There was a four-foot-wide concrete walkway abutting the outside of the fort wall, extending into the bay. "People live like pigs up there. Then they come here to convert us barbarians. Why is it that the ones who always screw up the most move to Key Rey?"

"You're doing a pretty good job changing subjects," Raleigh said. "You sure like a lot of sugar in this punch."

"Rots the roots. But I love it. You know, I was wondering when you were going to get around to coming to see me. Checking records, the way you've been doing. Interviewing people. Calls to Tampa. Calls to Washington. Why, even looking up on my little campaign contribution to our fine congressman. You're a one-man detective agency, Mr. Fixx. But I admire hard work." They were walking down a long dock. The cabin cruiser was a sixty-footer, with deep-sea fishing rods in place in back, reels gleaming, and a deckhand in cutoffs and a T-shirt watched them approach.

81

Quade said, "I don't mind any of it, 'cause I got nothing to hide. Like our good President Nixon said. I am not a crook. You want to know how I feel about something? Ask me. Bird Island? Nobody goes out there, Mr. Fixx. Couple of people every couple of weeks. What's going to happen out there is what happened to Miami and Key West, and everyplace else in Florida. That island is going to have homes on it in five years. The only question is, who's going to build them? Some kick-ass New Yorker who lives on Madison Avenue and never even visits here? Or a local man who's got the community on his mind? And friends to do the work. Who can provide jobs to the poor underpriviledged coconuts. Why do you think they call us coconuts, Mr. Fixx? Is my head shaped like a coconut? Or maybe they think when you crack it open, milk runs out instead of brains."

"Changing subjects again," Raleigh said dryly.

Quade had never altered his friendly, modulated tone. The sun glistened on the water. "You a fisherman, Mr. Fixx? I like to get those marlin. I like when you hook 'em and they swim all the way down and they hang there like this." Quade lowered his head into his shoulders. He extended his elbows like pectoral fins, parallel to the bottom to resist a pull from above. "Maybe we ought to go out sometime. The Cuba tournament's coming up." Raleigh noticed the man in the leisure suit and the man in the shorts sauntering up the dock toward the boat. Quade led Raleigh onto the deck, made of polished teak. Lots of brass instruments hung on walls. He said, going to the harbor side and putting his foot up on the railing, "I don't want to give the wrong idea. I like outsiders. They made me rich, and I like people like that. I bankrolled Johnny Coetzee's sound studio. I give five thousand a year to Professor Pete; he's an outsider, and son, that's charity, not investment. I must have sunk a hundred grand into that hole in the last fifteen years."

"I never had that kind of money," Raleigh said, "so maybe

this will sound like a funny question to you. But what do you need more for? Why don't you leave that place alone?"

Quade laughed softly. He picked at a bit of cheroot wrapper lodged betwen his front teeth. He called to the man in cutoffs, "Start 'er up, Charlie. We'll run around the harbor."

He said, as the engine coughed to life, "Being rich is like being old. Everyone expects you to stop doing things. Play golf. Hire servants." Behind them, Raleigh noticed the man in the leisure suit and the man in shorts had reached the boat. They were bending by the bow and stern lines, unwrapping them from the pilings. Quade said, "But what if you enjoy your business? Do you have to stop because you're good at it? I own the Rey Del Mar and the Swordfish Saloon and the Chevrolet dealership. I own half of Morgan Street. And that's just on this island. But of course you know that because you've spent so much time at the records at City Hall. That spy, whatever his name is. Wheeze. I could lie to you and tell you with this house I keep adding to and this ocean liner here, I have payments to make. But I don't. I pay cash. You want to know the real reason I'm going to take over that island?"

The smile dropped from his face. The cheroot stub waved at Raleigh like a bobbing finger.

"Because people stopped me from doing it last time," Quade said.

Quade looked directly into Raleigh's eyes. "What do you say?" he said. "Spin around the harbor?" It seemed more like a threat than an offer.

"Sure. I love boats."

At a hand signal from Quade, the men with the tie lines stepped on deck. Raleigh figured this boat was one of the biggest private yachts he'd ever boarded. He'd been on the presidential yacht *Sequoia* once, and Quade's was bigger. It had to be big enough to get to Europe. Slowly, the yacht began edging away from the dock, slicing the turquoise water. Another sailor in cutoffs had joined the first on the bow.

Raleigh fell into one of two fish-fighting chairs in the back of the boat. He hooked his hands behind his neck. He closed his eyes and turned his face toward the sun.

In his mind, he kept hearing the girl who was afraid to come out of her house. Go away, she was saying.

Raleigh said, without opening his eyes, "Is this what you did with the people who tried to fight you on Rey Del Mar? Offer to take them fishing?"

"Well, you're thinking there's a little ego involved here," Quade's voice said, a foot away. "And I can see how you might believe that, but there's a great deal at stake. We're talking about how you keep your place in the world. Five years ago, I needed the money and I was blocked from buying that island. I don't like the little jokes that spring up about it. See all those men around here. They listen to me because they're afraid of me. If they stop being afraid of me, they'll stop listening. Then they'll stop working. I want my son to take over the business one day. I'm thinking about the future, Mr. Fixx."

Raleigh opened his eyes. He could see the octagon-shaped Spanish fort receding across the long stretch of water. The boat was heading for the mouth of the harbor, passing little charter boats that were anchored by the tarpon channel, in a cluster. Raleigh wondered how far the cannon in the fort had been able to fire, three hundred years ago.

"You got any juice or water?" he said. When Quade went to get it, he turned lazily and saw that the man in the leisure suit and the man in shorts were not on the aft deck. Maybe they'd gone below. He'd been hoping Salinger might come up naturally in the conversation, but that had not been the case. When Quade came back with frosted pineapple juice on ice, Raleigh said, "A couple of days ago, I went to visit a man named Jay Salinger."

Quade swatted at a fly. Everybody on the island knew what had happened to Salinger. Quade and Raleigh lounged, side by side in the fishing chair, like old buddies. Fifty feet to port, the gray coast guard drug patrol passed, the sailors in blue caps waving. Raleigh tried to see Abel's face. "He wanted to talk about you," he said.

"Never met the man, but no harm in talk, Mr. Fixx."

"He wanted to talk about Rey Del Mar. He told me about some people who'd opposed you on that. A couple of them had trouble."

"Oh, that motorcycle thing again. That's history. The police checked that out. It was an accident."

"An accident."

"The homo took some poppers and drove his motorcycle into the swamp. Read the report."

"And Nan Grant?" Raleigh said. The sunlight glinted off the edges of Quade's glasses. It was impossible to see his eyes.

"Graham?" Quade said, turning the name over. "I don't recall a Graham."

They reached the mouth of the harbor and swept through the pincer-shaped headlands, into the blue waters of the channel outside. A single cloud hung high up, in the dazzling sky.

"Salinger told me he had proof of what happened back then," Raleigh said.

He was gratified to see the smile leave Quade's mouth. The face turned toward him. He could feel the sun on the sea side of his face.

"Well, if he had proof, I'd think you'd be at the police station, and not talking to me," Quade said more coldly. "Yes, I'd think you'd be with the police, Mr. Fixx." He turned back to the sun. "I'm starting to think you're interested in another one of those murder books. Not in Bird Island at all." The pineapple juice was sweet and delicious, with bits of crushed fruit that oozed down his throat. He heard Quade's voice growing harder. "People have accused me of many things, Mr. Fixx, but this is the first time of murder." When Quade heated up, it was with a slow, rich burn.

The sun was blotted out. Quade was looking down at him.

"I invite you to my house. I take you out on my boat. I offer you my friendship. I killed him, is that what you're saying?"

"I'm asking."

"Well, who are you to come here asking questions, anyway? You're not the police." The boat went over a big wave and Quade gripped the rail behind him.

"Oh, you want to be friends," Raleigh said. "You invited me here to be a buddy. To tell me how you're going to murder a couple of thousand animals to get revenge against people you don't respect in the first place."

But Quade wasn't listening. "He had proof," Quade said, as if Raleigh had not spoken. "He's a goddamn liar if he said he had proof, because I had nothing to do with that business years ago. I'm not sure whether to throw you over the side and let you swim back to shore. You didn't see that proof, did you?"

Raleigh couldn't figure out whether he was acting. "No."

"You're goddamn right you didn't see it, because it doesn't exist. I didn't know Jay Salinger. I never met Jay Salinger. Murder. *Murder.* Mr. Fixx, enjoy the ride."

Quade spun on his heel and strode into the cabin. Raleigh sucked the last pineapple pulp out of the glass. He was still thirsty. The man in the leisure suit and the man wearing shorts climbed up to the deck. They strolled out of the cabin, toward Raleigh. The man in the leisure suit nestled into the chair Quade had occupied. He was wearing sunglasses now.

"Abel's mad," said the one in shorts.

He didn't sound like whoever had threatened Diane, either.

Raleigh turned his back on them, stepping up to the railing, and gazed out to sea. The boat was making a loop, heading away from the island, toward the open sea. The sun was hotter here. It burned the inside of his eyes. But the yacht kept turning until it was headed back toward the harbor. The man in shorts lit up a cigarette. Raleigh saw a sea turtle, swimming. They cruised back between the headlands, slowing as they passed pleasure boats. A girl on a windsurfer with bright stripes on her sail blew them a kiss.

The secretary took Raleigh back toward the long twisting hallway. On the way, he passed a heavy woman in a magenta-colored sun dress who he figured was Mrs. Quade. Outside, the man in the KISS MY BASS T-shirt leaned against the Mustang. Raleigh got five blocks from the house before he saw the police light spinning in the rearview mirror. There weren't any curbs of concrete to pull over to, just the sandy fringe of the road. The patrolman who pushed Raleigh up against the Mustang was bigger than last time. Raleigh's face almost brushed the hot hood of the car. He felt the heat singeing his nose. He could not see who was behind him, but he heard the slow rhythmic tap of boots coming closer.

"I warned you," Sezar's voice said. The patrolman gave Raleigh's arm an extra shove, driving it up toward his shoulder blades. The pain was increasing. Sezar sighed. "Why did I know you wouldn't listen," he said.

SIX

"How can I be in your way?" Raleigh forced out between gritted teeth. "You said Salinger was selling drugs. You said it had to do with Tampa."

The cop behind him twisted his arm higher, bent him almost parallel to the hood. His face, reflected in the shiny simonized Mustang, looked distorted—the eye huge, the nose going on for yards out of his tiny peach-shaped head.

Heat drifted up off blue steel.

From close behind, Sezar used a soft, chiding tone, almost an affectionate singsong. "Obstructing justice, Raleigh. Interfering with an officer in the performance of his duty."

"Look, I can talk to people if I want to. There's no law I'm breaking."

Boots clicked on pavement as if Sezar was pacing around back there.

"That's a very interesting argument," the detective said. "I even think a judge might consider it. Well, maybe not a Key Rey judge. *After* we book you. After you spend some time in a cell." Sezar yawned. "The arraignment. Hiring an attorney.

I have a friend I can recommend. Is that the way you want to do this? We can do it that way if you want."

"Which way does Uncle Abel want it?"

He was shoved lower. His knees slammed into the car. The handcuffs jangled on the cop's belt behind him. Turning his face to keep it off the hood, Raleigh had a truncated view of a quiet Key Rey street. A bit of asphalt, shimmering and elongated, the sandy edge of road shoulder, a slice of lime-green saw grass that managed to flourish in the loose Florida earth. And now a little blonde girl stepped into the frame, licking blue ices as she came right up to the car.

The policeman gripping Raleigh's arm told Sezar, "No power for a big guy."

"Come around the house some night without your uniform," Raleigh said. "Anytime."

The cop pushed Raleigh's cheek onto the hood. His vision blanked from the heat; sweat poured from his face.

Good-naturedly, Sezar's voice warned, "Lester," and the force eased slightly. Raleigh pulled his face away. His eyes watered from pain. As his vision cleared, he tried to ignore the burning by concentrating on the little girl. She looked about six, with an apricot-colored plastic beret and matching sandals. Her white T-shirt read SWIM WITH THE PORPOISES.

Her enormous blue eyes matched the ices.

"Hi, Uncle Julius," she said. "Is that the murderer?"

Dungarees moved into view a few inches away, and the lower half of a paisley pearl-buttoned shirt. Sezar's belt buckle was a brass oval with a cowboy hanging on to a bucking bronco. "Sarah Jean, you little cat," the detective said delightedly. "Where'd you come from?"

The other cop said, "Sarah Jean, your daddy go shrimping today?"

The girl bit off the top of the ices. Her lips were blue. "You gonna beat him up?" she said.

"Julius Sezar?" Raleigh said in disbelief.

There was an odd comfort in recognition. Raleigh was treated to a full view of the detective's face, six inches away. The inverted V-shaped mustache, the sideburns, and diamond irises. The slight redness of the skin, patchy from broken blood vessels, from drinking, not uniform like a tan.

"I had trouble with that name in school," Sezar said.

"I bet you were a big hit in the Marines, in the brig," Raleigh said. His cheek throbbed where it had been pressed into the hood.

Sezar straightened back out of sight. Raleigh envisioned cold water running out of a tap, into a glass. Sezar said, "You know why Julius Caesar was a great man? Everybody knows about the big things, but it was the day-to-day decisions that made him memorable. He cleaned shit off the streets in ancient Rome. Not personally, but he drew up plans." There was a white ranch house in the distance, across a lawn. Sezar poked Raleigh's shoulder. "That's what I do. Clean shit off streets."

The girl inched closer, licking faster because the ice was melting onto her hand. "You know what my Daddy says you should do with the murderer? My Daddy says you should chop his cock off. Uncle Julius, isn't a cock a chicken?"

The uniformed cop guffawed. Since nobody was addressing the question, Raleigh told the girl, "I'm not the murderer."

"My daddy says you should whip criminals," she told Raleigh. "My daddy says you should throw them into the Gulf for sharks."

"That's an enlightened point of view, Sarah Jean," Sezar's voice said.

Then the detective's face was back, but the smile had disappeared. "I don't want to find out you been there first. I don't want to learn you snuck around after. I don't want to hear your name when I'm on the job, and I'm always on the job. Am I making myself clear? Maybe those New York cops let writers run all over their investigations, but not here."

The girl tugged at Sezar's belt, leaving a dot of smeared blue. "What will you do to him if he doesn't *have* a chicken?"

"Lester, you let him up a few inches, a little breathing space."

Sezar laid a hand on his shoulder. "You have to trust me, Raleigh." More people were gathering on the shoulder of the road, watching. A man in a tight bathing suit leaned against a hand-powered lawn mower. A fat woman in a grapefruit-yellow sunsuit held an aluminum sun reflector against her thigh. Two gay men came up the road, hands entwined.

Sezar said, "Next time, we won't be so gentle." He went singsong. "Drill time, troopers. Are we going to get in Sezar's way?"

The arm was jerked up. "For Christ's sake," Raleigh said.

"I didn't hear that. I didn't hear what you said." Sezar was putting on a show for the neighborhood. They were probably all his cousins and aunts, Raleigh thought. He was far enough away from the hood so that he had a clear view of Sezar now, hands on hips, head tilted slightly. Raleigh had not noticed the mole on the right side of the mouth before. And the tiny black hair growing out of it.

Sezar, the ex-Marine sergeant, crooned, "I caaaaan't heeear youuuuuu."

Raleigh forced a smile. "Hearing aids can help," he said. "They're small. People hardly notice them."

."Bob Hope," Sezar said. "Chevy Chase." But he pulled away when static erupted from inside the car, from the police radio. The Chevrolet rocked when he got inside. Raleigh could not make out the dispatcher's words but he heard Sezar say, "Again?"

Sezar called out, "Lester, Cubans on Rey Beach! Two boats!"

To Raleigh, he said, through the open passenger-seat window, "Better put something on that cheek. You got a sunburn there."

They were gone as quickly as they had come. The shiny, olive unmarked car disappeared around the corner, lights flashing. Its bumper sticker said, ARMS CONTROL MEANS AIMING RIGHT.

Raleigh massaged his arm. It felt longer, stretched out. The girl, unfazed by Uncle Julius's departure, licked the bottom inch of Popsicle, and her hand between thumb and forefinger. The crowd had grown. There was a boy astride a one-speed bicycle, a tatoo of a dragon on his forearm, and a girl with big glasses carrying a 7-Eleven bag. Woods lined one side of the road, small houses the other. An angry-looking woman in a peach halter top stomped toward them across a lawn. "Sarah Jean!" she rapped out, reaching for the girl's wrist.

Raleigh picked the last bit of ices off the road after the girl dropped it. The crowd was dissipating. He got into the Mustang. When he touched his face, heat rolled off it. The ices felt cool against the burn.

Raleigh took his time walking around the outside of the house, checking strands of dental floss he'd wedged between doors and windows, and the jambs. Precautions felt melodramatic until he had a memory of a man in a Santa Claus suit charging out of his bedroom closet in New York, butcher knife held high. "The Christmas Murders" had been a successful series in the *News*.

Everything was in place. Inside, he took a cold Carling Black Label can and half a salami and cheese sandwich from the refrigerator. He hadn't eaten since breakfast and he was hungry. He took the snack to his writing table. The ceiling fan was on, so was a desktop one beside the computer. A small rubber suction cup was attached to the telephone receiver on the desk. A wire ran from the cup to a Sony tape recorder. He left the machine off when he dialed the Customs House. Wheeze answered on the first ring.

"I need a favor," Raleigh said. "A name. Nina something. She called Salinger when I was there. Do you know her?"

He pressed the can against the cheek. The cold numbed the

throbbing. An Audubon poster of a great blue heron hung above the computer. The heron's head was turned so only one eye was visible. It seemed to follow Raleigh when he moved.

Wheeze snapped, "Go to the store yourself, Lucy! I'm busy!"

"There's people there? Whisper it."

Wheeze shouted, "Cupcakes give you cancer, man!"

Raleigh envisioned Wheeze in his work clothes, brown pressed slacks and faded, crumpled maroon tie. He would be at a wooden desk behind a long steel counter. Raleigh leaned back in the chair, tipped it back. "I won't call you there anymore after this. Come on. It's important."

Wheeze whispered, "Esterhoff." Then he said, "It's not my problem!" Then he hung up.

The beer tasted icy and refreshing. Raleigh snapped his Royal Highland bagpipe cassette into the stereo and turned the volume low. The swelling music began. For some reason, the orchestra was playing "Moonlight in Vermont." By the time Raleigh returned from the kitchen with the telephone directory, the phone was ringing. He pressed the Record button on the Sony. Casually, he said, "Hello."

"Hi, Tonto," Diane said. "They installed a phone in First Class. Can you hear me?"

"Where are you?"

"Sunny, fun-filled Yugoslavia. Some kind of Atlantic City hotel owners' tour on board. Lots of bald drunk guys with silk shirts and pinky rings. Hold on. A passenger's coming."

Raleigh switched off the recorder. He made out a man's voice over the line, slightly fainter than Diane's. "Hi, Diane," the man said.

"Can I help you, sir?" Raleigh rewound the tape.

"Yeah." The man flirted. "You can help me. You? Me? Dubrovnik? Dinner? Tonight?"

"No thanks."

"No *thanks*?" There was a shocked pause. Then, milder, "Well, um, can I have a Coke?"

She was back an instant later. "I finished the play," she said. "From a dream last night. Coco gives birth to little Charles. It's in a cottage with a fire going and snow outside. There's a midwife in the room." Diane was getting emotional. She made her voice resonant. "I predict this child will be the president of France," she said.

"A midwife?"

"I'm sending the play to New York, with the copilot. His uncle is a producer, the Italian producer, Dino Rosco."

Raleigh said, feigning more casualness, "When are you coming home?"

"I couldn't switch routes, so you're stuck with me earlier. In two days." She went coy. "My aching body." A moment later she said, "You don't sound too excited about it."

"No, I'm excited. But couldn't you switch with Roslyn? Or Matt? Matt always likes to switch."

There was a pause. The heron seemed to stare at him. "What's the matter there?" she demanded.

"Nothing. Work. Two Department of Interior guys are here from Washington. They might hold up the sale of the island. Isn't that great?"

"It's the phone call you got before I left, isn't it? It's Salinger."

Raleigh hoped he sounded sincere. "That was just Wheeze that time. I'm telling you. It's work."

A faint dinging noise came over the line. And a baritone voice said, "Please fasten your seat belts. We've got turbulence coming up."

"I'm not waiting two days," Diane snapped. "I couldn't switch to a later trip but I can come earlier. Tomorrow."

"That's blackmail!"

Raleigh took the top off the sandwich. It needed mustard. "Terrific," Diane said. "I tell my lover I'm coming home early. 'Blackmail,' he says."

Raleigh cursed under his breath. "All right, but if I tell you what's going on, you have to promise something. You have to promise not to come back until Tuesday."

"I promise."

Raleigh told her.

"I'm coming now," she said, and hung up.

Raleigh stared at the buzzing receiver. Great, he thought. On the desk, he looked over the document Wheeze had given him, the Department of Interior recommendation that Bird Island be privatized. Atlanta Office, read the letterhead. And the signature, "Mark Politowsky."

Raleigh took the number from the paper and dialed. The operator at the Department of Interior office didn't know any Politowsky, neither did the personnel office. He tried again, calling from scratch, just to be sure. This time, an older-sounding man answered. "Mark? Sure? He retired. You can reach him at his retirement home."

"Where's that?" Raleigh said.

"Poland."

"Excuse me?"

"Look," the voice said. "The zloty goes a long way, I mean dollarwise. Lots of people are going back to the old country when they retire. You can live like a king on the pension. Mark's dad came from Warsaw."

"When's he coming back?"

"What for? You ever eat tripe soup, the good stuff?"

Raleigh hung up. Thought a minute. Wondered how much Politowsky had taken out of the bank. He smiled, checked his Rolodex, and tried a number in Washington, D.C. He went through more voices and finally reached one with a thick Bronx accent. "IRS. Munoz."

Raleigh made his voice jovial. "It's me, Jesse. Here's that chance to do the favor you owe me."

"Is it illegal?" the voice said.

"Absolutely," Raleigh said.

"Then fuck you," the voice said, and hung up.

Why is it, Raleigh wondered, pulling the Mustang to the curb, that everyone involved in this murder lives on Drake or Morgan Street. It was a cool tropical night. The three-quarter moon rose over the geiger trees beside Nina Esterhoff's house, an out-of-place Cape Cod with a steeply pitched roof and an overextended porch out front. The shutters were open, but the only light shone from behind the drawn downstairs curtain. Three women's bicycles leaned against the side of the porch. An old red pickup, a Firebird with a racing stripe, and a battered yellow Escort were parked outside.

Nina lived half a mile from the main strip. The music and traffic hum from downtown formed the bare edge of noise on Raleigh's consciousness. A reddish glow lit the sky to the north, beyond fireflies blinking in the palms and geigers.

A stunningly beautiful blonde answered the door in a green muumuu that showed her long tanned arms. She was even better looking in person than she'd been in Salinger's photograph, and Raleigh realized he'd seen her in town, riding her bicycle. And in the Coetzee Rocks 'n' Socks store, selling T-shirts, Hawaiian-print bathing suits, and wraparound sunglasses to tourists. Long hair cascaded down her back. She was a tiny girl. The big muumuu had large rust-colored orchids printed on it.

"You're Raleigh, right? Wheeze said you'd call." The voice was gentle, a surprise after the angry crying Raleigh had heard on Salinger's answering machine. A cat bolted up the stairs as she led him along a narrow hallway lined with photographs he could not make out in the dim light. The house smelled of mint. The hallway opened up on the right into a living room. He saw four or five women looking back at him. A bony woman with her black hair in a high ponytail sat curled on the velvet couch, lips tight and mouth turned down. Two women with identical cropped dyed red haircuts, faded dungarees, and work boots sprawled across oval throw rugs on the wooden floor. He recognized a tall strawberry blonde in a peasant dress as the midnight-to-three bartender at La Margarita. The diving instructor from the shrimp pier waved at him with a hand holding a smoldering cigarette. She lay on one hip at the foot of the couch, in faded denim cutoffs and a sleeveless maroon shirt.

"Our women's group meets every Wednesday," Nina said, folding down into a lotus position in the armchair, waving to indicate Raleigh should make himself comfortable. "Nobody minds if you sit in on the end of it." There was a snort from the frail-looking girl on the couch. Raleigh looked around the room. Lobster-trap table. Cinder-block—supported shelves filled with books and flower vases. Plastic glasses beside the women held dark liquid that might have been iced tea or rum or Coca-Cola.

A match flared as the diving instructor lit another cigarette, illuminating the bottom half of a Gauguin poster that showed nude South Sea island women braiding their hair.

Although the couch was empty beside the frail-looking woman, Raleigh chose the floor, like the others. He sat against the wall, four feet from Nina's left, halfway across the room from the spike-haired twins. Cut flowers decorated the room, in vases, in juice bottles, floating in a china bowl.

Nina was so small that her knees barely touched the arms of the chair. The lamp beside her was cast in the form of a devil. But on closer inspection, it seemed more cherubic, a Woolworth's devil. A little fat angel with horns and a grin.

Nina's voice pulled Raleigh back. "We were talking about guardian angels. You can join in if you want. Do you have one? Do you know him?"

By the curtain, Raleigh saw the outline of a plastic lawn flamingo, legs implanted in a flowerpot.

97

"What's a guardian angel?" he said.

The girl on the couch snorted again. "Everyone has one," she said. She looked at Nina as she spoke, not at Raleigh.

More kindly, the bartender from La Margarita said, "It's hard to get in touch with them. But they help you, guide you. They're spirits, roaming." She waved a hand vaguely, to encompass all the places spirits could roam. She had a flat *a* midwestern accent. Chicago or Iowa.

"My guardian angel is an Ethiopian pirate," she said. "He died fighting Roman slavers in Atlantis. He was brave."

Raleigh nodded. The spike-haired girl on the left said in a surprisingly sweet voice, "Mine are two Cheyenne Indians. They were lovers. The woman gave birth on horseback. She gives me stock tips."

"An ancient crone," the diving instructor volunteered, stubbing out the cigarette in an aluminum ashtray. "I saw a picture of her in a book, in a painting of the marketplace in Sumaria. She was talking to me." The diving instructor sat up slightly. "It was intense."

As the cat crept into the room, eyeing Raleigh every halfsecond, ready to bolt, another woman came into the room, smiled at him, and put one of the plastic glasses down beside Raleigh. It smelled like seaweed. He sipped. It was awful.

Nina was saying, "Feel your way back, Raleigh. Past being born. Close your eyes. Drift. I bet he's trying to reach you. My guardian warns me when things are wrong for me. I can feel her, here." Nina touched the back of her neck.

Raleigh closed his eyes. He heard the diving instructor say, "The thing I love about Key Rey is that people are really open to new experiences." A picture came into his mind. It was Frank eating a smoked chicken sandwich.

When he looked at the room again, the women were smiling with approval. "Well," Nina said, trying to console him, "few people make contact on the first try." She turned her attention back to the others. "We're pretty much finished except for the reading. Linda was about to read Sarah, Raleigh. That's how we end each week."

The cat wandered toward Raleigh, sniffed at his glass, and jerked away. It ran out of the room. "Persia's sensitive," Nina said. "Linda? Ready? Sarah? Raleigh?"

The diving instructor sat up straighter against the couch. She extended her legs in front of her, flat, like a nine-year-old. Her long hair brushed the floor. She held something silvery in her fist—Sarah's watch.

Raleigh glanced at the couch. The bony woman was absolutely still, staring at Linda. The already deep lines on her face were etched with tension.

Linda squeezed her eyes shut. She held the watch up to her breast. She said, in a whispery voice, "I see a castle." The others strained to hear. Linda added, "Like I saw in a movie once."

Her eyes opened and closed. "I see a garden. It was also in the movie."

There was a sob from the couch. Sarah leaned forward, her shoulders heaved violently. She fell back.

"I see a princess walking in the garden. The princess is carrying a little baby Jesus. She comes to a pond filled with lily pads. She was in the movie. So was the pond."

The sobbing started again. It grew worse.

"The pond is filled with pads with yellow flowers. The princess carries the baby into the pond, but it's shallow. Now it's kind of like the end of the movie, like the camera is pulling back, you know? Like it's going into the sky and everything is getting smaller."

She formed her hands into an imaginary camera lens and drew it toward her face. The watchband dangled from her fingers. Raleigh waited for her to list credits. Best boy. Gaffer. But the reading was over. On the couch, Sarah sobbed hysterically, shoulders heaving, tears washing down her face. She buried her head in her hands.

"Wow," Linda breathed, looking at Sarah.

Still in the lotus position, Nina leaned forward. She watched Linda but addressed the group. "Linda," she said softly, "you don't know this, but you have touched upon one of Sarah's former lives."

"Wow," repeated the girl on the floor. "You were a princess?"

Sarah was too upset to answer. Nina said, "Yes, she was a princess. And it was one of her former lives." She paused. She said, "Wasn't it, Sarah?"

Sarah shrieked, "It was the best one! But it ended so quickly!"

After the women filed out, twenty minutes later, and Nina closed the door, she told Raleigh, "That was a big breakthrough for Sarah. She's been depressed."

"It looked emotional, all right."

The cars started up outside. With the women gone, the sparse light in the living room seemed more intimate, less mysterious. The devil base of the lamp grinned obscenely. The hem of green muumuu brushed the floor as Nina walked to the easy chair, settled back into it. Her toes extended from the edges, tiny, pink.

Raleigh cast about for a gentle way to ease into Salinger. "I'm sorry about . . ."

"Jay. You want to talk about Jay. I know." She maintained the calm helpful attitude, nodding for him to continue, when she had to be grieving inside. She said, "Wheeze said the police took you in." Her frown formed as the slightest rearrangement of lines on her forehead. It did not effect the soft, small mouth. "Sezar," she said. "He talked to me, too. I felt sorry for him. He doesn't believe anything people tell him."

"I noticed that." Raleigh still felt throbbing in his shoulder socket.

"You have to trust people more," Nina said. Again, she divined Raleigh's thoughts. "You're worried about Wheeze. You think he tells your secrets." She shook her head. "We're on the Bird Island committee, so he tells me things." Her laugh was unexpected, light. "Actually, we're the whole committee. Pete's in Tampa or Miami every Thursday at his coin meetings, raising money. Ike White signed on but never comes. He's scared. The other two members are New Yorkers; they own an import store. They only spend three months a year here. They went home in March."

Raleigh had to admire her composure. The pain beneath the calm exterior had to be acute. They sat diagonally from each other, she on the sitting chair, he on the lumpy couch.

The plastic flamingo in the flowerpot seemed to be looking at Raleigh. "I only met Jay for a few minutes, but he struck me as a good person, a person I would have liked," Raleigh said softly. "When was the wedding supposed to be?"

"What wedding?"

"*Your* wedding." She was rearranging her body beneath the muumuu; there were slight shiftings beneath the outer folds of the garment. Her breasts seemed larger. The tiny curved arch of one foot was visible. She slid her hand down the devil lamp. She looked puzzled. Raleigh said, "He said you were his fiancée."

Nina started to laugh. "His fiancée," she said, and laughed harder. "Jay, you are such a liar, a miserable liar."

Raleigh sipped the tea again. Dead fish. That was what it reminded him of. He didn't want to ask what was in it. He said, "I was on the houseboat when you called. Salinger's answering machine was turned up."

The words propelled her out of the chair. He had not noticed how smoothly she moved before. Even agitated, not going anywhere, just crossing the room, she flowed, back arched, toes pressing into the throw rugs.

She stopped on Raleigh's left, a foot away from the plastic flamingo and beside a china bowl filled with floating lilies. A poster on the wall showed a child's drawing of stick figures holding hands, circling the earth: PEACE DAY. There were daisies in a wine carafe on the lobster-trap table.

"I was upset, angry." She looked away, into the hall. "He

101

liked women." She turned back, pain in the smile now. "I should have known what would happen when I saw those pictures on his shelves. He didn't hide them. I guess that's his warning." She shook her head. "You never think bad things will happen to you."

This time, she halted directly in front of Raleigh and sank down into the lotus position at his feet. Her eyes were huge, fixed on him. He had not noticed the perfect curves of her lips before, the edges sculpted, the center full.

"He used to come to the store and have T-shirts made with funny sayings. He'd invite me to the boat. He said he was a great cook. The first time I went over, he had Vivaldi playing." A slight floral odor came up from her, drifting. "I never heard Vivaldi after that first night," she said. "After that, it was, 'Let's watch a tape of the show.' But that first time . . ." she trailed off, smiling. "Scallopini. Champagne."

Slowly and dreamily, she reached between Raleigh's calves, touched the velvet couch and rubbed it, up and down. She imitated Salinger with her voice, referring to the pictures on the shelves. "Her? She came here from Texas a couple of years ago. She's just a friend. Her? I used to go out with her, in Vermont." Raleigh remembered Nina's photo. It had been on the shelf of music tapes beside the picture of the Chinese girl in the red negligee. Nina had been shot from the waist up, in a cameo frame, her head tilted slightly, the same muumuu on. The smile had been warm and happy.

"I even recognized some of the women in the photos," she said. "Tourists who came into the shop. Raleigh, do you think I'm ugly?"

"Are you kidding?" Raleigh said. The hand was still moving up and down. "You're beautiful."

"I know I'm not ugly, but he could make you feel that way. Make you feel horrible about yourself. Once he got your picture up." She pulled her hands back, rubbed the floor instead, the polished wood. "He shut off. No phone calls. Nothing. If

I went over, asked him what was wrong, he'd be abrupt. He didn't smile anymore. I'd see him in town with other girls. It's hard to believe I let myself get sucked into that."

The light flickered above the devil, a bad bulb starting to die. It grew strong again.

"The day he was killed, I was at the store," she said. "Two girls came in, barely teenagers. They were trying on bikinis, if you want to call them that. Adam 'n' Eve line. You need talent to wear those. They were giggling like they had some kind of secret. Then they couldn't hold it in anymore. They'd met this fantastic man who lived on a houseboat." Her voice grew lower. "They'd stayed with him the night before, both of them." She stopped. Her grief seemed to raise her out of the lotus position and onto her knees. It was so quiet in the house, he heard the cloth of the muumuu rub against her legs. The floral odor grew stronger. She was closer now.

She said, "I was devastated. I went to the back of the store. I have an office there. I closed the door and cried. I haven't cried like that for a long time. I . . . I liked him, even after things went bad. I guess the girls could hear me, but I didn't care. I phoned him. That's what you heard." The hand stopped. "So he was there. That's what I thought."

She smiled with only one side of her mouth. "The girls were gone when I got back. So was a bathing suit."

"Why would he tell me you were his fiancée?"

She reached behind her neck, brushing away an insect. "He must have figured that was the way to make a good impression. It depends what he wanted from you."

Raleigh had been wrong about the insect. As the front of the muumuu dropped away, uncovering her breasts, he saw the aureoles swelling, growing as he watched. She stood up. Venus stepping from a muumuu, perfectly proportioned, a tiny doll statue.

"Raleigh," she said.

The living room seemed to have become smaller. It was hot. Raleigh was sweating. He was touched by the extent of her hurt.

Wanting a delicate way out of it, he began, "You're beautiful." She said, "Don't say anything." But he said, "I live with someone. I love her."

Nina's dreamy smile remained in place. Her logic seemed independent of outside influences. When she settled onto his lap, he felt the twin moons of her buttocks press his thighs. The flower smell was overpowering. She said, circling his neck with her arms, "That's a lovely thought, a lovely feeling."

"Nina," he said, "I live with someone."

"I heard you." She stood up, moved away a few steps, half in dance, arms out. She shrugged. "I like to walk around the house like this. Where else can you do it if not in your house?" Raleigh wiped his forehead. She grinned. "If you want to ask questions, you have to put up with it. That's not so bad, is it? Is it so bad?"

She seated herself on the chair and crossed her legs. The lamplight created a line of shadow across her chest. "Raleigh's a beautiful name," she remarked. "Like Sir Walter Raleigh. Maybe you were a knight in one of your former lives. Maybe you were him."

Outside, he heard a man singing, on the street. Drunk. Slurring the words. "Anna-belle Louuuuuu, you make me bluuue."

Raleigh reached for the tea and drained the glass without tasting it. He stood. He leaned against the arm of the couch. He folded his arms. He asked, wondering if he sounded normal, "Did he have any enemies?"

"Name somebody."

"No, people who hated him, really hated him."

"Are you really going to keep asking questions?" She shifted around a bit. "Raleigh, I can't reach this itch. Can you scratch my back, please?"

He let out a breath. In the Gauguin poster, two brown South

Sea island women sat on their knees, breasts small, free. Lush green jungle plants filled the background. Nina rubbed her hand and forearm across the arm of the easy chair. It was a habit of hers, rubbing things.

Raleigh said, "Tell me. People who hated him enough to kill him."

She sighed. "Sezar asked me that. I don't want to name names. They don't mean anything."

"Name them. You're not accusing them. It's just a lead."

"I told you. Lots of people didn't like him. There's nothing special I can tell you." For the first time, she seemed petulant.

Raleigh tried a different tack. "Did he sell drugs?"

"Everybody sells drugs. A few dollars, that's all. He did it from the bar. Lots of bartenders do it. Ask Harold, the other bartender at Cap'n Bob's. Tell him you know me. Harold Wong."

"Did he have any run-ins with professionals? Drug people? Did you ever hear him talk about Tampa?"

"One of his women was from Tampa. The Chinese girl, I think."

She uncrossed her legs. Raleigh could see the tiniest fold of flesh below her belly button. There was a dark freckle on the curve of her right hip. He said, "What was her name?"

"I don't know. Maybe it wasn't the Chinese one. Maybe it was the lawyer in the Camaro. One of them was from Tampa. One was from any city you can name."

The room was really stifling. Raleigh glanced at the plastic flamingo in the flowerpot. It seemed to be inspecting the curtain. He said, "Do you have a lot of those?"

"Jay gave me that. He named it Clarence. It was a joke. He would put it out at night, like a cat. Or he'd throw rolled up socks and order Clarence to fetch them. You think I killed him?"

"No."

She smiled. "Somebody was with me at the store all day. Check it, you'll see. I don't mind if you think I did it. You don't know me. Why shouldn't you think that?"

Raleigh got back to the drug dealers from Tampa. "Did he say anything about them?"

A subtle change had transformed her. She'd accepted his lack of interest. "I don't know anything about professionals," she said. Now she became curious. "Why are you even interested in Jay? You hardly knew him."

"I write about murders sometimes. I had a call from my editor in New York."

Her head shook back and forth. The slow smile appeared. "Not the reason," she said.

"Okay, Sezar thinks maybe I did it. I have a personal interest." When she didn't buy that, Raleigh told her about the threatening phone call. If she was behind it, he figured, she'd know anyway.

"Oh," she said, "You feel threatened." The smile widened. She understood now. "You want to know the real reason you're asking these questions," she said. The hand touched her knee, slid toward her upper thigh again. "You like it. Is that so bad? Doing something you like?" She was heating up again. Her voice was dropping. She shifted around in the chair, went into the lotus position again, knees out, legs folded over the blond patch. Her long lustrous hair showered the thin shoulders.

She said, "If you were really worried about your friend, you'd leave. But you're not doing that. You could live in Miami and write about Bird Island. Or New York and make trips. But you like it here, you like it." Her legs began to unfold. She got out of the chair. "Is that so bad? Doing what you like? Someone's got to investigate murders." Her voice was getting whispery. "You like it."

She came across the room at him, swaying. The floral smell was all over the place. It seemed ludicrous to back away from this tiny woman. Her breasts brushed his shirt; he felt the nipples through the fabric. She looked up into his face. Her long arms hooked over his shoulders. "Kiss me," she said. "One time."

She was so small he could lift her away using just his hands.

He put her down a few feet away. "I'm sorry," he said. "It has nothing to do with you."

But his head swam with the smell of flowers. The air seemed thinner when he got outside. The touch of the Mustang's seat against his crotch was sweet and excruciating. He felt like his balls had swelled to elephant size.

Raleigh was too preoccupied to check all the doors and windows before entering the house. He could still feel the press of her against his thigh, still feel the heat of her on his palms and where she had touched his shoulders. He locked the door behind him and went upstairs in the dark. He made his way through the silent hall into the moonlit bedroom. He flicked on the stereo, which played his bagpipe tape. He stripped off his clothes and lay on top of the cool covers.

A shaft of moonlight bathed a photo on the dresser beneath a wide mirror. It showed Raleigh and Diane on the stoop of their West Side brownstone in New York. Diane sat one step above Raleigh, with her arms around his neck. She pressed her chin against the top of his head, buried it in his hair.

Raleigh's skull felt drained, a vacuum pounding with heated-up blood. He still smelled the lilies floating in the china bowl. In his mind, Nina said, "Kiss me," and reached up, her face coming closer. Then he saw Diane in the tangerine-colored bathing suit, lying in the channel at Bird Island. The images came faster. The tide was running over her neck.

Raleigh came in a flood that spattered his belly, chest, thighs, and hand.

He lay back, breathing.

He half-raised his head so that he watched the offending member, limp between his thighs. "You like it," Nina had said. "You could leave but you like it." Raleigh pointed an accusing finger between his legs. "Traitor," he said. "Can't you even wait five days?"

S E V E N
▼ ▼ ▼ ▼ ▼ ▼ ▼ ▼ ▼

"Buckley, BUCKLEY, MANHATTAN SOUTH," shouted the voice that answered on the first ring. Raleigh heard sirens in the background, and a man yelling, "Venus did it! Not me, Venus!"

"Having a quiet morning, Dave?" Raleigh's feet were on his desk. A breeze came into the living room through the open kitchen sliding doors. He wore a plain white bathing suit.

"Fuck you, asshole. What do you want at 6 A.M.?" The sirens grew louder. There were more of them now.

"Had to reach you before your shift was over. What's going on there? Russians attacking?"

"Fuckin' fire across the street. Fuckin' sirens. Fuckin' fire department."

"I'm glad I got you when you're calm." As Raleigh talked, he switched on the computer, punched in a code word, *Eskimo*, which he figured Sezar would never guess. On the amber screen, names of suspects glowed. A chart.

The voice on the other end sighed. "I wrote down what you wanted somewhere. So where's the thing? *Hustler Magazine? Who put this here?* Goddamn toilets went out this morning.

Can't even take a leak where you work. You gotta go to the Greek joint."

"Come to Florida, Dave. We have the finest urinals here. Michelangelo designs. Gold plating."

"And get skin cancer lying in the sun? Mosquitoes carry diseases. No thanks, pally." Raleigh's breakfast of a spice doughnut and mug of espresso sat between the In Basket and the computer. He pictured the chief of detectives in an olive-drab room with a tiny electric fan atop a file cabinet dented from being kicked. Buckley's voice said, "Got it. I checked with Bobby Cortazar; he joined Tampa when his dad got sick down there. You were right. It's Cubans. They cut off a piece of left earlobe in a little triangle. Cortazar says how come you know? Only police are supposed to. He says it's some kind of gang war in Tampa, but no place else. He doesn't think they'd move away without consolidating their territory, and if they did move, it would be to another city. Cortazar had to look up where Key Rey is. P.S., he fucked up the taxi case, remember?"

"You find anything on Wheeze?" he asked.

"Creedmore had a patient named Francis Johnson, called himself Wheeze. Asthma, right?"

"Violent stuff?"

"Martian stuff. Spy stuff. The voice made a pulsating noise like a spaceship landing."

"What about Jay Salinger?" Raleigh said, typing information into the chart. Columns for each suspect read, "motivation," "location," "history."

"Bigamy. Whaddaya make me run around if you know the answers? He did his time."

Raleigh had one last question. "You check the National? Professor Randolph Pete? Nan Grant? Quade or White?"

"Big zero on those. Hey Raleigh, is Diane ready to come back to civilization yet? I got a spare room she could use. It has a lava lamp. She can look at it while I whisper in her ear."

"I'll tell her your offer, but you have to clean up the language for her, Dave."

"What's wrong with my fuckin' language?" Hoarse laughter came over the line. Then, more seriously, "Plastic flamingos rang a bell, reminded me of something important. I better tell you."

Raleigh leaned forward. "What?"

The voice rang out, "Keep your dooooors locked. HAha-hahahaha!"

Raleigh hung up. The computer wasn't helping. Stretching, he went into the kitchen and poured more espresso. Diane would be back tonight and he felt no closer to figuring out who had killed Salinger than he had when he started thinking about it. The answer's there, he told himself. He took the espresso onto the back lawn. The wet grass cooled his bare feet. The doughnut was fresh. The coffee throbbed in his toes.

The property sloped down to the partially eroded water-front. The thickly grassed area at the shoreline was shaded by sapodilla and Spanish lime trees.

Raleigh left the mug on land and stepped into the water, sinking inches into the smooth cool sand. Dawn banded the horizon orange on bottom, translucent purple-blue above, where the moon was still chalky and a last star visible. The slow purring of a boat came to him across the water. A quarter-mile off, a twenty-five-foot gray coast guard patrol had stopped a double-decked fishing boat. The guard seldom bothered people leaving Key Rey but showed special interest in returnees, especially at dawn and dusk. Shielding his eyes from the rising sun, he made out the tiny figures of two guardsmen on the fishing boat, one gesturing at the captain, one searching the prow. Other guardsmen stood alert on the foredeck of the patrol boat—in blue caps, ready to intervene if trouble erupted.

Raleigh dived into the water. With lazy, powerful strokes he swam toward the two boats, simply because they formed an arbitrary point in a surface without landmarks. He loved the water cascading against his skin. The bay, aquamarine at the surface, deepened into jade in the depths. He saw a ray, beneath him black wings flapping. A porpoise shot past in an upwardly curving arc and barracudas hung, watching him pass. Raleigh kept swimming until his body began to ache pleasantly.

When he got back to the house, he showered and changed into shorts and a Key Rey T-shirt. He poured a third mug of espresso. It made sweat break out on his brow. This time when he punched a number into the phone, a woman's voice answered. Slow and southern. "*Herald.* Isabel Craft."

"Hi, Isabel."

"Lover! You've come to your senses. I have vacation time coming and I'll clean out the big closet in back for you."

"You wouldn't want me if I left her. I'd be a wreck."

The faintest note of sadness came into the voice. "Try me." Then, brighter. "Okay. What?"

"Abel Quade."

"We don't have much on him. We ran a series on Keys developers a couple years back. Different builders. Same story. Accusations and no proof. Cars run off roads. Broken legs. Nothing went to court and Quade made money."

"And the police here?"

"Small-town police." He sensed her shrug. Her voice grew concerned. "So you're into crime again. Go back with Frank. He'll do anything for you. He'll back you if something happens."

Lots of bartenders sell drugs. Ask Harold Wong, Nina had said. Raleigh lied, "I'll think about it." Nobody answered at Cap'n Bob's bar. Too early. No Wong was listed in the directory or with the operator. Raleigh would drop by tonight.

He cross-referenced information on the computer. Everyone's alibi checked out. He typed *Eskimo* into the keyboard an hour later and the screen cleared. At a thunk by the front door, he whirled, but it was only mail falling through the slot. The first few envelopes were bills. A *Time* magazine. An *Environmentalist.*

He stopped at a white envelope addressed in red ink. No return address but a Key Rey postmark.

Feeling a rising tide of excitement, Raleigh tore the flap open. He unfolded a single sheet of paper inside.

It took a second for the contents to register. A sick, leaden feeling came into his stomach.

Two words were scrawled over and over: *Raped me.* In violent script. The words ran into each other, over each other, off the page. There was no signature, and ink was smeared in spots. The writer had been crying. He remembered the closed shutters at Nan Grant's house. He took the letter when he went for the Mustang. A pickup truck with QUADE CONSTRUCTION on the side was delivering two-by-fours next door.

He reached Drake Street in minutes. He kept his finger on her bell.

After awhile, although he'd heard no footsteps, he sensed that the quality of silence had changed, deepened, on her side of the door. She was there.

Softly, he said, "It's Raleigh. I got your letter. Thanks for sending it."

In the street, shaded by the big banyan tree, the two boys were back, circling on their bikes, watching him.

Raleigh pressed his lips near the door. He could smell the pine. "Can we talk? I need to know more." No answer. "Hey, it's tough talking to a door."

He sighed. "I know how hard this must be for you, so I'm just going to sit on the porch awhile, not say anything." He settled down. "You decide, it's nice in the sun here. I'm just leaning against this porch."

A line of black ants marched across the buckled walkway. The bartender from La Margarita rode by on her bicycle, saw him, and waved. Across the street, a bald man in an undershirt took in mail and stared at Raleigh a long time. Raleigh went back to the bell.

"Guess who?" he joked. "Ever play that game when you were

a kid? Someone says, 'I'll give you a dollar if you can shut up five minutes.' I was bad at it. I had to pay them." He heard a vague sliding sound and imagined hands running down the door.

Raleigh mopped his forehead from the heat. "Quade has two men," he said. "A tall thin man, with dark hair, shiny hair. A bigger man, not fat. Heavy." Raleigh's cheek brushed the warm wood. "Does that sound like them? Give me a clue."

He paced the porch. He shouted, "You sent me the letter! What did you think was going to happen!"

Suddenly he felt an emptiness. He knew she had gone.

She'd looked pretty in the picture he had seen at the *Sunfish*, with her pageboy haircut and small upturned nose.

The day felt hotter as he walked to the car. In the distance, silver and cranberry balloons rose into the Gulf sky, growing smaller, tiny. Someone was having a party.

LITTLE CARNIVAL WEEK, announced the banner across Morgan Street. The whole town seemed to be celebrating. At 11 P.M., the Coconut Head torchlight parade was in full swing. There were coconut-head nuns, baseball players, gorillas, aliens. Spectators lined the bar balconies, howling with laughter. Raleigh saw a twenty-foot-tall drag queen float going by. A line of dinosaurs playing kazoos. A dozen fan dancers.

Raleigh ducked down a cobblestone alley near the Morgan Street pier. T-shirt and souvenir shops lined one side, woods and the cemetery on the other. When Raleigh pushed open the door to Cap'n Bob's, a burst of salsa music hit him. The bar was packed. Lights on the bay blinked green and red beyond plate-glass windows. The wallpaper showed sunken treasure galleons, masts broken, rudders in sand. Photos of Professor Pete holding up treasure with Jake hung behind the bar.

"Brazil, Brazil," pulsated from the jukebox. Raleigh grabbed an empty stool at the bar, over a reinforced glass strip of floor that looked down into the water below. Fish swam upside down beneath him, mistaking lights below for the sun.

"Hey, the bagpiper!" called a voice to his left. Raleigh had not recognized Kazanjian without his marine patrol uniform. The big man was on the next stool, in jeans and a T-shirt, nursing a Budweiser in a long-necked bottle. On the wall over his head was a black and white picture of Professor Pete, in a diving suit, clutching booty from the *Isabella* as he bobbed on the surface of the sea. Kazanjian waved the bartender over. He told the man, who did not look like a Harold Wong, "Whatever he wants."

Raleigh glimpsed one of Quade's men—the thin one who had been on the boat—on the far side of the bar, talking with two men in South Sea islander grass skirts. The honey-haired woman, Linda, who had been at Nina's meeting yesterday, sat alone at a corner, by the plastic tray of drink condiments— olives and orange peels—sipping a drink with lime, ignoring the enraptured gaze of the tattooed man beside her. Raleigh had seen the man driving a black Suzuki around town.

"Get the goods on Abel?" Kazanjian asked. Even off duty he looked like a cop, with the perfect black hair and mustache.

Raleigh told him as the Bud arrived, "I'm always open for ideas."

"Talk to the guy by the jukebox. He works for Quade."

"I met him. Cheers."

Kazanjian's brows rose. "In the daylight? I didn't think they came out in the day."

Raleigh had a flash of Diane in her Trans Europe uniform, blue top with bronze wings on the left pocket. Blue skirt and pumps. She would be driving up from Key West in an hour, if her plane got in on time.

"So you and Sezar had another talk," Kazanjian said with amusement. "Getting to be old friends."

The beer was ice-cold. "Is everyone in this town related to everyone else, or just the people I run into?"

"One happy family." Kazanjian grinned, lifting his bottle with two fingers, at the neck. The music changed to "Heart Like a Wheel." Raleigh said sourly, "Who are you then? Sezar's brother? His grandfather?"

"He gets things done his own way." Someone bumped Raleigh on the right, and a hand went into his pocket. He turned. Two grinning coconut faces bobbed a foot away, with thick red lips and painted green hair. The women holding the coconuts in front of their faces wore Egyptian harem suits.

Raleigh glimpsed Wheeze slinking toward the door, through the space between the coconut heads.

He felt in his pocket. A paper was there.

"New Yorkers." He grinned at Kazanjian, turning back. "You get jostled, you think it's a pickpocket."

"I came from Chicago twelve years ago," Kazanjian said. "I'm a pilgrim, like you. I like it. It's different. A little nutsy but interesting. And you can't beat the bonefishing."

Once again, Raleigh wondered if Kazanjian was pumping him for information. "The marine patrol and the police are in the same building," he said casually. It was a question. The music grew louder. Kazanjian winked. "So we are." He took a long drink. "Can you play, 'When Irish Eyes Are Smiling?' My grandfather played it when I was a kid, but he called it 'Armenian Eyes.' "

"I can play it." Raleigh lifted his left arm, cradled an imaginary bagpipe. He ran his fingers down the pipe and moved his head jauntily. He had an urge to be out in the boat, alone, on the water, playing.

Raleigh noticed Jake Pete about ten feet off, on the same side of the bar. The diver had his arm around a girl's shoulder. With the index finger of his free hand, he jabbed at a photograph of himself on the wall.

Kazanjian followed Raleigh's gaze and asked more quietly, "You get that gun yet?"

"No."

115

The patrolman shook his head. He pulled a pack of Carltons from his pocket and laid them on the bar, but he did not take out a cigarette. "That guy's watching you," he said, raising his index finger just a fraction off the counter. Quade's man had moved against the far wall. He was looking at Raleigh as he sipped a blue drink.

"I'll never get to hear the bagpiper if he has an accident," Kazanjian said. They drank in silence, liking each other. The closest photo, on a column on Raleigh's right, showed Professor Pete bobbing in the ocean, diving mask perched on his head, beads of water dripping from his beard. He was grinning toward a gold chain that dangled from his fist into the sea.

"Next time I take out the pipes, come along," Raleigh said. "All four of us'll go. Bring your wife."

The goodwill oozed from Kazanjian's face. He looked away from Raleigh, at the bottle. His head withdrew an inch into his shoulders. "She's not here." He played with the pack of Carltons, not opening it, just moving it between fingers. "She's sick," Kazanjian said, looking at Raleigh again. His face was expressionless. There was heartbreak in his voice.

Raleigh said, "I'm sorry."

"Me, too." The big patrolman shook his head. "She never looked like she had anything," he said dully. "She didn't even feel bad. It was one of those checkups." He pushed his bottle away. "She's at a clinic," he said. More to himself than to Raleigh, he said, "She's going to die."

Raleigh repeated that he was sorry, very sorry. Kazanjian finished the beer. He squeezed Raleigh's shoulder when he stood up. "Got a four A.M. patrol," he said. "Call me if you're out there, remember." He leaned close. "Get a gun."

Kazanjian called to the blond bartender, "Take it easy, Wong."

"Harold Wong?" Raleigh said when the man asked him whether he wanted another Bud.

The bartender leaned close. He had a pleasant, open, midwestern face, smooth shaven, with light brown eyes. He screwed up his expression. In ridiculous pidgin English he said, "Whatsamatta you! No likeee Wong name?" With a New York accent, he called to a tall curly-haired man trying to pick up Linda by the condiment tray. "Weber, take the bar for ten minutes." Then, to Raleigh, "Fixx. Bird Island. Right?"

Why did everybody know him here? Wong led Raleigh toward a back wall. A band had climbed onstage, a local group Raleigh had often seen in Key Rey. The leader's denim vest was open at the chest to show his pectoral muscles. Two long-haired women took up electric guitars behind him as he weaved to the mike, clutching a half-empty bottle of rum. "I'm dedicating this song to Johnny Coetzee," he slurred. "A great musician. A real friend."

A roar of approval went up for Key Rey's foremost citizen. The band launched into reggae. "I-lands, I-lands," the singer crooned, two guitarists flanking him gyrating in sync. Harold Wong took a round table from three girls who were leaving. He tipped his chair back so his hair brushed the wall. He pointed his index finger at Raleigh, like a gun. "*Daily News*, right? I bet you heard of me, too. Wong? Sunday *Times Magazine?*"

"You're that Wong?"

"Yep. Scandal Wong." The man switched to a W. C. Fields voice. "A promising career, destroyed." Raleigh remembered a Sunday magazine cover, a photograph of a woman with black braids in the jungle, wearing military fatigues, rifle in hand.

"The bitch fooled me." Wong grinned. "How did I know that picture was taken in the Everglades? 'My Life with the Guerrillas.' Ha. She never even left Florida." He'd bought a three-quarter-filled milk shake—sized glass with Scotch on the rocks. He took a pull of the drink. "Sleeping with her didn't help my judgment, either. Oh well, this place isn't bad. All I can drink. All I can squeeze. I don't miss the paper, I really don't."

117

The chair tipped back down. "I don't," Wong repeated.

"I can see that."

"I'm curious," Wong said. "Don't answer if it's personal. How much can you make on one of your books? A lot?"

"I do all right."

Wong burst into laughter at what he regarded as an understatement. "All right. I worked with Jay four, five months. That's what you're here for, isn't it? Not the island. What do you want to know?"

With a journalist, Raleigh figured the direct approach would be best. "Did he sell drugs?"

Up went Wong's palms. "Whoa," he said, looking around. "What are you trying to do to me?"

"To you? Nothing."

Wong pulled at the Scotch. A new look flickered over his face, a more furtive expression of a man with a hidden agenda. He said, more quietly, "How much did you say you make on one of those books?"

Raleigh was surprised. Journalists never touched you for money. But he pulled out a twenty and passed it along the table. He hoped Wong had something to sell.

"Fifty?"

"Twenty."

Wong drank more Scotch. "Twenty, what's that? A tank of gas?"

Raleigh put a ten on the table but held on to it when Wong tried to pick it up.

Wong said, "He didn't sell hard stuff."

"The police think professionals hit him."

"The police," Wong said with disdain. "He couldn't pay rent on what he made from it. He had maybe five or six regular customers; it was beer money, that's all." His eyes, roving around the room, fixed on Jake Pete for an instant and moved away.

"Him?" Raleigh said. Jake was gulping beer from a bottle.

Wong snapped his attention back. "Who?"

Raleigh looked from Wong to Jake. Wong gave a little half-smile, pursed his lips, and leaned forward confidentially. "Look, Salinger's dead. I don't mind talking about him. I don't want to get anyone in trouble."

"No more money."

Wong shrugged. "That's fine," he said. "There's plenty else to talk about."

Raleigh nodded. "I guess I'll ask Jake and tell him you sent me over."

The bartender went pale, sat absolutely still. "You'd tell him that? It isn't true," he said. "The guy's an animal."

Raleigh gave a consoling look. "How big a customer was he, Harold?"

Wong looked into his eyes, deciding if Raleigh would really do it. "You're digging in the knife," he said. He rolled his eyes like he was doing Raleigh a favor. Wong lowered his voice. "He bought a lot. Remember. I'm trusting you."

"Who were other customers?"

Wong shook his head. "Here's your money back."

Looking over at Jake, Raleigh started to get up. Wong said quickly, "Wheeze, sometimes. Nina. She told me you'd be here. Mike 'n' Eddie. They run the Mobil on Morgan and Conch."

Raleigh sat down again. Someone in a spacesuit and glass helmet was walking around near the bar, broadcasting over the din, "Earthlings! I come to warn you!" "Who took over selling the drugs after Salinger died?" Raleigh said.

Wong leaned back and took a long drink. "Let's get one thing straight. I didn't have any gripe against Salinger, and I was here all day the day he died. There's eighty, a hundred witnesses. And between you and me, what if I told you I took over? Who cares? What would it mean?" He leaned forward, over his glass. "Anyway, I'm getting out of it. I'm tired of looking over my shoulder all the time. What the hell did I talk to you for anyway?"

"Thirty dollars." Raleigh could come back to Wong as a subject later. "Nina was pretty mad at Salinger," he said.

"You'd be, too, if somebody gave you AIDS."

A sick feeling began in Raleigh's stomach. He remembered Nina's arms wrapped around his neck. He remembered the squirm of her buttocks on his lap. "She has AIDS?"

Wong finished his Scotch. "He got tested for it. He came back scared. A lot of people have it here. He would never talk about it; I bet he gave it to her."

"But you don't know for sure," Raleigh said, only slightly relieved.

"I haven't seen the test results, if that's what you mean."

He still smelled her perfume. In the black and white photograph on the wall near the bar, a heavyset, tight-jawed Florida marine patrolman cradled a shotgun, standing guard on a dock while Pete and Jake carried silver bars off the shrimp boat. The professor's shoulders hunched from the load, but he was smiling. Wong said, "She picks up lots of guys now, takes them home. She didn't used to do that."

Raleigh kept looking at the photograph of Jake's face. The long downturn of the mustache. The dirty hair, the wide shoulders. He wondered what Jake's voice would sound like on the phone, with a handkerchief over the receiver. His father had brought him up here, teaching him how terrific pirates were. "How could he afford all that coke? I thought they're broke."

"I don't know. He always has rich girlfriends. Then he beats them up and finds another."

Jake, Raleigh thought. Did Jake kill him?

"He was arrested four, five years ago," Wong continued, growing self-righteous as long as he had to talk anyway. "A girl from Texas, a runaway. He beat the daylights out of her, broke her jaw."

Raleigh remembered the girl with the welt on her face, fleeing the shrimp boat. "What happened to him?" he asked.

"She didn't press charges. Changed her story, I think. But he did it. He picks weak ones. I got to get back to the bar."

Wong stood up. He said, putting his hand out, taking the ten, "Brother journalists, right?"

When he was gone, Raleigh remembered Wheeze's note, pulled the crumpled sheet from his pocket and spread it out under light. "The eagle flies in cloudy weather. The orange grows sweet," it said. "Cemetery. 12:14. James Bond."

Raleigh chuckled, checked the flamingo clock over the bar. 12:50. On the dance floor, Jake Pete was squeezing against his girlfriend during a slow song, working his hands around in the back of her pink shorts. Raleigh watched Jake for a moment and then pushed toward the door, through the press of bodies. The cool air outside was a relief. The parade was over. One or two tourists strolled past the mouth of the alley, forty yards away, and a little red scooter zipped by. The late night Shark-mobile passed, loudspeaker echoing. " . . . escaped convicts hid out in Key Rey after the prison break-in. . . ."

The cemetery sent a lush, fragrant smell of willows and geiger trees across to him. There was no path, only haphazardly arranged headstones, worn by age and tilting in the loose soil. The moon was so bright, the first inscription was visible: I TOLD YOU I WAS SICK.

"Wheeze?" The graveyard was L-shaped, so Raleigh only saw the front part of it, and Wheeze wasn't in it. Wheeze might have gone home. Even in the brief period they'd known each other, half the time his information was worthless anyway.

Behind him, in the alley, the door to Cap'n Bob's opened and two men lurched out, waving coconuts. They were having a laughing, drunken argument. One said, loud enough for Raleigh to hear, "It does *not* look like Harry Truman, it looks like a goddamned coconut!"

Raleigh reached the junction of the L and turned right to proceed into the rear of the cemetery, which was slightly darker, blocked from the lights from the alley. Another in-scription read, AT LEAST I KNOW WHERE YOU'RE SLEEPING TO-NIGHT. He was surprised to spot Wheeze, from behind, sitting on a concrete bench at the edge of the grounds, below a line of sapodilla trees and facing the woods.

"Okay, 007. I'm here."

Wheeze didn't turn. Raleigh got closer. Maybe he'd fallen asleep. His head tilted against his shoulder. His back slumped a bit.

Raleigh stopped as he saw the atomizer on the ground, the moonlight accentuating its whiteness.

"Wheeze?"

A sick, cloying odor came to him. He recognized it.

"Oh God," he said.

Wheeze's eyes were open, fixed sideways and down, at a pebble on the ground. The lips were parted. A stain spread across the front of the shirt in a mass. It was thick with insects and it gleamed sickly in the yellow light. Raleigh made out pieces of white bone through rips in the fabric.

"Oh, Wheeze." The chest didn't move. He knew he should not touch the body, that he should get away from it, not mess up footprints on the ground. The drum beating from Cap'n Bob's seemed a thousand miles away, and the singer was belting out a muffled "She moooves me."

Raleigh heard the faintest snap behind him, in the sapodilla trees. He threw himself left without turning, already rolling as he struck the ground, feeling the puffs of dirt burst behind him, hearing the whiz of bullets flying past his head and the smack of one hitting a gravestone. He kept moving, scrambling diagonally for the woods, glimpsing a man with a beard rising from behind a headstone, wide-shouldered, a cap on his head. A stranger. Raleigh had the thought, He looks like Hemingway. Orange flame spat from the outstretched fist. Dirt mushroomed a foot away.

Raleigh, hearing the man coming, dove into the trees. There

122

was a grunt back there. Crashing in the brush behind him, which stopped. The man was listening. Raleigh lay still. The earth was moist beneath him, and sent up a loamy smell. He heard himself breathing. He heard people coming up the alley, singing. Two or three people, just beyond the trees.

The footsteps started up nearby, but moved off in the other direction.

Raleigh bolted toward the singing, reached the alley. A man and woman in I LOVE KEY REY shirts recoiled as he ran out of the trees. Raleigh couldn't hear what they said to him, the blood pounded so loud in his head. He pushed the door to Cap'n Bob's open. Jake Pete was coming through the other way, with his girl. Raleigh squeezed through the crowd headed for the phone. The singer was crooning "I love you soooooo much."

E I G H T
▼▼▼▼▼▼▼▼▼

"Were you and Wheeze lovers?" asked Detective Blaney.

"Yeah," said Detective Shaw. "How come you were meeting at the cemetery after midnight?"

Raleigh was back in the little interrogation room at City Hall, with the tiny lopsided window and the white steel medicine cabinet. This time only two detectives grilled him. The black guy who'd blown on his neck and dropped phone books last time was gone.

"I told you six times," Raleigh said, voice rising. "Why are you wasting time with me? He's going to get away!"

Shaw smiled. "You mean the man who looks like Hemingway?" He sneered.

"*Ernest* Hemingway," grinned Blaney.

"Yes, Ernest Hemingway. What's so funny about that? A man with a beard. A big guy. A white beard."

The sudden, crisp sound of a gunshot crackled outside. Everybody rushed to the window. Below, Raleigh saw people fanning into Morgan Street from Cap'n George's Bar. They ran slowly, heads down, scanning the ground. They carried mason jars.

Cap'n George held a half-raised smoking starter pistol just outside the door of the bar.

"Palmetto Bug Tournament," he cried, looking up. "Biggest find wins margaritas."

Back in the undersized wooden chair, Raleigh faced a new addition to the room, a black and white poster of an empty electric chair tacked to the paneling. Straps dangled from the chair in the picture. The caption read, REGULAR OR EXTRA CRISPY?

Detective Shaw paced when he asked questions. He shook Wheeze's note at Raleigh.

"What does this mean?" he demanded. "*The orange grows sweet.*"

"I told you! He played games! I don't know why he wanted to meet me. He was going to tell me there. Look, why don't you set up roadblocks on the bridge? He's getting away!"

They'd been at it two hours. Shaw pulled a small brown kit from the steel cabinet and unsnapped it on the writing arm of Raleigh's chair. There were test tubes and cotton swabs inside. He dabbed Raleigh's right hand, left hand, index fingers, and palms with a Q-tip dipped in chemicals. He sealed the results in a vial.

"Antimony, barium, and lead, that's what we're looking for," said Blaney, perched on the side of the chair. "We'll send it to Miami. If you're clean, I guess you didn't fire the shots."

"Terrific. When will you have results?"

"Three months," Shaw said as the door opened. "They're slow."

A little Hispanic man came into the room. He had woolly hair and a red silk Caribbean shirt with a print of a flamingo in sunglasses on it. He carried a clipboard. Shaw introduced him as Cruz, the sketch artist.

"He says the man who tried to shoot him looks like Hemingway," Blaney said.

Cruz's mouth fell open. He looked as if he was holding back a laugh. "Erneeeest Hemingway?"

Cruz sketched quickly. A face took shape. The questions never stopped. Did someone really try to kill you? Shaw asked. How many times have you spoken with Wheeze before? Did he always pass you notes first? You met him in Ohio?

"I told you," Raleigh said. "I met him here. Let me call Diane. She's supposed to be home by now."

"We sent an officer to check," Shaw soothed. "She's not there. We called Trans Europe. The flight's delayed."

The questions started again. How many shots were fired? Blaney wanted to know. You're pretty clean for a guy who was rolling around on the ground. Where did the shooter stand? What kind of weapon did you use in Vietnam again? Were you facing Wheeze when he got shot?

"What are you, deaf?" Raleigh said. "I came into the cemetery afterward." He yelled toward the door. "Sezar, I know you're back there. Get me out of here."

"How about taking a polygraph test, Bubba?" Blaney asked. "Any objections?"

"Good. Great. It'll get me home."

"Erneeest Hemingway," sang Cruz. "Is this heem?"

Shaw said, "The polygraph's busted. He'll have to take it tomorrow."

New carvings had been gouged into the desk: HINDU 15 and DORKS.

"Why not bring out the cherry Kool-Aid and the hypodermic?" Raleigh said.

He could not rid himself of the vision of Wheeze slumped sideways, head on shoulder. And of the white van doors closing on his green plastic-wrapped form.

He'd been kept at the cemetery an hour before being brought here, watching while police scoured the woods and found nobody, while ballistics men checked headstones for ricochet marks and lead traces. The volunteer ambulance crew had finally arrived.

Now the door opened and Sezar sauntered into the room.

He seemed to fill it up. He looked fresh in a light green checkered cotton shirt, jeans, and tan cowboy boots. He flicked his index finger at Blaney. "Johnson's house," he ordered. And at Shaw—"Wong's." When the detectives left, he pulled a chair around backward and sat, arms draped over the top, facing Raleigh, two feet away. He didn't say anything. He just looked. They heard the throb of the Beatles' "Revolution" from Morgan Street. The ceiling fan made regular thumping noises.

Raleigh said, "He's probably in Miami by now. He could be in Cairo by now."

Sezar shifted in the seat, getting comfortable. "You'll just have to excuse our plodding coconut minds," he said. "We don't have your experience with this kind of thing. Maybe if you stick around and we have four or five more murders, we'll learn to do it right. Did they tell you your girlfriend's flight's socked in, in London? Come on, I'll drive you home."

"No thanks. I can walk from here."

Sezar stood up and stretched. "I insist."

"Where we going this time?" Raleigh sighed. "The swamp again? You want to show me more crocodiles?"

Sezar locked the door to the interrogation room when they got into the hall. "Alligators," he corrected. "We don't have crocodiles in Key Rey. I thought a naturalist like you would know that. I thought you had a great interest in our animal life." The hallway was decorated with color photos of Key Rey leaders, hands folded on their shiny desks, American and Florida flags at their backs. MAYOR JOSHUA QUADE, read the nameplate in the middle photo. Unlike Abel, Joshua had black hair and wore a suit and tie. Sezar put a penny in the Lions Club gum-ball machine and popped three pieces in his mouth.

"Actually, you're right about not going *directly* home," he admitted when they were in the unmarked Chevrolet. "I thought you might need a drink. That room makes you thirsty."

Sezar was at his kindest before springing hidden information. They rolled down Morgan Street. After Wheeze's death, the forced cheeriness of the town depressed Raleigh. He looked over the inflatable plastic palm trees and smiling alligator ashtrays in the souvenir shop windows. Leather hoods and edible underwear displays were featured at the sex shop. Lounge music tinkled from an open-air patio bar, beneath a thatched roof, and soft laughter floated out to them at a light. Scooters zipped past. They were heading back toward the cemetery at 3 A.M.

The police radio crackled. "It's Lester, at the bridge. I still haven't seen any drivers fitting his description." Raleigh glanced at Sezar with surprise, but the detective drove easily, one hand on the wheel, eyes straight ahead. At the upcoming corner, a drunken boy in a Northwestern T-shirt weaved a foot off the curb, pointing to his crotch every time a car with girls went by. He drank from an oversized can of Australian beer.

Sezar stopped and leaned out toward the boy, who grinned back with bloodshot eyes.

"Son," Sezar said, "I see you need satisfaction. We got some big hefty takers at the jail."

The boy scuttled back into The Treasure House. Sezar started rolling again. When they'd almost reached the alley, he turned right, away from Cap'n Bob's, bumped down a narrow cobblestone street along the waterfront, cut left back up a narrower palmetto-lined alley, and pulled up in front of a large ramshackle bar Raleigh had seen but never gone into. It was a Spanish-style stucco building with regular openings into the street.

"Buy you a beer," Sezar said. Leaping marlins and swordfish were painted in blue and red on the yellow outside walls.

"You're wasting your time on me."

"Wasting time? *Wasting* time on an expert like you?" Sezar threw his arm around Raleigh's shoulder so that Raleigh felt the muscles. Lots of shouting was coming from inside the bar. "I want to consult you," Sezar said. "I want to get your opinion."

Raleigh took two steps into the Billfisher and stopped.

"Oh, Jesus," he said.

He was looking at another banner over the round bar in the middle of the floor. It said: HEMINGWAY LOOK-ALIKE CONTEST!

There were Hemingways all over the place. Everybody in the bar looked like Hemingway. Hemingways lined the bar stools and leaned against the jukebox. They stood admiring souvenirs on the walls—Hemingway's old skis, fishing rods, typewriter ribbons. On one wall, Raleigh recognized the poster he'd seen on Salinger's boat, of Hemingway in a lowered cap. Another black and white blowup showed the writer on a country road, kicking a can. There were photos of Hemingway on docks, beside Marlins. On boats. On a beach looking out to sea.

Sezar said, pleasantly, "Will the real Ernest Hemingway please stand up?"

The men in the bar all had real hair and beards like Hemingway, but the contest apparently didn't cover how they dressed. Neck down, they were a cross section of Key Rey tourists.

A thin, tall Hemingway in matching sage-colored cotton pants and shirt lurched up to Raleigh, drink in hand. He wore an L. L. Bean boat hat with the brim turned up. "Which stool did Hemingway sit on when he was here?" he said. He had a Chicago accent. "I'm having an argument with my friend."

"Which one were you on?" Sezar asked.

"That one."

"Isn't that something," Sezar said. "That's the one!"

The man beamed and hurried back toward a shorter, fatter Hemingway in a safari shirt at the bar. "You probably never knew Hemingway visited here once, did you Raleigh?" Sezar said, reaching for a bar stool. "Back in thirty-seven or thirty-eight. He was fishing out of Key West. He lived there, you know. A storm came up. They put in here. He was at the Billfisher a couple of hours. That's his bar bill on the wall over there."

Raleigh stared at the skis, rods, stuffed fish. "All this happened because of two hours?"

"Well, Key West does a pretty good job with their Hemingway Festival, so Josh Quade thought we'd try one here Little Carnival Week. We like to pack 'em in."

An announcement on the wall read, HEMINGWAY BOXING MATCH TOMORROW. HEMINGWAY FISHING TOURNAMENT.

Raleigh noticed uniformed police scattered around the bar, talking quietly with Hemingways, writing notes.

"So which one took a shot at you?" Sezar remarked. "That skinny one with the glasses over there? How about the one leaving? He looks suspicious to me. He look suspicious to you, Raleigh?"

"You're right," Raleigh said. "I need a drink."

They sat at the bar, surrounded by Hemingways. At a tap on his shoulder, Raleigh turned to see an immense red-faced Hemingway with a receding hairline and an extra-thick beard. The man struck a dramatic pose, like a high school actor. He recited, in a deep resonant voice, "He was an old man. He lived near the sea."

"That's for the contest tomorrow," he told Raleigh. "You're a civilian. What do you think?"

"You could be him," Raleigh said.

"Not bad," Sezar told Raleigh. "You're getting the hang of it."

Beside them, a short Hemingway in a Lacoste shirt argued with a Hemingway in wire-rimmed glasses held in place with a string. "He drank rum runners!" said one man. "Oh yeah? The bill on the wall says beers!"

Sezar suddenly leaned close. The good humor went out of his face.

"I got two goddamn murders on my hands and I need to know what you know. How come every time there's a murder, you pop up?"

"Don't you think I want to know the answer to that?"

"No, I think you know the answer. I don't believe in

130

coincidences. I believe in planning. You're in deep shit, Raleigh."

They drained their beers. The bartender, a thin bald man with a gold earring and a teardrop tattoo beneath his left eye, put two more beers in front of them without being asked.

"In deep shit with you or with Uncle Abel?" Raleigh asked.

Sezar sat back. "Why'd you give Harold Wong money tonight?"

Raleigh jerked. Shaw and Blaney hadn't asked that. Then anger filled him. "If you knew I was in Cap'n Bob's when he got killed, what was all that crap back there?"

"Thirty dollars. You buy a little coke from him?"

"If I'd bought coke, you'd have me in jail by now. Your undercover guy would have told you. I was paying off a bet."

"What bet?"

"Mets game."

"Which one?"

"Tonight's."

Sezar smiled. "They weren't playing tonight."

"Yeah? Ask the St. Louis Cardinals. They lost."

"What score?" Sezar said.

"Ten to five. Two hundred to three. Arrest me because I don't know the score."

Sezar finished the second beer. He relaxed a little. He said, "In the old days, there was a policy in the Caribbean. It was how they dealt with pirates. Every once in a while, limited time only as they say on TV, an amnesty. Stop being a pirate and you get to go home." Sezar ran his finger down his empty glass. "Now you and I, maybe we want the same thing. I know you've been poking around into Salinger. You know it. Maybe you're thinking if you admit it, I'll throw you in jail. Interfering." Sezar leaned close. The edges of his mustache formed points. Somewhere behind them, a man with a high-pitched voice was reciting, "Robert Cohn was a boxing champion." Sezar said, "One time only. Amnesty."

He sat back.

Raleigh said, "Strawberry hit a homer in the third. Towering fly. Right-field fence."

Sezar smiled and nodded, changing tack. "You want to try something good, something really good? You like rum? Barban Court, it's the best. Elliot! Two Barbans!"

Raleigh eyed the detective with understanding. A slow grin spread over his face, too. He called to the bartender, "Doubles, Elliot."

"Cheers."

"Up yours."

"Two more," Sezar remarked to Elliot ten minutes later.

"Skol."

"French toast."

"Another round," Raleigh called out a short time after that. "You know what?" he confided to Sezar, hearing the slur in his words. He nodded at his own wisdom. "You are one of the biggest assholes I ever met." He whispered, "And I met a lot."

Sezar's head rolled a little. "If you have to be an asshole, you should be the biggest," he said. "You know, you could look like Hemingway if you put on a beard and wig."

Raleigh clutched his shirt at the chest. His forehead was starting to hurt. "You found me out," he said. "I tried to shoot myself but missed. Then I chased myself through the trees. What police work!" Raleigh focused on the bar. "What's this?"

"Another rum."

"Who put it there? I didn't see anyone put it there?"

"L' Chaim!"

"Rashcolnokov!"

"Getting a little dizzy, Raleigh? Getting a stomachache?"

A Hemingway behind them was looking intently into the face of a small blonde woman in a green dress. "Are you my first wife, my third wife, or my fifth wife?" he said.

"Stomachache!" Raleigh snorted. "Elliot!"

More soberly, he said, "He was a good guy. He was a nut

but so what? He wanted to help those birds, that's all. A gentle guy. An old hippie. He . . . I mean . . . he couldn't even breathe like a normal person." Raleigh squeezed his thumb and index finger up and down. "That atomizer," he said.

"Time to go."

In the car, Raleigh shouted as they drove up Morgan Street, "You're drunk and you're driving! This is a citizen's arrest! Stop this car, do you hear me? I said stop it!"

When it did stop, Raleigh saw they'd reached his driveway. The lights were off in the house. Diane was due around five, Sezar had said.

Sezar shut the motor, which clicked as it cooled. The night was brilliant and starry, the moon a sliver. Raleigh said, "I want a chocolate doughnut."

"Harold Wong told me you never gave him any money," Sezar said.

Raleigh started to get out of the car. "Then he's a liar. I told you. The Mets."

Sezar leaned toward him, halfway across the seat. He blinked more when he was drunk and his upper lip protruded slightly. His diamond irises seemed to have rotated sideways, so that they almost ran southwest to northeast now, instead of lying flat. In a slow voice he said, "The only reason you're here instead of El Jailo is that you had a bad night. Next time, you'll be trying to reach Ed Quade."

"Who's *Ed* Quade?" Raleigh held on to the roof of the car for support.

"The only bail bondsman on Key Rey." Sezar grinned.

Raleigh turned to go into the house but there was a long blast on the horn. Lights went on next door. A woman's voice shouted, "It's three-thirty! Shrimpers!"

Sezar had put the car in gear, Raleigh could tell from the way the motor raced. The detective leaned on one hand, on the front seat. "One last question," he said. "I have to ask you one last question."

133

What's it going to be this time? Raleigh thought. He caught a glimpse, through the driver's window, of a white Toyota across the street. There was something familiar about it but he could not remember what.

"How come there's dental floss hanging from your windows?" Sezar said.

"To clean my teeth if I get stuck outside," Raleigh said. As he turned away, he saw the slightest movement inside the Toyota. The lawn spun slightly. Within minutes of getting into the house, he was asleep.

NINE

The more Raleigh looked, the pinker Rey Del Mar seemed. Four stories high, it rose in twin wings extending in a wedge shape from a Parthenon replica in the center. Small fountains fronted the condo, with sculpted nymphs spewing water from their mouths. The balconies were enclosed by pink picket fences and pink begonias in flowerpots. Raleigh had seen a pink Rey Del Mar brochure at Abel Quade's house. "No two units are alike," it had said.

The Wells Fargo guard leaned out of the guardhouse, to hand Raleigh back his license. "Treasure meeting's in the Pizarro Room," the man said with a slight stutter, over the drumming rain. "Park in the visitor's lot." In the rearview mirror, Raleigh caught sight of the white Toyota, with Detective Blaney in it, pulling up on the shoulder of Conch Boulevard, behind him. An arm came out of the driver's window and waved.

The Wells Fargo guard waved back.

Key Rey storms were swift and brutal. Raleigh sprinted through the hot drops, past the parked Cadillacs and Lincolns. His squeaking sneakers attracted irritated glances from the clerk in the pink sports jacket behind the lobby desk. Plaster of Paris Ponce de León statues occupied alcoves near potted palms. Travel and real estate offices off the lobby were opening for the day.

Raleigh hoped Jake would be at Professor Pete's presentation. He wanted to hear Jake's voice again.

He followed signs and slipped into the Pizarro Room. Pete's voice was saying, "Let's look at the next slide." Raleigh stood in back, beneath a chandelier, letting his eyes adjust to the darkness. The projector glow made silhouettes of roughly two dozen spectators scattered in rows of folding chairs, legs crossed or leaning forward, blue cigarette haze above a few heads. The screen showed a sixteenth-century pen-and-ink drawing of Indians wielding picks underground, in a tunnel, while Spanish pikemen prodded them with lances. In the foreground, an Indian wearing a loincloth lay sprawled on the ground while a guard raised a truncheon in the air over his head.

The professor's round glasses glinted. He stood at a podium to the right of the screen. "Ten thousand Incas died mining silver at Potosí," he said. The projector clicked and now Raleigh looked at the Marquis: the Van Dyke beard above the white lace collar. The detatched brown eyes, liquid, haughty.

"He cheated his friends as well as his king," Pete said. He used the same hushed tones whenever the Marquis came up.

The rain must have picked up outside. The battering sound increased on the other side of the drawn shades. Moving down the far aisle, Raleigh tried to make out the spectators' faces. A match flared in the sixth row and Raleigh stopped. In the glow, he saw a tall man with broad shoulders. Raleigh took two steps into the row and someone whispered, "Get out of the way!" He saw the man wasn't Jake.

On the screen, divers in black suits hung a foot off the sea bottom, their hands hidden in swirling sand as they groped for treasure. Tiny zebra-colored fish seemed oblivious to the searchers, near waving fan-shaped plants.

"The search is scientific, systematic," Pete told his potential investors. "We set up baselines on the ocean floor. Mark points along the baselines every thirty feet. A diver swims out a ways and forms the third point of a triangle we explore thoroughly. We've gridded thousands of square miles of ocean. We get results. It's not magic."

Just for an instant, Raleigh wondered how much money he could make if he bought a single share of Pete's business and Pete found the *Nuevo Mundo*. He kept moving.

A collective ahhh from the audience pulled his attention back to the screen. He recognized the picture of *Isabella* treasure. Gold coins. Bars shaped like Milky Ways. The rain stopped. From a sudden infusion of light in the room, Raleigh knew the back door had opened. A tall figure was framed back there, advancing into the room. It wasn't Jake.

The projector clicked faster. A jaguar design had been cut into the center of a silver plate. The jaguar's claws were embedded in the neck of a fleeing deer, and its teeth ripped at the throat.

A silver bowl featured a design of a human heart pierced by an arrow. It had been dripping blood for three hundred years.

Raleigh had been tempted to go back to The Billfisher this morning for the Hemingway look-alike boxing matches. "Take one step into that bar," Sezar had warned last night, "and you'll be in jail."

Pete's enthusiasm seemed genuine, no matter how many times he had done the show. "The fleet always took the same route," he told the crowd, narrowing down the area in which the wreck could be found. An old parchment map filled the screen. "North past Key Rey to Monkey Island. Right turn to Bird Island. Right turn to Spain. The odds of finding the *Nuevo*? Long. We know that." His voice smoothed. "But if we find her this year, and rest assured, we *will* find her. Maybe not tomorrow or next week. Maybe not by Labor Day. But we're closing in." His voice rose a little. "When we find those two tons of treasure, the investors will be paid not only in cash *but in objects.* In bars and coins and jewelery. Our friends who funded the *Isabella* search own many of the objects you've been looking at. Why, I found the ship and I had to get their permission to show these slides to you!"

The audience seemed to like the idea of getting the treasure away from Pete. Raleigh wondered what the jaguar would feel like under his fingers. Cool, he thought. No. Hot.

He caught sight of a Hemingway look-alike, a man with a white beard staring at him from an aisle seat. When the man saw Raleigh looking back, he turned away and put his arm around his woman companion.

The lights came on.

Raleigh heard disappointed "ohs" that the slide show had ended. But nobody made a move to leave. He recognized Harold Wong in the third row, staring at the blank screen. There was a sense of hunger and incompletion in the room. Of appetites whetted. Raleigh was surprised to see Pete was wearing a sports jacket and tie at the lectern. He let the silence fill the room a moment. Then he leaned forward and said, "A photo's a poor substitute for real treasure. That's why I brought some along with me today."

A murmur went through the room. Two Wells Fargo guards were carrying in a glass display case. As they set it down near the podium, people craned to see, and Pete said, "We'll open it in a bit. Come up. Ask questions. I'll be around."

The guards stepped back, attendants who would hover close to satisfy Pete's next whim. The professor swept his hand low, toward the table, but no one was looking at him anymore. "The treasure of the *Isabella*," he announced.

Raleigh drifted forward with the others. He would give Jake a few more minutes, then try the shrimp boat. But before he reached the outer perimeter of the crowd, Pete pushed through from the other direction, reached with both hands, pumped Raleigh's hand.

"I knew I'd found a kindred spirit when I met you. A fellow dreamer." Pete winked. "Or should I say, another man who knows dreams come true."

"I wanted to hear what you had to say."

"And see the real stuff, eh? It's hard to stay away. It even brought you away from your murder investigation." More confidentially and gossipy, Pete whispered, "Who did it? Who do you think?" Raleigh demurred. He would have to be careful how he brought up Jake. He noticed, close up, that Pete's jacket was frayed at the collar. The ironed white shirt had yellowed with use. The faint smell of fried potatoes came off the man, despite the cologne.

Pete took Raleigh's elbow to steer him toward the case. "The heart with the arrow in it was my favorite. Those Indians were like Rembrandts the Spanish made into slaves."

"You know," Raleigh said, stopping, "you look a little like the Marquis, with that beard."

"Do you think so? Yes! You see it?" Pete clapped his hands together. "I'm a kid when it comes to him." He drew closer. "Sometimes I feel him next to me, trying to tell me where the ship went down. Oh, I know he's not really there. Only a crazy old professor could be friends with a dead man, eh, Mr. Fixx?"

"You should see some of *my* friends," Raleigh joked. He looked around casually. "Doesn't Jake give the talk with you?"

"Jake? Ha! He doesn't have the image investors react to. Well, they react, but not the way I want." Raleigh heard a woman gasp and say, "Exquisite. They're glorious." Pete frowned. "Besides, he had to go to Marathon today. That engine."

Then he brightened. "But I have good news." He indicated a man in a seersucker jacket near the display case. "Department of Interior," Pete said. "Harbaugh's his name. He owns a condo

139

here. I talked to him about Bird Island." Pete's grip tightened. "He thinks he might be able to swing a review of the whole process to block Abel." Pete's grin widened. "And people say I'm too busy to work with the committee."

"The guy scratching his head, with the bald spot?"

"He wants to talk to you," Pete said.

Raleigh asked how long Harbaugh was staying. "I'll call him later."

Pete looked surprised when Raleigh left without talking to Harbaugh. In the lobby, he leaned against the wall, a dull throbbing in his stomach. He kept seeing Wheeze as he had been in the bar last night. A last glimpse of the man, disappearing between revelers.

Who followed you out of the bar to the cemetery, Wheeze? The question had gone around and around in Raleigh's head since last night.

In his mind, Wheeze grinned. "SMERSH has been after me for years. Bolivia. Istanbul. They finally caught up. Maybe they saw me pass you the note in the bar. Maybe they waited outside. KGB disguised as tourists."

What were you going to tell me, Wheeze?

But Wheeze was gone. A slim redhead came up to him in the lobby, a gold dubloon sparkling in a lanyard around her neck, the coin resting on the vermilion silk of her Chinese collar. "Are you the man who wanted the buying price of the Drake Street house?" she asked. She giggled when Raleigh said no. "Whoops, better keep track of my customers. Two weeks out of Camden and I'm a mindless slut by eleven in the morning."

He excused himself and at a pay phone called Trans Europe. Diane wasn't due until midafternoon. This time, the jet had developed "engine trouble." He called Coconut Cabs and told the dispatcher what he needed, giving a phony name in case the man he was talking to was related to Quade, or Sezar, or the police. Through the lobby window, he watched a lone fisherman on the flats battling a bonefish. The storm was over. The fish was running hard, bending the angler's rod nearly in two. The sky had gone a deep blue.

Ten minutes later, a pink Chevy cab pulled to the side entrance. Raleigh ran out and ducked inside, hoping Blaney was still on Conch Boulevard, watching the front.

"Blaney's not following you, he's *protecting* you," Sezar had said on the phone that morning when Raleigh complained.

"Mr. Harbaugh?" the driver asked, checking to be sure he had the right fare.

Raleigh groaned and nodded, sinking down on the backseat. "What a night." He leaned down farther. "I'll just lie . . . mmmmmm."

"You're not gonna be sick or nuthin'?"

"Just tired." Lying on his back, Raleigh told the man where he wanted to go. The man whistled.

"Johnny Coetzee? You a friend of his?" From the back seat, the driver was a long neck, greasy prematurely gray hair, and a gold earring. "I lived here eight years but I never met him. I seen him play at Cap'n Bob's." He put the taxi in gear. Raleigh heard the swish of tires in puddles. "He's a genius. 'Coconut Paradise' made me move here," the driver said. "I'm working in Cleveland, right, in a shoe factory. Listening to Coetzee's music on the assembly line. I'm thinking, What am I doing here? I could be there. And he was right. Key Rey is Paradise. You ought to move here."

"I'm only visiting for a few days," Raleigh said.

"Well, it's an honor driving someone to his place. Like a circle coming around. I mean, I moved here because of him and now I'm driving you to his house. Very mysterious."

Raleigh watched the top of the guardhouse go by. He wondered whether the guard had seen him and was signaling Blaney. A poster on the back of the driver's seat showed a flamingo grinding out a cigarette butt with its foot. PLEASE DON'T SMOKE, the flamingo was saying.

"The Beach Boys. Ronstadt. They visit him," the driver said. "The Hazy Days album came out of those sessions. What am I telling you for? You a musician?"

"An agent," Raleigh said.

"An agent. I bet you know a lot of those famous guys. David Bowie. I had his sister in the cab once. At least she said she was his sister."

The car swung left. They were on Conch Boulevard.

Raleigh felt his excitement rising at the idea of meeting Johnny Coetzee. He remembered a small figure in denim at Madison Square Garden, alone onstage, bathed in crimson light, playing a guitar. In those days, Raleigh had lived in Greenwich Village. He'd bought the tickets from a scalper because the concert had been sold out. He'd sat all the way up top.

Bits of information he'd read over the years came to him. Coetzee and his movie-star girlfriends. Coetzee the shrimp fisherman's son, and his rise to fame. The European tour. The audience with the Queen.

"I always wanted to go to his house but it takes guts," the driver said. "I remember those tourists, New Yorkers, they were. Coetzee's dogs ripped 'em apart."

"Dogs?" Raleigh said, suddenly interested in what the driver was saying.

"You know. The Dobes. Everybody knows this story. I guess if I was famous, I wouldn't want people bothering me, either."

Raleigh repeated, sitting up, "Dobes?" Behind them, the Toyota was nowhere in sight. Conch Boulevard unwound, deserted except for the Sharkmobile coming in their direction. They cruised past houseboat row. Plastic flamingos still decorated Salinger's upper deck, but Raleigh saw the potted palms had died. A wooden board was nailed across the front door.

The driver said, "Then there were those other guys. That band a couple years back. They went out to his house to play for him. Maybe you heard of this."

"I wasn't here."

"They figured they'd creep around at night, quiet. Set up their equipment. In the morning, they'd start playing. Maybe he'd give them a break, they thought."

"The dogs again?"

"Ruff," the driver growled. "Ruffff."

They were still on the undeveloped side of Key Rey. The cab swung off Conch Boulevard and onto a pitted dirt lane so narrow Raleigh was unsure whether it was a driveway. They pitched into potholes, sending up spray. The roadside exploded in floral color. The storm had knocked thousands of bougainvillea petals off the bushes and they carpeted their path in orange flame.

The driver switched on the radio. As if on cue, Coetzee's voice floated out to them, reggae style, "Aye aye ayyyye got de rock fe-ver. . . ."

Raleigh swallowed. "Is the property walled or do the dogs run free?"

"What are you asking me for? You're his friend. I never go near the place."

Abruptly, the vista opened up and they stopped. Raleigh had expected music, noise, dogs, cars. But the house sat quiet, a New Orleans—style mansion of aquamarine stucco, set squarely in the center of a lush mowed lawn. More flowers bordered the property. Passionflowers with crimson petals and purple and white filaments. White moth orchids. Red lobster claws.

"I don't see any Dobermans," Raleigh said. "Besides, there's no fence. If he had Dobes, he'd have a fence."

"Maybe they're inside."

Raleigh asked the driver to wait. He walked gingerly along a flagstone path toward the house, expecting to need to bolt any minute. Thin wrought-iron columns rose from the downstairs porch, through the second-story balcony to the overhanging roof. Purple cut-glass parrots were set into the double

143

arched doors of polished mahogany, lining both floors. The doorbell made a sound like a snare drum. It swung open. The rock star himself stood there.

Coetzee looked like he did on album covers. He was a tall man with copper-colored plastic glasses, watery blue eyes, and a white Indian cotton shirt that billowed out. He wore a straw hat even though he'd been in the house. A single black dreadlock fell down across his cheek. He blinked out at Raleigh, smiling slightly. He held a twelve-ounce glass filled to the brim with amber liquid. "Hi."

Feeling like a boy asking for an autograph, Raleigh heard himself say, awkwardly, "My name is Fixx. I'm sorry to bother . . ."

"Fixx! I know that name!" The dreadlock fell free as Coetzee leaned forward, two inches away, gazing into Raleigh's face. "Got it! You were the backup drummer for Heavy Metal. How'd you get rid of that scar?"

"I'm not . . ."

"Don't say it. Don't. Say it." Coetzee waved the glass. "The auto supply store! You're Earl!" He shook his head. "But you said your name was Fixx."

Coetzee grew quiet. He looked out beyond Raleigh and caught sight of the cab. He looked back at Raleigh. The magnified eyes narrowed behind the thick round lenses.

"You're the one the police say killed Salinger," he said in a flatter voice.

"I didn't kill him."

But Coetzee grinned enormously. "Well, if you did, you're always welcome here!" He threw the door open the rest of the way. "But you probably didn't do it," he said. "If the Keystone Kops think you did it, you have to be innocent. Sezar said to tell him if you came. Fat chance. Want a drink?"

"What is it?"

Coetzee peered affectionately into the tall glass. "Coetzee punch. A delicate mix. Barbados rum. Cuban rum. Bahamian rum. Haitian rum and," he said, holding up one index finger as he disclosed the coup-de-grace ingredient, "Puerto Rican rum. You want to talk about Salinger, right? You're writing a book."

Close enough, Raleigh thought. Coetzee's flip-flop slippers and Raleigh's sopping sneakers made a symphony of sucking noises as the singer led him through the living room. "When I first moved here, the cops used to come once a week. Looking for drugs, they said. Give 'em twenty bucks and they'd go away until the next Saturday."

The house was white—white walls, white wicker furniture on teak floors, rows of rotating ceiling fans, and a huge six-foot painting of Coetzee's first album cover over the white Steinway. In the painting, the singer reclined on the deck of a sailboat, guitar in hand, glass of rum at his side, trousers rolled so his bare feet brushed the blue glassy sea.

"Nice house," Raleigh said.

"Quiet. I like quiet. I used to have a poodle but he OD'd at a party. Everybody in town thinks I have Dobermans out here. We made up this story about . . . never mind. But it keeps more pain-in-the-ass tourists away than an alarm system would."

In the patio, the temperature rose at least ten degrees. The air was humid and sweet from more flowers. Blood red chaconias. Peach angels, with their bell shapes flaring in yellow-pink. Raleigh eased into a reclining chair near a pink povi tree and by a small pool of green water. A cornflake-shaped blossom fell, touched the pool, sent out ripples.

Coetzee brushed the dreadlock from his face.

"Sezar was right," Raleigh began. "I want to ask you about Salinger." A thrashing in the pool interrupted him. The petal was gone and a small brown fin sank out of sight. Coetzee said, "I keep them a little hungry. Baby sharks. Whoever did it, more power to him."

"Whoever did it killed someone else last night. A friend of mine. Maybe you knew him. Wheeze."

145

The dreadlock jerked. "Wheeze?" Coetzee took off his glasses and squeezed his forehead. The brim of the straw hat made it hard to see his eyes. "He was like a kid," Coetzee said. "Who would hurt Wheeze?" His shock seemed real. "My God, what's happening here?"

Raleigh told him about last night. Coetzee sat stunned.

"Salinger, I can understand Salinger," Coetzee said. "But Wheeze?"

Coetzee stood up and went to the pool. Joining him, Raleigh counted three little sharks down there, babies. "Nurse sharks," the singer said. Their gills opened and closed, revealing bright red slits. Their spineless backs wriggled as they slid bellies along the bottom.

"You name them?" Raleigh said.

Coetzee drank deeply. "Fish. You know where you stand with fish. They're too dumb to fuck around with you."

He looked up. "You want that rum? I'm going to make myself another."

"How about juice?"

Raleigh watched the sharks until Coetzee returned with two glasses piled high with ice. Coetzee said, "The first time I met Wheeze, I was playing at Cap'n Bob's. He came over during a break. Told me he was a 'music spy.' Music spy? I thought he was a nut." Coetzee shrugged affectionately. "And he was, totally off his rocker. He told me he was going to protect me. He used to call me up when anyone was writing music on the island. Tell me they were stealing my stuff. They weren't." Coetzee's voice hardened. "But I liked him. He never wanted anything. Sezar was mad at you because you're getting in his way, I think." Coetzee seemed to find this amusing. "I'll tell you something. I might as well. Half the country knows it."

He beckoned Raleigh to follow him. "I don't know if this will do any good, but maybe you can help Wheeze. Not help him, I mean you can't really help him, but you know what I mean." He led Raleigh into a sunny downstairs room looking

146

out on the patio. The room was completely empty. "Used to be a big table here. Redwood. And chairs." In an adjacent and equally empty room, squarish spots had faded on walls where pictures had once hung. Coetzee said, "The den." The empty rooms went on, one after the other. Shocked, Raleigh realized the only furnished room in the house was the living room.

"Pretty good facade, huh? You should have seen this place four, five years ago," Coetzee said wistfully, leading Raleigh onto the second-story balcony. "Parties. Jam sessions." He trailed off. He leaned over the railing and gazed out toward the cab. A humid smell came to them after the rainstorm, and drops still glistened on the grass.

"Mind if I ask you a question?" Coetzee said, softer. "Do you like my music? I don't mind if you don't, but do you have a favorite?"

Coetzee nodded when Raleigh said, "Coconut Paradise." "That was Nineteen-seventy-nine," the singer said. Raleigh told him "Diver Girl." Coetzee smiled. "I like that one, too. Nineteen-eighty. 'My Marquesa'? Eighty. 'Turtle Kraal'? Seventy-nine. See the pattern?"

Hearing the names of the old songs, Raleigh had a vision of his old Manhattan balcony, overlooking Mercer Street in Greenwich Village. He remembered a blonde sculptress with spiky hair and a black tank top slipping off high heels to dance barefoot with him. He could still hear Coetzee's soft voice coming from the stereo inside, mingling with the traffic noise on a Saturday night.

"Salinger was my friend, at least at first," Coetzee said. "He had me on his show. It wasn't any money but he was funny. He knew the greatest jokes. He always had mushrooms."

Raleigh had not been aware of the anger building in him against Salinger, but now it exploded inside him, ballooning in his chest, hammering in his temple. For phoning him in the first place. For drawing him into this. Another Salinger story was beginning, another story by someone he'd hurt.

147

"One night I made a mistake," Coetzee said. "We were on his boat, after a party. Watching some movie on the video, *Eraserhead*, I think. I told him I'd been having trouble writing, hell, trouble." Coetzee made a face. "I hadn't been able to write in four years. I'd just told people I was taking it easy."

"Jay was good about it. He went into the other room for more beer, but he came back with a tape recorder too, in his pocket. I didn't know he had it. I told him everything. The depression. The days sitting with the guitar with nothing coming." Coetzee looked down at the lawn. "Next day, he calls me up," Coetzee said. "Come on over," he says. "He's flying, really up. When I get there he plays the tape. At first, I think it's some kind of joke. Yeah, sure, I tell him. You're going to play it on your show. But then I see he means it. He tells me he needs money to make payments on his Celica." Coetzee's voice dropped. He looked Raleigh full in the face. "I paid him."

"I don't understand. If you paid, how did the story get out?"

"Well, I paid the first time." Coetzee's hat shook back and forth. "I still remember what happened to him when he found out I'd pay. He started dancing around the boat. Singing. Making these weird 'King of the Keys' jokes. Manic."

In Raleigh's chest, a ticking started, an excitement.

Coetzee said, "The guy was crazy, I mean sick." He drank more rum, drained the glass. "A couple months later, he shows up at the house. He wanted more. I guess he figured it was easy. But I'd been brooding about it. I told him to go to hell. I said I wasn't going to spend my life paying him." Below, the cabdriver had gotten out of the Chevy, seeing Coetzee, and he was waving and smiling.

Coetzee waved back. "He went nuts. He started screaming. Crazy, I tell you, when he didn't get what he wanted. I've never seen anybody change like that." Now the driver was holding up a pad and pen, making signs like he wanted an autograph. The pulse was rising in Raleigh's throat, constricting it. He drank the juice but didn't taste it. There was the sense of the truth starting to break open. Coetzee tried to suck more rum from the glass but only ice was left. The singer motioned the driver to come up. The driver started running across the lawn.

Coetzee said, "He sold the story, up north. In a week it was on every TV show. 'Entertainment Tonight.' I guess he made a few bucks. I stopped getting bookings, good ones. My friends . . . I guess they weren't friends . . . stopped calling. The only way I'll keep this house is if Pete finds the *Nuevo Mundo* this year. I'm in for five shares. I'm a sucker for that guy."

There were running footsteps inside the house. Coetzee said, "Salinger ruined me."

"Did you kill him?"

The footsteps grew louder. The singer seemed to rouse himself off the railing, to blink out from behind the glasses. He took off the straw sombrero. More dreadlocks fell out. "Me? Kill someone?" His laughter echoed across the lawn. In the distance, Raleigh saw a white-tipped osprey, diving over the trees.

"Use it if it does you any good," Coetzee said.

The driver's face was bright with sweat when he reached the balcony. "Man, I am such a fan of yours," he said. He extended the pad. "It's for my sister. Hey Johnny, where are the Dobes?"

T E N
▾ ▾ ▾ ▾ ▾

"Another highball, my dear?" the old man asked. His liver-spotted hand reached to raise the seat partition separating him from Diane. "No, thank you," Diane said. Even off duty, stewardesses had to be nice to passengers. The plane banked left, broke from the thunderhead into clear sky. Tinged in purple from the storm behind them, she saw the smooth Gulf below. And Key West, construction cranes towering over the town.

The partition slid all the way up. The old man leaned close. "You still have a chance," he said as the NO SMOKING sign lit. "My son runs the store but I can get you furniture at cost. Hassocks," he whispered. "Love seats."

Diane stared at the blank pad of paper on her lap. She couldn't concentrate on the new play. She'd stopped being angry at Raleigh yesterday, and pushed the worry for him from her mind. There was nothing she could do about it anyway. But she wanted him. It was always this way after a trip. She thought of the way his fingertips felt squeezing her nipples. He smelled of spice when he lay on her, and she would trace tendons in his shoulders with her lips.

Diane spotted the veiny hands creeping across the gap between seats, crawling on knotty fingers. The old man's voice grew higher, childlike.

"Inky dinky, inky dinky," he singsonged. "The gooooood spider and the baaaad spider. The good spider would never bite a little girl but the bad spider . . ."

Diane dropped her hardback *Tropic of Cancer* on the nearest spider. Other passengers in first class turned at the yelp. The old man yanked away and extracted a flight magazine from the seat pouch in front of him. Diane put the book back below the window and against the arm of her seat. The man muttered something about women's libbers.

Her heart quickened as the jet touched the runway. She saw the leaping blue marlin atop the Key West terminal. The delays had made the trip so very long, and she was tired. In minutes, she was driving the Firebird out of the lot. When she wanted Raleigh, her skin grew more sensitive. Clothing bothered her as it rubbed against her body. Raleigh was especially energetic during investigations. Sex was more exciting when any minute attackers or police might burst into the house. "Make the best of things, Diane," her mother, a former Miss Montana, had always said.

It took only forty minutes to drive to Key Rey, but when she reached the driveway, Raleigh's Mustang was gone. She was disappointed but not surprised. His dental floss was wedged around downstairs doors and windows, so he had left the house safely. The doughnut crumbs on the plate by his word processor were still moist. Either things were breaking on the Salinger killing or Trans Europe had told him the wrong arrival time.

Diane couldn't wait to share the treats she'd brought home. Two bottles of Dom Perignon from Paris. Chocolate, raspberry, and champagne truffles. Raleigh liked to mash them between their bellies when they made love and lick them up afterward. She'd brought eclairs for tomorrow morning, croissants and *chèvre* cheese for tonight. Bright blue bath crystals that tickled when they blew into bubbles, and black perfumed soap. Raleigh insisted he hated cornichons, but whenever he worked late, the jars would be empty the next morning.

She put the food in the refrigerator and brought one bottle of Dom Perignon upstairs, with a long-stemmed glass. She left the flask of lotion from the Frankfurt airport's sex shop on the night table near the bed. The plane smell was on her, stale recirculated air and cigarette smoke. Her uniform stuck to her skin. She peeled it off in the bedroom; it fell around her. Naked, she uncorked the champagne and drank a warm glass. She went into the bathroom and stood in the tub. Diane upended the bottle above her head so the Dom Perignon spilled down her hair, cheeks, breasts, running onto her belly and legs in rivulets. She liked the bubbles bursting on her skin. Then she chose the striped bikini.

There was no way to tell when Raleigh would be home. After long periods without diving, her muscles ached and she craved the sea. The air tank was always full in the closet by the front door. In the car, with the top down, she listened to the Rolling Stones sing "Can't Get No Satisfaction." The salt smell seemed sharper on Conch Boulevard, tangy and electric, but the sun in Key Rey was out.

Diane's favorite beach was on the west point of the island. She lugged the tank and weights along a foot-wide path threading mangroves. She frowned at a discarded Coors can, a half-empty Dewar's bottle, a red foil wrapper that had held a condom.

But familiar peacefulness suffused her when she stepped onto the beach—white, clean, and crescent-shaped, made up of hot granular sand, not the normal Key Rey powdery variety. At her back, a half-standing wall of an old Spanish blockhouse protruded from the edge of the forest. Sometimes teenagers came to this beach, but today it was empty, deliciously private. The thick smell of vegetation mixed with the warm ocean odor.

On the cove, a small fish jumped, slapped the surface, and was gone.

She experienced the welcome cutoff of peripheral vision when the mask came on. The flippers rubbed at her feet and she tasted salt on the mouthpiece. Trans Europe seemed a thousand miles away. So did Raleigh. Key Rey. She balanced against the surf and stepped down a three-foot drop. Then she was under, swimming through aquamarine light along the bottom of a ridge, fire-coral ledges swelling away on either side. She felt her muscles expand and contract. A yellow angelfish hung watching her, pancake-thin with a crimson fringe on its tail. On the curving expanse of green brain coral below, the striations looked like the cortex of a human brain. Calmly, the fish turned away.

She wished Raleigh would take up diving, but he grew nervous at the idea of going underwater. Claustrophobic.

Diane probed under a ledge, inserted both hands, and gently withdrew a puffed-up porcupine fish, a balloon shape with yellow spines, the points still soft because she had not alarmed it, the tiny fins swishing back and forth. When she let it go, it hung suspended in the water. After a second, it built up speed and shot away.

That was when Diane caught sight of another diver approaching from the right, along the ridge. He'd probably come from the brushy woods flanking the beach. Underwater, he looked big, coming steadily. Diane figured he was hunting for dinner because the long, thin shape of a spear gun jutted at his side.

He never took his eyes off her. After a moment, she felt a tremor of unease at the purposefulness of his movements, at the absolute straight line in which he came. When he grew close, she saw a fringe of dirty blond hair above the mask, although she could not see his features. Diane pointed to the ledge where the porcupine fish had disappeared, wanting to show him what she had found. But the gun came up, pointed at her chest.

Angry, Diane waved for the man to aim elsewhere. She swam off a couple of feet, but the steel point followed her. Her breathing seemed louder. The man jerked a thumb over his back, indicating she should swim in that direction, toward the shore on the side of the cove.

To hell with you, Diane thought. She fled toward the beach, kicking hard, using her hands to scoop the water. But something streaked by her ear, left it tingling. The spear left a churning wake as it disappeared. She glanced back. He had already inserted another spear into the gun, and when he jerked the thumb again, more angrily this time, she complied.

Her throat burned. Underwater, she had to keep breathing steadily. She tried to get a better look at the man when she passed. He looked fit, muscled, and he swam without extra movements.

Diane kicked slowly. Her fists clenched. Tears of rage collected inside her mask. I won't be afraid, she thought.

Raleigh stared out of the back window of the taxi but scarcely saw the mangrove swamp going by outside. He was heading back toward Rey Del Mar. The thick feeling in his throat, the sense of a pattern forming was getting stronger. In his mind, he saw Professor Pete walking down the dock of Salinger's boat. He still heard Johnny Coetzee's words, "As soon as Salinger found out I'd pay, he started dancing around."

Raleigh imagined Salinger in his ridiculous pink pith helmet. A red-faced, red-bearded man in an aloha shirt. Sneakers thudding on the carpet as he jumped up and down.

Half-turning, the driver grinned, waving a paper above the seat. "Johnny Coetzee's autograph! Those sleazeballs at the garage'll believe I met him now."

Raleigh went back over Pete's speech at Rey Del Mar. He

154

remembered the professor taking a check from a woman who had been admiring the *Isabella* jewelry.

I don't know where Jake gets his money, Harold Wong had said.

The sun burned puddles off Conch Boulevard. The driver was saying, "So he says, 'Call me *Johnny*.' And I say, '*Call me Nick.*'"

A police car shot by from the other direction, two Hemingway look-alikes in back.

He tried to remember what Pete had told him about raising money for the *Nuevo Mundo*. A thousand dollars a point. Abel Quade had bought five points. Coetzee, five. How many points did Pete sell a year? A hundred? A thousand?

"When I wouldn't pay, Salinger went nuts," Coetzee had said.

"I said, what's wrong with collecting autographs?" the driver demanded, half-turning.

"What?" Raleigh said. "Nothing."

"Then what are you making that face for? You think it's bullshit? Kids do it?" The driver shook his finger, watching Raleigh instead of the road. "I have news for you. My uncle sold DiMaggio's autograph for two hundred bucks."

"I don't care if you collect autographs. I was thinking about something else."

They missed a palm tree and veered back onto the road. The driver muttered, "You think you're great because you know Johnny Coetzee?"

Detective Blaney's Toyota was gone from Rey Del Mar. Raleigh noticed the logo on the gate guard's hat, pelicans flanking the Hapsburg shield. The guard's eyes widened when they met Raleigh's. He waved the cab ahead with elaborate casualness. Looking back, Raleigh saw the man already on the phone.

Pete had left an hour ago, but for what Raleigh needed to know, that was fine. At the front desk he asked to speak to whoever arranged Pete's talks. The pink-jacketed clerk ushered him into an overly air-conditioned office overlooking the Gulf. The woman behind the frail-looking French desk wore a thin wedding band and a calf-length Laura Ashley dress. Her long mouth turned down at the edges. A Wharton Business School degree hung between original lithographs of Chicago 1890s architecture. The pearly conch on the desk was the only concession to Florida.

Feigning embarrassment, Raleigh explained that he had attended Pete's talk and had been intrigued enough to consider investing. "But I've read about, well, con artists," he said. "I don't mean to . . ." He fumbled for the proper word, ". . . accuse him of anything. It's just that Rey Del Mar has such a good reputation, and I don't have much money. I was wondering if there are any safeguards."

The name on the business degree read, *Anna Lasser*. She wore no jewelry except a thin gold watch. "There are no guarantees in treasure hunting," she said severely. "Surely you realize that."

"Yes, of course. I don't mind the risk of not finding the ship. I'm just concerned about, well, the *con* artists. I'd feel better if Rey Del Mar were involved, if there was some connection between you and Pete."

From the strict posture, Raleigh had the feeling Anna Lasser disapproved of treasure investing. "We're not part of the business but we do keep records of investments made here," she said. She moved her index finger up and down inside the conch as she talked. "You may remember three years ago Pete had some trouble with the government."

Raleigh feigned horror, but she waved a hand to dismiss his concern. "All kinds of tax examiners came down, looking for fraud, for anything that might enable them to seize the find. They made things unpleasant," she said. "For him and for us. Since Pete uses Rey Del Mar as a base for his fundraising, they went through our books as well." She grimaced. "They found no improprieties but I advised our association president, Mr. Abel Quade, that we should safeguard ourselves against a reoccurrence." She sighed. "Mr. Quade is quite generous with the professor." Too generous, she seemed to say. "He donates the space the professor uses. He regards the professor as a quaint, er, tourist draw."

The finger tapped the pearly inside of the conch. "It was the professor's idea to maintain his books here. He thought it would make investors feel easier, and the association, too. The books are open if you would care to see them. The professor raised several thousand dollars just today. Of course," she added, looking at the lithographs of Chicago's art museum, "investing in treasure isn't like putting money in blue chips."

"Wharton," Raleigh said admiringly, inclining his head toward the diploma on the wall.

As she rose to bring the books, Anna Lasser said, "Mr. Quade insists on exceptional quality in his workers. Mr. Quade doesn't forgive mistakes."

At the Key Rey *Sunfish*, Raleigh found Ike White at his upstairs desk, beneath his San Francisco posters, addressing a pile of silver envelopes with monogrammed motorcycles on the flaps.

The thin, balding editor grinned. "I was just sending one to you," he said. "To get to know you better. Just a few friends. Barbequed steaks and snapper. Piña coladas."

"Can I bring Diane?"

Some of the glow went out of White's eyes. "Diane?"

Raleigh let him off the hook. "The fifteenth? We have to be in Miami the fifteenth." White did a good job of looking disappointed. An eight-by-ten photo of the editor sat beside the old Royal typewriter. In the picture, White sat sideways, astride his black motorcycle. He wore a black jacket, black cap, black jeans, and black leather wristbands with studs. His chin was spotted with silver glitter.

157

"I'm writing a feature for the *News* on Professor Pete," Raleigh said. "And I was hoping you'd let me look at your old clips."

White brushed the hair back on the sides of his head. "Anytime."

"Also, I was curious. I know Pete had all that trouble with the IRS three years ago, but what about since then? Any more examiners come down?"

White shook his head. "He embarrassed them, believe me. All the publicity, and they never found a dime out of place. But the *Miami Herald's* come down a couple of times. They find a disgruntled investor, check Pete's books, trace the money."

"Disgruntled?"

White made a face. "Tell some people a hundred times they'll probably lose money on something, and when they do, they'll still scream you tricked them."

Raleigh nodded. In the poster of the Golden Gate Bridge, a line of men danced the rhumba along the walkway.

"How about the money he raises at coin fairs?" Raleigh said. "Does the *Herald* trace that, too?"

"Same books, isn't it?"

"Probably." But it was something to check. Raleigh had also copied down names of investors at Rey Del Mar. He would phone and randomly try to find out if the numbers in the book matched the figures the investors would say they paid. Ten thousand from a Cleveland investor. Two thousand from Orlando. Eight thousand. Six. One. Eleven.

White's manuscript in the typewriter was headlined BARGAINS IN PARADISE. White went back to licking envelopes as Raleigh stood to check the clips, and Raleigh noticed a photograph flat on the desk, by the In Box. In the snapshot, a young girl in a cloth coat held a puppy in her arms in front of a brick house. It was autumn in the photo. Oak and maple leaves lay piled on the lawn. The edge of a letter protruded from under the silver envelopes. Raleigh made out the childish scrawl on powder-blue stationery. "When are you coming home, Daddy?"

Raleigh walked down the shrimp dock toward Professor Pete's boat. The *Sunfish* clips on the treasure hunter had held nothing new. The other boats were gone. "Professor?" Raleigh called, looking up at the pilothouse. No answer. The cabin was locked. He rapped on the window.

When he stepped back on the pier, he saw the honey-haired diving instructor sauntering toward him, past a gray and white pelican preening himself on a piling.

"No class today?" Raleigh said.

"Maybe I told them to come back later," she said. The sun glinted rusty streaks in her waist-length hair. "Maybe I was waiting for something more exciting."

Her polka-dot bikini was tied so tight it left white marks on her pelvis. One knee was extended outward, provocatively, two inches from Raleigh's legs. Too bad she and Ike White couldn't hit it off, he thought.

"I haven't seen Pete all morning," she said. "But you can wait for him in the shop if you like." She moved closer. "I have Carta Blancas in the fridge."

Raleigh looked over the four-foot-wide elbow-shaped pipes suspended from the winch in back of the trawler. In Pete's show, he'd seen the blowers shoot water into the sea bottom, forming holes searchers could explore. Jake had been at the control winches on deck, his long hair raggedly brushing the tops of his shoulders.

"How about Jake?" Raleigh asked. "He around?"

"I saw him about forty minutes ago. I don't know where he went. He took the Ford." Her knee brushed Raleigh's trousers. "What do you say? A cold beer in the shop?"

A fiberglass Boston Whaler shot across the inlet, its outboard emitting a high, thin buzz. Wheeze's boat had been the same color green.

Jake is in Marathon, Pete had said.

The thickening feeling spread to Raleigh's jaw.

Raleigh rushed into the house and grabbed the phone on the third ring.

"Getting *bored* lying in the sun?" Frank said. "Tired of birds? I got a call from a friend of yours. Sezar. He said you're pretty active down there. Writing a story for somebody else, Raleigh? *Esquire? GQ?*"

"If I were going to write for anyone, it would be you." Raleigh spotted Diane's duty-free canvas tote bag on the dining room table. His breath caught. "Hold on." Pressing his hand against the receiver, he called, "Diane!"

Damn Trans Europe, he thought. They always get the schedules wrong.

"Why are you investigating a murder if there's no story?" Frank said.

"Oh, I asked a couple of questions, that's all. It's the birds I'm working on, Frank. Today I heard that the Department of Interior is—"

"Fuck the birds," Frank said. "Listen to this. 'Dear Sirs.'" He made his voice all wobbly, like an old woman's. "'I am an invalid and a widow living in Larchmont, and a great fan of Raleigh Fixx. I look forward to his grisly tales in your otherwise worthless—'"

"Frank."

"Another one? 'Dear editor. My name is Emil and I am nine years old. I like Raleigh Fixx. I especially liked the man who pushed people on IRT tracks.'"

"Frank, I'm busy right now."

"From Flushing. Riverdale. Harlem." Raleigh heard Frank flipping pages by the receiver to show him how many letters had come. "Here's one in Portuguese, for Chrissakes. I don't even know what it says except your name. Chinatown! The woman wants to subscribe to the *new* paper you're writing for. She figures you must be writing for a *new* paper and she wants to know what it is."

"I'm not writing for any paper. I'll call you tonight."

Diane wasn't upstairs but her uniform lay on the bedroom floor. A faint perfumy sandalwood odor came to him. He started to get aroused. He smiled at the empty bottle of Dom Perignon she'd left on the sink. Champagne showers again.

Downstairs, he opened a jar of cornichons, munched one, and said, "Egh." When the coffee was brewing, Raleigh took the last spice doughnut from the refrigerator. He snapped the bagpipe tape into the stereo, low, so the sound wouldn't interrupt him on the phone. He put his Adidas up on the makeshift desk. It took four rings before Isabel answered the phone at the *Herald*.

"I'm on deadline, Ace. What can I do for you?"

"Coin fairs in Florida. And how treasure is sold. How the companies finance themselves. Shares. Investments. Whatever they do."

"Is that all? How about all the clips on El Salvador, too?"

"Could you read me what you have on Professor Pete?"

"*Read* you?" Despite her rush, the journalist in her was intrigued. "Why the hurry?"

"If there's a story here, I'll give it to you first. I promise."

There was a click on the line, another caller trying to get through. Raleigh ignored it. The coffee machine beeped in the kitchen and the room filled with a fresh-brewed smell.

"When do you need it?" Isabel asked.

"Now."

The cassette, which was playing "You Take the High Road," started skipping but smoothed out again.

Isabel started laughing. "I'll switch you to the library. Tell Roman you're working for me, freelancing. Otherwise, he won't help you. And remember, I get the story first. Before Frank."

On the Gulf, Raleigh watched a teenage boy on a windsurfer skimming toward the open sea. The board tilted far left, the purple sail a triangle filled with wind.

Roman sounded like an old man, and hoarse, like a smoker. He had a New England accent, clipped vowels.

"I'm not supposed to do work for freelancers," he complained as the music started skipping again. "I'd be on the phone all day if freelancers could call."

Raleigh pulled out the cassette, held it up. It looked okay. He shoved it in his shirt pocket.

They started with financial stories. Roman read a series on structuring treasure companies. The idea seemed to be the one Pete had explained. You sold shares. You paid off if you found a wreck.

They moved to fraud. "In one swindle," Roman read, "three New Yorkers stole a million dollars from investors in Dallas and Fort Worth. They claimed to be looking for a sunken British privateer. They outfitted a trawler in the Gulf of Mexico and brought investors on board. They showed false maps and a ship manifest they said they'd found in London. Most of the money went into a Swiss bank account. The pair was finally arrested when an Austrian investor grew suspicious of their lavish lifestyle. They were sentenced to fifteen years."

Phony maps, Raleigh wrote.

Roman groaned when Raleigh told him, "Keep reading."

"In another swindle, a New Orleans man named Stockbridge announced he'd found the wreck of a galleon off St. Martin. He planted coins he'd bought at the site. He told investors he needed special equipment to bring up the rest of the find. He stole over six million dollars."

"What happened to Stockbridge?"

"He was buying the coins from a dealer on St. Martin. The man found out what he was doing and tried to blackmail him."

Raleigh's breathing quickened.

162

"Stockbridge tried to kill the dealer," Roman read. "The man turned him in."

"Blackmail," Raleigh wrote. Roman growled, "Do you mind if I eat my lunch now?"

Raleigh munched on the doughnut. The information on Pete was a disappointing rehash. The professor's roots in Minnesota. His years at the University. The battle over the *Isabella* treasure.

"This the guy you're doing the story on?" Roman asked.

"Story? Right! The story!"

The boy on the windsurfer was having trouble turning against the wind to head back to shore. He stepped around the front of the sail. It toppled.

"Here's something on his son," Roman said. "Arrested in Tampa."

Raleigh felt a chill. He glanced at the tote bag Diane had left. The closet door was half-open and her diving gear was gone.

Roman was getting hoarser, losing his voice, so he read the highlights only. "Beat her up . . . two witnesses but the lawyer got him off. . . . You know what we would have done to someone like that in Manchester? Chopped his cock off, that's what. There was this Jewish guy . . ."

The boy on the windsurfer stood up. He was waving for help.

Raleigh said, "Go to the last file, Roman. Read me about the coin fairs."

"What are you writing, a story or a book? I have real staffers around here, you know, who want things, too. And my toast is ruined." Raleigh envisioned a lean man surrounded by cigarette smoke, upending a six-inch-long manila envelope so news clips spilled on a table.

"Only one article in here," Roman said jubilantly.

He read fast now. "Two big fairs. Tampa and Miami. Buyers come from all over the country." Roman grunted. "Here's a coin went for three hundred thousand. These people crazy or what? Here's a picture of Pete. He's selling a silver plate to a South American diplomat."

As Raleigh hung up, a small coast guard outboard came into view, heading for the windsurfer.

The phone rang. "Frank." Raleigh sighed, picking it up.

But it wasn't Frank. A deep Italian-accented voice, quavery with emotion, demanded, "Where is she? Where is that genius, that Madonna? She made me cry. She made me cryyyyy."

"You mean Diane?"

"Don't toy with me! I must speak to her, *immediatamente!* I tell my cousin all the time, *don't bring me plays! If you want to come on to stewardesses, do it without me!* I take it back! Eduardo, bring me anything! And Charles de Gaulle!" Lecturing, the voice said, "Until the artist brings truth to our attention, we do not see it in front of our face."

It was Rosco, the famous Dino Rosco, the producer in New York.

Tenderly, the voice said, "When the baby is born, the bambino, and it is snowing, the wind, the howling wind and the trees blowing." Rosco grew breathy. "Will the bambino survive? Is the bambino doomed? Aren't we all the little bambino, all of us, oh, the feeling, the feeling."

"She'll want to talk to you," Raleigh said.

The voice grew suspicious. "Where is she?"

"Diving."

The voice grew frantic. "Diving! Something could happen to her! You let her go diving!" Rosco did not wait for a reply. "I will produce the play! No one else must have it! I will fly her to New York! She will be as famous as she is talented. Are you her lover, her husband? I will put the publicity woman on. You must tell the publicity woman everything, everything for the campaign. Do not neglect personal details." The voice rapped out, "Your name, please."

Raleigh said it and Rosco grew quiet. "Not the writer of murders?"

"Yes, but I stopped that. I'm doing a book on an island now, Bird Island, near . . ."

"Birds?" the voice cried. "I will call back at four. Have her ready!"

Raleigh heard humming on the receiver.

Whooping, he leaped into the air. "Broadway!"

Over an hour had elapsed since he'd arrived at the house. Diane had enough air in her tank for a forty-minute dive. Ten minutes to any beach on the island. Twenty minutes of lying in the sun. She'd probably be home any minute.

Raleigh called the University of Minnesota, told the publicity office he was writing a profile of Pete and promised to send a copy. He verified that Pete had resigned from the faculty in good standing.

He switched on his computer. Next to Wheeze, he had typed "Creedmore" and "Drugs." Next to Coetzee, "Blackmail." Next to Quade, "Rape." Next to Nina, "Aids."

The greatest place in the world, Raleigh thought.

So Pete had lied to him. Did that make him a murderer? Everybody lies.

And what about the nick on the earlobes? And what about the man who looked like Hemingway?

Raleigh reached for the phone again. It never hurt to make the extra call.

A sexy-sounding operator gave him the number he wanted in Tampa, of the coin dealer the *Herald* had mentioned. A man answered with a booming southern accent.

"Coin auctions? That's us," the man said enthusiastically when Raleigh mentioned he was considering investing. "Every Thursday afternoon. Biggest operation in the state. Old coins. New coins. Spanish coins. Treasure. Come up, take a peek. Fly up a day early. I'll show you around, explain how it works."

Raleigh told him it sounded like a good idea. "Say," he said, "doesn't Professor Pete, that professor who found the *Isabella,* doesn't he look for investors at your fair?"

"Used to, that's for sure. Haven't seen him in months, though," the man boomed.

The phone seemed lighter in Raleigh's hand. He said, "I'd heard he gives a talk there every week."

"We were wonderin' about him the other day. Maybe he got the money he was lookin' for and didn't need to come up here anymore."

"How much *was* he looking for?" Raleigh's throat was dry.

"Plenteee, I'll tell you. He coulda been a millionaire after the *Isabella,* but he plowed it back into that *Nuevo Mundo* search. Me, I woulda stopped right there. Gone fishing for the next twenty years. My wife thinks he's a little touched anyway, like he's some kind of reincarnation of that Marquis he always talks about. Thirty years of frustration'd crack me up, too."

Raleigh squeezed his forehead. He thanked the man and said he'd think about coming for a visit. He punched the number of the Miami Coin Center, where the owner was a retired doctor, Roman had told him.

"Pete dropped off the face of the earth," she told him. The cheap phone she was using made her sound like she was in a steel tank. "If you talk to him, tell him to get in touch."

If he doesn't go to Tampa every Thursday, where does he go?

Raleigh rose and moved across the room and sank into the chair by the picture window. He shut his eyes. He did not want to miss anything. He forced himself to breathe slowly, to slow down his thoughts.

He remembered everything he could think of about Pete. He remembered how Pete had said, "The Marquis is all I think about." He remembered the way Pete tapped his forehead when he talked about what a genius the Marquis had been.

Raleigh remembered Jake's belligerence on the trawler. "The

166

fuck are you?" Jake had growled, and then gone oddly meek in his father's office, refusing to look up from the floor.

Think of little things, even if they don't seem important.

He remembered asking Pete, in the cramped office of the trawler why Salinger would try to blackmail him. "You don't exactly look like a target for blackmail," Raleigh had said.

The enormity of the answer drove Raleigh out of the chair. He stood frozen. In awe and disbelief, he said, "That?"

Again the ringing phone jolted him into the present. From the brittle orange light, he realized he'd been in the chair over an hour. Diane still wasn't back.

Something's wrong, he thought.

Raleigh grabbed the phone.

"I warned you, Bubba," said the slow, easy voice. "Her legs are long and tasty. Her tits are swell. She smells nice, Bubba. How come women smell so nice?"

"Where is she?" Raleigh said. He could scarcely get the words out. Air was oozing from his lungs without his exhaling it.

"You know those little red dabs on her toenails? I could suck that curly little toe for hours."

"I'll kill you," Raleigh said. He switched on the tape recorder.

The voice grew cheerier. "One day with us, Bubba, then we'll let her go. 'Course she might not want to go back to you after that. No police. Stay in the house. We're watching. One day."

Sluggish, the cassette spun. Raleigh remembered the Quade construction crew that always seemed to be roofing next door. He was squeezing the receiver so hard he'd lost feeling in his hand. His senses were roaring. "I know your voice, Jake," he said between clenched teeth. "I know it. You hear me? You let her go."

There was a pause on the other end.

The pause went on a couple of seconds.

The caller hung up.

Raleigh stared at the phone. His heart sounded huge. He rewound the recorder, but it had started late and the only voice on it was his own.

In an agony of self-blame, he thought, Suppose Jake panics? Suppose I was wrong, and it wasn't Jake?

The shrimp boat, Raleigh thought.

He ran for the keys on the kitchen table. When he yanked open the front door, Detective Blaney was marching up the walk between two uniformed officers, the duo who had arrested Raleigh after Salinger died. The big cop named Hank and his woman partner with the oversized cap.

Raleigh ran toward them, happy to see them. "They have Diane!" But instead of listening, Hank moved in like a wrestler, arms opening, crablike, that stupid grin on his face. The woman was going for her holster. Raleigh had startled her, running at them. Raleigh cried, "What are you doing?" as Hank grabbed Raleigh's wrist, caught it, and started to yank. But this time, Raleigh wasn't having it. Less than two seconds had passed. He spun left, his right knee slamming into the soft flesh of the policeman's groin. Hank was falling back, mouth dropping open, bellow beginning, and the woman's gun was almost clear of the holster. Raleigh lowered his shoulder, bulled into her, knocking her sideways. She was light and he was turning to run, to get to the Mustang, when Blaney's face swam up at him and he saw the fist at the last minute. He thought, as the pain exploded in his belly, I don't believe this.

On the lawn, face and knees pressed into the warm grass, Raleigh saw Hank lying sideways a few feet off, curled and cupping himself, groaning.

Blaney cuffed Raleigh's hands behind him. "Hank, there're people watching," the detective hissed. "Get your hands off yourself! Moira, pick him up, come on, do I have to do everything?"

Raleigh was gasping. "It was Jake. Jake killed him, do you hear me?"

Hank and Moira half-carried, half-pushed him toward the squad car. The usual crowd of onlookers watched. He knew Blaney was right behind them, from the voice, calm now and professional. "Section eight-four-three-oh-two. Whoever shall obstruct or oppose an officer in the lawful execution of legal duty . . ."

"Would you listen to what I'm trying to tell you!"

Hank shoved him. Blaney was saying, ". . .guilty of a . . ."

It was unreal, a nightmare. Hank pushed Raleigh's head down when they put him in the car. The locks clicked shut. He gripped the screen. He smelled fish, piss, and Lysol.

Raleigh shook the screen, raging. "Let me out of here!"

Blaney sat between the two uniformed police in front. He smelled of English Leather cologne. "Sezar said not to talk to you," he said. He seemed happy almost. Obstructing an investigation was a lowly misdemeanor, but attacking three officers, well, that was the real thing. Hank's breathing was still a bit ragged. In the rearview mirror, Raleigh saw the button nose on the woman cop beneath the shiny visor that hid her eyes. Raleigh wanted to grab Blaney's shoulder, which was only six inches away. To shake it, to yank the man around.

"I know who killed Salinger!"

The car started moving, leaving the neighbors behind. Blaney half-inclined his head in Raleigh's direction. On the staticky radio, the dispatcher's voice was saying, "Bring me a large fries, Shaw." Hank drove carefully, glancing both ways at the first intersection. The woman looked straight ahead. "Right." Blaney yawned. "Sezar said you'd say that, too."

ELEVEN

▼ ▼ ▼ ▼ ▼ ▼ ▼ ▼ ▼ ▼ ▼

"But Frank couldn't have gone on vacation," Raleigh said. "I just talked to him."

It was shift-change time at City Hall. Police went in and out, punching a time clock. Raleigh's wrists throbbed where the cuffs had pinched. His stomach still ached from Blaney's blow. The detective eyed him, holding a nightstick, leaning against the bulletin board beside the "Dangerous Substances" chart and a softball schedule. CRACK. MARIJUANA, read tags over plastic packets filled with samples.

Under "Know Your Goofballs," someone had written, "Sezar."

"Mr. Ledbetter left twenty minutes ago for Kennedy Airport," the girl on the other end said. She sounded chatty, happy. "His secretary's out, too. I'm a temp."

Raleigh asked what airline Frank was flying, but the girl laughed. "Oh no. He said for once in thirty-five years no one would reach him. He's on his second honeymoon, going to Venice. It's so romantic. Can somebody else help?"

Raleigh's jaw hurt from the vehemence of his rage. City Hall was only five minutes from Pete's trawler, but Blaney had refused to go there on the way to jail. And Frank. Frank never went on vacation.

He told the girl, "I've been doing a story, in Florida. But I've been arrested. Switch me to Kelley."

The only two attorneys in the Yellow Pages had been named Quade and Blaney. He'd take the job with Frank, he'd decided, or at least write the series. Frank would get a lawyer here fast. And call the FBI about Diane.

"Jail?" The girl sounded unsure. "You are a reporter here, right?"

"Right. Hurry. Right." Kelley was the seventy-five-year-old editor in chief of the paper, who could generally be found asleep at his desk in the city room, where staff members feared to wake him up. As soon as Kelley heard Raleigh wanted to come back, he'd be hired anyway. But when the girl returned, her friendliness was gone, replaced by cool accusation. "I talked to Tina, Mr. Kelley's secretary. She said you used to work here but you quit."

"Frank's been trying to hire me back. I'm going to do it."

"Well." She huffed. "If it's a question of a job, I should give you personnel." He could almost see her reaching for the Hold button, ready to hang up, to get rid of him.

"No! Look! I'm sorry." He imagined the finger poised. "I really have been working on a story with Frank. It's important. Tina doesn't know about it but Kelley does." She didn't say anything. He said, "It's a kidnapping. Tell him I'm on the line. Just tell him. He'll want to know."

"Well." She wavered, slightly mollified. She said, "I'll ask Tina. Let's see. I keep getting mixed up on these phones. First I push hold . . ."

The line went dead.

Raleigh reached to redial, but Blaney's finger slammed down the button, cutting off the tone.

"One phone call," Blaney said. "One."

"But I got disconnected!"

Blaney tapped his palm lightly with the nightstick. "Talk to Sezar about it. You were on ten minutes, anyway."

"I'll pay for it," Raleigh said. But when he reached for the receiver, the nightstick stretched out, hovered above his knuckles. "I said no," Blaney said.

There was only one cell in the building and two men already occupied it. A shiny-faced man with a big stomach and the white hair and beard of Ernest Hemingway. And a dark lean man on a folding cot, who wore green hospital clothes, a shower cap, no belt, no buttons, and thick athletic socks without shoes. Mental patient or suicide attempt, Raleigh thought.

"Joe Bump," Hemingway said, rising off his cot and shaking hands vigorously, as if he was at a convention and not in a cell. He wore plaid Bermuda shorts and black leather penny loafers. "I would have won that contest. What kind of police do they have in this town, anyway? The cop drives up to me on Morgan Street. Would I volunteer to be in a lineup," he says. Bump followed Raleigh as Raleigh went to the window. "No way, I tell him. I didn't come here to spend my vacation in a police station. Uh, you're not in here for anything dangerous, are you?"

"Murder."

"HAHAHAHA! What'd they get you for, jaywalking? Littering! That was my crime. After I told that cop no, this Snickers wrapper must have fallen out of my pocket. Whoa! Cops all over! Who am I, Charles Manson? Hands on the car! My big chance and I never reached the contest. Between you and me, I'm tired of selling cars. Acting, that's my calling. Like Hal Holbrook. Mark Twain, that's all he does. You gotta have a gimmick."

The lean man on the cot sat up and smiled, concentrating on Bump like he was having trouble understanding the words.

"Me, I decided to be Hemingway," Bump said. Raleigh tested the bars on the window and in front of the cell. Otherwise

172

the room was a duplicate of the detectives' offices. Cramped. Paneled like a basement. Smelling of alkaline.

Bump said, "I saw all the movies. *Old Man and the Sea. The Sun Also Rises.* I can talk like . . . listen! Gertrude!" he barked with a voice like a man with throat cancer, "*Sandwich de fromage, s'vous plaît!*"

"Aunt Sylvia lives in Queens," said the man in the shower cap, nodding seriously, staring into Raleigh's eyes.

Raleigh gripped the bars. "I want to make my phone call!" he yelled. "I didn't tell her what town I'm in!"

At a sting, Raleigh slapped the back of his neck. He came away with a squashed, bloody mosquito.

"He's a defector," Joe Bump said, jerking his thumb at the swarthy man. "A goddamned captain in the Cuban Air Force. Stole a helicopter. Landed near Rey Del Mar. They deloused him, took away his clothes. Welcome to America, you feisty son of a bitch!"

The man in the shower cap grinned. "I am fine. Would you like a cupcake?" he asked.

Since the cell was situated on the fourth and highest floor of City Hall, the window provided an unobstructed view of town. Beyond the steeple of the Spanish church, Raleigh saw FUN REPUBLIC flags fluttering up and down Main Street, above pastel-colored bars and boutiques. Each flag showed a girl in a string bikini blowing on a conch. The LITTLE CARNIVAL banner still hung near shore, the Sharkmobile passing beneath it. On the water, to the northwest, a Cunard liner eased toward Key Rey.

Raleigh batted down terror. He remembered Jake swaggering from the trawler's bunk room. He remembered the welt on Jake's girlfriend's face.

He concentrated on the shrimp dock. A lone jogger ran past an empty berth where Professor Pete's trawler should be. Other trawlers were coming in for the day, docking.

"Now that you're in America, you're going to need a car," Joe Bump was telling the Cuban in an overly loud voice.

173

In the east, where the sea was tinged purple by gathering thunderheads, sail and speedboats had brought spectators to watch races. Cigarette boats roared around a red buoy on a late lap of the Key Rey to Isla Mirada qualifier.

"When we get out of here, you see me." Joe Bump was giving the Cuban a card. "The Fiero, with lots of extras. That's for you. Me, Senhor Bump," he said, poking his chest.

"Do you mind if I borrow your cot?" Raleigh asked Bump. Raleigh folded the blanket and laid it on the floor. Then he folded the cot as well. He slammed it into the bars as hard as he could, over and over.

"Sezar," he screamed above the clanging. "I know you're there!"

The door opened a minute later, but it was Hank standing there, in uniform, steam rising from plastic bowls on his tray. "Break it, pay for it," he said. "And sleep on the floor." Raleigh put down the cot. Sweat poured down his face; he was exhausted. Hank slid the tray into the cell.

"Soup?" Bump protested. "It's ninety degrees in here."

"State says hot meals. My sister made it," Hank said.

When the cigarette boats returned, Raleigh spotted a trawler against the horizon and his spirits rose. But as it grew closer, he saw nets on deck. Pete had no nets on his boat.

By the time the cigarette boats rounded the buoy the third time, all the trawlers except Pete's had docked and were unloading shrimp. Charter fishing boats were trickling in from the reef and flats.

He heard the creak of the door opening, but he kept looking at the town. A breeze had come up, washing his face with the honey smell of bougainvillea.

He heard Sezar's voice say, "Ready for a talk, Raleigh?"

Sezar's office had a more homey, lived-in feeling, an air of having been occupied a long time. Photographs and citizenship awards hung on the paneling. There was a Lions Club certificate commending Sezar's work with crippled children, and a Chamber of Commerce scroll for addressing the high school on drug abuse. A proud, young-looking Sezar, no mustache in the photo, stood ramrod straight beside a jacked-up 1960 Le Mans. The face seemed more oval without the mustache, and he wore a Marine uniform. A Sezar with a shaggy Serpico-like beard stood in a firing range in another picture, pistol held in both hands, flame erupting from the muzzle.

Raleigh fixed on the smallest picture. A man rolled on the ground, wrestling an alligator as dust rose around them. The alligator's tail was raised, about to slam the earth. The man's arms wrapped the snout, closing it, and there were tiny cheering people in the back. But the head was turned from the camera. There might have been a Marine tattoo on the forearm, but dust flew too thick for Raleigh to be sure.

Sezar eased into his swivel chair. "Striking an officer," he said. "Damaging city property."

Raleigh's insides were grinding. He towered over the detective, who put his boots up on the desk. Raleigh leaned across at him, knuckles on the desk like a football lineman ready to charge. "I told Blaney who did it! Why aren't you doing anything!"

"You told him," Sezar repeated, pleasant, like he always was when Raleigh was in custody.

"It's Pete."

"Professor Pete," Sezar nodded.

"He's gone," Raleigh shouted. "They took Diane! What's the matter with everyone around here?"

Sezar wore a red and blue checkered cowboy shirt, pearl buttons down the front and on the pockets. His oxblood pointed-toe boots had swirled patterns on the stitching. He leaned way back, his head almost touching the map of the sea on the wall.

"Want to see something disgusting?" Sezar said. He tossed some snapshots on the desk. "Here."

Raleigh grabbed them. The first showed a man-sized dummy, straw sticking out of a Florida State sweat shirt and baggy dungarees. Lipstick painted the eyes and mouth. A clothesline noose wrapped the neck, trailing off on the ground.

"A bum made it," Sezar said. "Some kind of engineering genius, but sick." Sezar twirled his index finger near his forehead. "He lived under the overpass, that little bridge near houseboat row."

The second close-up showed a man's half-crushed head turned toward the camera, bloodied bone and gristle protruding from the shattered remains. One eye stared, the iris cracked like glass. A slightly out-of-focus cinder block rested in grass, more rope around it.

"He rigs up the pulley system so he can lie on the ground under the cinder block," Sezar said. "He hauls the block into the air, suspends it over his head, with the rope." Sezar raised his arms as if grasping the rope. "He let's go." Sezar's brows went up and down. "We located the family in Montreal. Rich, too. They'd been looking for him."

Raleigh threw the photos down. "What does this have to do with Diane?" he demanded.

"Nothing. I just thought you'd be interested, being a writer and all."

Raleigh sat down in the wooden chair beside the desk. He folded his arms. A spike of pain was driving through the top of his head, into his brain, and down the side of his neck. "What do you want?" he said. And then, lower, "What do you want?"

Sezar rearranged pencils on the desk, picking one out of a group of five, placing it behind the others, reaching for the next one. "Nothing," he said. "You already told us who did it. Ernest Hemingway. Rose from the dead, up from the grave like Jesus, but less kind."

"It was Professor Pete."

Sezar laughed. Somewhere in the station, a radio played Linda Ronstadt singing "Blue Bayou." "Not Hemingway anymore?" Sezar asked. Every photograph on the wall was Sezar. No women. No children. No friends. One alligator. "How about Liberace? Or Mickey Mantle?" A hint of bitterness had come into the voice. It occurred to Raleigh that Sezar had ordered the whole department out, looking for Hemingway.

"You know what I think?" Raleigh snapped, aware of the burning intensity flowing from him. "I think you know I had nothing to do with Salinger. You feel lucky I'm here, *lucky*," he repeated, "because you're not used to dealing with murder." Sezar played with the pencils. Raleigh drove on. "You want help but you're too proud to admit it. All you have to do is ask me. No, you have to play games. If you think I'm making everything up, how come you arrested that salesman up there?" Raleigh thrust a finger toward the jail cell.

Sezar slid his boots back a fraction on the desk, making himself comfortable. "You're absolutely right," he drawled, "and I want to thank you. Us poor dumb coconuts can never figure anything out ourselves. Putting gas in cars, for instance. Where is that little hole?" He laced his fingers behind his head. "Professor Pete. Skinny, sixty-five-year-old Professor Pete. Maybe you can tell me, explain how he did it. Maybe he stood on stilts and wore shoulder pads, that's why you thought he was so much bigger last night." Sezar's voice hardened a fraction. "Everything, Raleigh. Or do you want to go back to the cell? Walk me through it. From the beginning. Maybe slow old me, maybe I'll understand."

Raleigh thought wildly, Maybe Sezar has people out already, looking for him. He said, "I've been trying to tell it to you for three hours." But he slowed himself. *This is her chance. Tell it right*. He tried not to look at the clock.

Raleigh began by reminding Sezar how Pete had been leaving Salinger's boat the day of the killing, as Raleigh arrived. Sezar said dryly, "I remember."

He explained how Pete had claimed he'd refused to go along with Salinger's blackmail. "But what if he was lying?" Raleigh said.

177

Four-thirty, the digital clock read. Sezar picked up a ball-point pen and started clicking it, either out of interest, agitation, or boredom. He nodded at the part about Jake and coke. Tell me something new, he seemed to say.

But there was absorption in his impatience. Raleigh felt a shift in the room, of control. He was the storyteller. His voice picked up strength. Did Sezar know, Raleigh asked, that Pete had not attended a single coin auction in Florida in months? "Where was he on Thursdays if he wasn't in Tampa? You can make the same calls I did, check this in fifteen minutes."

Clickclickclickclick. Sezar's left eye narrowed and he rubbed it. He dropped the pen and reached to pull a thin panatela from a glass humidor on the desk. It was hard for him to listen and not interrupt. When he lit up, the room reeked with the raw odor of overly dried tobacco. Raleigh kept himself from screaming, from reaching to shake Sezar.

"I know Jake's voice," Raleigh said. "And the way he paused. I felt him on the other end."

"You'd spoken to him once before, you said. That's all?"

"Once," Raleigh said, meeting the gaze fully, letting his certainty show.

Sezar sighed. "Raleigh, cut the bullshit and tell me something. Did someone who looked like Hemingway take a shot at you last night or didn't he?"

"I'm getting to that. Yes."

Sezar's heels scraped across the desk and thumped on the floor. He poked the air with the panatela. "Then who was he, or isn't he part of this anymore? Pete's too small. Jake was in Cap'n Bob's."

Raleigh would have preferred to work around to this point on his own. But he couldn't hold it back now. "A third man," he said. "There's got to be a third man involved."

Sezar took a long draw on the cigar. "Oh," he said, nodding. "The *third* man. The third man was Hemingway. Why didn't I

178

think of that? And how about the fifth man, what did he do? Drive the car? How about the ninety-first man?"

"The fifth man was the detective who made jokes while they got away," Raleigh replied.

Blue-white smoke swirled above the map of the sea, collected in a pool midway to the ceiling. "I always had trouble understanding things," Sezar said. "Bad gene pool. Why didn't you tell me any of this before?"

"I just figured it out."

"Um hmmm." From the corridor came Joe Bump's voice. "You're letting me go?" he was saying. "The contest was two hours ago. I'm never coming back to this island again."

"You're making lots of accusations but I'm still looking for a little motivation," Sezar said. "I can speed this up. You're saying Pete got involved in drugs in Tampa. He traveled back and forth, so he was a perfect courier for them. That's why Jake had drugs, huh? That's why Pete stopped going to auctions. He didn't need money anymore." Sezar grew more agitated. "How'm I doing? And the business with the ears? Pete's Tampa friends getting rid of opposition. That's your theory, is that it?"

"No." Raleigh shook his head. "Pete stopped going to Tampa altogether, so he couldn't have been a courier. And if he had been into drugs, he would have had money to fix his boat. Plus, Jake wouldn't have to buy them. But he was broke. The engines were never running."

"Then why did he stop going to Tampa?" Sezar demanded, exasperated finally.

Raleigh said quietly, "Because he'd found the *Nuevo Mundo*."

In the corridor, "Blue Bayou" ended and an announcer's deep voice cried, "The erotic hot-dog-eating contest! Tonight at Doggy Palace!"

Sezar's mouth remained open but nothing came out. The panatela was suspended, smoked almost to a stub.

Raleigh heard the distant drone of the cigarette boats back for another lap.

He repeated softly, "He found it. That's what this is all about. Three. Hundred. Million. Dollars of treasure. The Marquis's boat. Pete looked for it for thirty-two years, and six months ago he found it. When did he fire his crew? Six months ago. When did he stop going to Tampa? He didn't need money for the search because it was over, Sezar. Over." Raleigh stood up. "He kept the pretense going in Key Rey, kept trying to raise money for expenses, because he didn't want anyone to suspect him. But on Thursdays, when he was supposed to be out of town, he was there." Raleigh jerked his thumb toward the map of the sea, toward the town beyond, and the harbor and the islands. "Collecting his loot," he said. "The rest of the week, they dived at the phony site, where they took investors. On Thursdays they went to the real wreck."

The diamond-shaped irises fixed on Raleigh. There were white flecks in Sezar's pale blue eyes.

"But Salinger found out about it," Raleigh said. "Maybe because Jake had money for coke when he was supposed to be broke. Maybe somebody said something, I don't know. Salinger tried to blackmail them. Pete pretended to go along with it, but they killed him."

The radio in the station was playing Willie Nelson singing "Moonlight in Vermont." Sezar tapped the panatela over the ashtray. A glowing mass of ash dropped. Raleigh said, "Pete knew when I reached Cap'n Bob's I'd make the connection between Jake and Salinger. He knew Wheeze passed me information. Everybody knew that. They saw him give me the note in the bar and they followed him to the cemetery."

"Guesses," Sezar said.

Raleigh drove at him, coming closer. "But it sounds true, admit it, true enough to check. Every Thursday. Every Thursday when he told everyone he'd be out of town, when he couldn't go to the Bird Island meetings, he was at the site with Jake. Diving. Using those winches on the back of the trawler. Blowing holes in the sand on the bottom and bringing up gold, jewels, silver. Piling it up. Hiding it on the trawler, and all the while pretending to keep looking for it because *he didn't want to pay off the investors.*

"Look what happened when he found the *Isabella!*" Raleigh said. "First the government tried to take his treasure away. Then investors got seventy percent, the actual find! The man's been in love with a pirate for thirty-two years. You ever hear him talk about the Marquis? A genius! The greatest guy who ever lived, hell, that Marquis stole from his friends and almost wiped out the Spanish empire."

Raleigh could still imagine Jake staring at the deck in Pete's workroom on the trawler. Not shy, as Raleigh had thought that day. Greedy. Looking at the floor beneath which the treasure was hidden.

"That's why Pete was always asking me how the investigation was going," Raleigh said. "That's why Pete always tried to sidetrack me with Bird Island."

Sezar stubbed out the last half-inch of cigar in a nickle ashtray with leaping dolphins in the middle. "You're good," he said. "I can see how you sold all those books, convinced all those people."

"I didn't convince people, facts did. You checked me out in New York," Raleigh said, "talked to police, my editor. He must have told you I turned down a job writing about Salinger. Wouldn't that have been my motivation if I was involved? Maybe you can't figure out why I'm always around when things happen, but you don't think I killed them."

"You don't know what I think," Sezar retorted.

There was a knock at the door. Sezar called out, "I'm busy!" He licked a shred of tobacco from his lip and ground it between thumb and forefinger. "You still left out one thing," he said. "The ears. The earlobes. If Pete did it, how would he know about the ears?"

Raleigh paused, and Sezar said, jumping on the hesitation, "Well? Didn't you figure out that part? Only cops are supposed to know about the ears. Tell me. I don't know what could be harder to believe than what you've said so far. I've known Pete since I was a teenager. He took me fishing. Let me dive with them," Sezar said, working himself up. "Why are you hesitating? Tell me what's harder to believe than Pete killing people, Pete stealing from his friends?"

"How about this?" Raleigh said. "The third man is a cop."

Sezar stood up.

Raleigh spoke quickly. "You said it yourself. Only cops know. It makes sense. Check it. Pete needed a little more time; he was almost finished salvaging when he killed Salinger. He wanted to throw you off the track, keep you busy. *Check* it."

"Except you saw through it. You."

"The caller told me not to contact you for a day," Raleigh said. "Pete's leaving. Whatever he's planning, he's doing it now!"

Sezar strode back and forth in the office. Three steps to the file cabinet. Two to the alligator picture. A burst of laughter came from the corridor.

Low and angry, Sezar muttered, "A cop." His fists were closed. Raleigh saw the agony in him for the first time. He had hired these men. He had trained them. He came up to Raleigh and leaned very close. "Maybe you think I did it," Sezar said.

Raleigh shook his head. He spoke more softly. "You had a chance to take me in last night, get me out of the way, and you let me go. What about your other people? Three hundred million dollars! Your undercover man at Cap'n Bob's saw Wheeze leave, didn't he? Where were your other people last night?"

"Fuck you. It's a lot of guesswork," Sezar snapped.

They were both standing. Close up, Raleigh could make out the old acne scars on Sezar's cheeks, and the bristling graying ends of the mustache. The odor of Old Spice came off the man. Raleigh said, "What can you lose? Find Pete's boat. I'm in custody." Sezar said nothing. Raleigh said, "That woman's the most important thing in my life. I don't know if she's even alive. We're not just talking about Salinger here, not just about who killed him." He wanted to smash the clock, to stop time. He said, "Look, if you're wrong, nothing happens. You don't even have to tell anyone you're checking. If I'm wrong, she'll be, she'll be dead."

Sezar looked into his face. "I know my guys," he said. He wasn't going to check anything.

Raleigh had only one card left to pay. "Okay," he said. "But what'll Uncle Abel do when he finds out you did nothing while Pete ran off with his money?"

Sezar reached for the phone. Outside, the sky was growing orange; soon it would be dark. The detective gripped the receiver so hard that tendons beneath the Marine tattoo clenched. He never took his eyes off Raleigh's face, even when he punched in numbers. Raleigh heard faint ringing on the other end, then an answering voice: "Coast guard. Midshipman King."

Sezar asked to speak to the watch commander. Raleigh was remembering a Sunday morning in New York. The first time he had slept with Diane. They'd not fallen asleep until four in the morning. They were in her brownstone apartment on Seventy-ninth Street. It had been raining outside, drops battering the window, and the ringing phone had awakened them at 10 A.M. She'd reached for it, emerging from the quilt naked, on all fours, one leg bent, the other stretched behind her, the hair a mane over her shoulders and arms, the long fingers extending past Raleigh. A musk smell had come off her. He'd tackled her on the bed, pulled her from the phone. I wonder who was calling, he thought now.

What if the coast guard found the trawler and Diane wasn't on it? She had to be on it, Raleigh thought. He couldn't bear to imagine where she was if she wasn't on board.

"Chuck? Jules," Sezar said, breaking Raleigh's train of thought. "Little favor." The detective sounded friendly, almost cheery. "I'm trying to get hold of Randolph Pete. Professor Pete. Any of your boats run into him this afternoon?" Raleigh could not make out the reply. "No, it's nothing serious," Sezar said, and waved Raleigh away when he started to interrupt. "I need to ask him a couple of questions about something. I don't want to radio him; I just want to know where he is."

The map of the Gulf was filled with wavy purple lines connoting depth and current. Islands appeared as olive-colored blobs in the blue.

"Sure, I'll hold," Sezar said.

He glanced at Raleigh. "I tried to find Pete while you were down the hall," he said. "The trawler left about one, two hours ago. Nobody saw Diane. No neighbors saw her leave your house, either."

The watch commander came back on the line. "Sure, I'm still here," Sezar said. He listened a few moments and his brow furrowed. He half-turned away so that Raleigh could not see his face and could no longer hear the commander's murmur from the telephone. "It was raining pretty badly here, too," Sezar said. Raleigh whispered, "What's the matter?" Sezar kept talking on the phone. "How low in the water?" he asked.

"Oh Jesus," Raleigh said.

A puff of smoke rose from the ashtray. Last gasp of the panatela.

"Sure, let me know as soon as you find out," Sezar said.

He replaced the receiver in the cradle slowly and swung back toward Raleigh. There was a new expression on his face. He'd drawn in his lips in concentration. His eyes had narrowed and he exhaled a long, tired breath.

"They're already looking for Pete," he told Raleigh, but he didn't seem gratified by it. He reached for the humidor again but changed his mind and withdrew his hand. More delicately he said, "The coast guard got a distress call from Pete twenty minutes ago. He was in deep water. Beyond the reef. In a storm. And his engines were out." Raleigh felt dizzy. Sezar said, "Chuck's got the big cutter out looking for them, but it's too rough for the little boats. And blowing too hard for the planes. But everything's ready to go as soon as the storm passes."

"Storm," Raleigh said dully. In Key Rey it was still sunny. Pete would be miles away.

He did not want to believe what he was hearing.

"Pete was sinking, Raleigh. They haven't been able to reach him since his first transmission. Chuck thinks he went down."

All sound faded in the room except for the pounding in Raleigh's head. A cold wind blew in through the window. Sezar seemed to be sitting far away. Raleigh felt a horrible tightening in his chest. His lungs were constricting. His breathing was going to stop. He swallowed and the sound seemed enormous.

Diane had to be on the boat, he told himself. It was his best hope for her. Raleigh looked down at the linoleum, which was the dull green color of seawater. He imagined the door crashing inward in the trawler's hold, saw the rush of ocean pouring in at Diane as the deck tilted, the furniture slid, cabinets smashing into bulkheads, thunder roaring outside. The trawler would go down fast, weighted down by all that treasure.

Beyond the reef, he knew, the ocean was sometimes two hundred feet deep.

Raleigh tried to convince himself that maybe Pete *had* left her behind, locked up somewhere. Maybe Jake had never touched her. She was in an empty house. In the woods. Safe.

But he didn't believe it. For Raleigh, a void was opening— crushing grief poised to crash in. Then he heard Sezar say, "Raleigh?" Slowly he looked up. The detective's expression had gone distant, abstract. He was looking at Raleigh but not seeing him. Always before in Sezar's presence, Raleigh had felt like he stood in a spotlight. Now he was a bystander.

The puzzlement cleared off Sezar's face.

The detective said, "At least Pete *said* he was sinking."

Raleigh felt the pulse start up in his throat again. A trickle. A flow.

"The coast guard hasn't been able to raise him since his first SOS," Sezar mused. "One more transmission and they'd be able to confirm his location."

"You believe me," Raleigh said.

"But with only one transmission," Sezar continued, "the coast guard has to take Pete's word for it, where he is."

Together they stood by the map of the Keys, looking at the colored islands, the depth marks, the cute, yellow, leaping swordfish by the distance index. One inch equaled fifteen miles.

"A lot of ocean," Sezar said.

Raleigh's heart was beating steady, strong. The dizziness was gone. "Show me where Pete said he was sinking," he said. The detective's finger touched the map south of Key Rey, two and a half inches away, in the middle of an expanse of blue, by purple lines that swirled like fingerprints.

"Ten, twelve miles an hour, that's what a trawler does," Sezar said. "Maximum."

Raleigh reached out, felt the cool, smooth paper, ran the tip of his finger from Key Rey, north past Monkey Island, right turn, east to Bird Island, left turn, north toward Miami. He said, not wanting to lose contact with the map, "Twelve knots an hour. Figure thirty-five miles along this route."

The detective indicated a point west of a hook-shaped island, a spit of land with the words *Ann Island* on it.

"He's here," Raleigh said. "About now." His finger pressed the map, but he felt more than just paper. He felt the boat there, moving, low, weighted down. The winches. The cabin. The diesel engines throbbing.

"How do you know he's there?" Sezar said.

Raleigh batted away doubt. *What if I guess wrong?*

"Because this is the way the Marquis would have gone," he said.

186

TWELVE
▼ ▼ ▼ ▼ ▼ ▼ ▼ ▼ ▼ ▼ ▼

It was like someone had taken a jewelry box the size of a car and spilled the contents all over the floor. Tarnished silver bricks as big as bread loaves leaned against the file cabinets. Knives with emerald-encrusted handles nestled in piles of gold. From the bulkhead to the door, coins were everywhere, scattered near the open trapdoor, flowing from the couch to the sitting chair, spilling out of the golden punch bowl with jaguars on the handles.

I have to get out of here, Diane thought.

She was handcuffed to a water pipe.

Diane lay on the lumpy, mildewed couch, gripping the rim of the cuff with her free hand and trying to pull the other through. Her wrist went raw. Pete didn't look up. He sat, legs folded in the treasure. She had to strain to hear him over the engine roar.

"Spaniards didn't pay taxes on jewelry. But if they transported gold as straight bullion, they had to pay the king a fifth. That's why they made jewelry so big."

From his eagerness, he might have been addressing a class. Diane could scarcely believe the length of the necklace he held up. The links spilled to the floor, snaked to the engine room door and over to the couch. Light glinted from the bare bulb on the ceiling, twisting shadow strings across his face. Each link must have been half an inch long.

"They wrapped chains around their waists, like money belts," he said. "This could have been someone's entire fortune. It must have dragged him down in the hurricane. Must have drowned him."

Diane shuddered. "What are you going to do with me?"

Pete discarded the necklace and crawled in the treasure, scattering coins. They clinked as he moved past the maps, the microfilm machine, the desk. Emeralds as big as thimbles crunched beneath him. Pete reached past a pile of gold bars to run his hand over silver bricks. He was like a blind man memorizing contours.

"Silver's not like gold, oh no, it goes black under the sea. We'll put it in sodium hydroxide and water, run current through it. Shiny again!"

A wasp buzzed angrily between mesh bags of potatoes hanging from the ceiling. There were no portholes, and she did not know how it had gotten down here. The trawler wallowed. The coughing engine spat oily blue smoke under the door. The earthy potato smell mixed with the metallic, acrid odor of gold and the whiff of shrimp that never went away. And there was a fishy smell from the food on the barely touched paper plate beside her. Breaded grouper and mashed potatoes, with a yellow glob of butter melting in a pool. The wasp landed on the potatoes, its stinger pulsating.

"Everybody knows your boat," Diane shouted. "People will recognize it."

Pete dangled an earring shaped like a llama, of gold, between thumb and forefinger. "Incan," he said. Diane raised her voice over the pounding engine next door. "You think Raleigh's going to stop? You don't know him!" Pete purred with delight, holding up the matching earring. "Ruby eyes," he said.

The wasp, freed from the potatoes, landed on his shoulder. *Sting him.*

The wasp took off again, slammed into the bulkhead, and fell on the floor. It walked in dazed circles on the flat part of a rusty sword.

"I don't think they'll find us," Pete said, surprising her that he'd been listening. I just have a feeling." He looked up at her. "We pushed the blowers into the sea. Hoisted nets up top and hammered on a new name. The coast guard doesn't stop ships going out, just in." She saw the reflected buttery light of the gold rippling on his face, a face pleased with itself. "We're moving as fast as *his* ship did," Pete said. "You want to go home?"

For a moment, she thought he was talking to her. Then, dumbfounded, she realized he addressed the earrings.

"You'll like your new owner," he said, like a man fussing over a pet dog. "*His* cousin, well, distantly. I sold him gold from the *Isabella*. When we get to Spain, you'll have a nice velvet box."

"Spain?" Diane said, horrified.

She turned as the door opened. The engine noise grew thunderous. Jake had to duck, stepping into the cabin. A pain shot from her groin to her chest. His shirt was off and he wore skimpy cutoffs. The upper rim of his mustache curled upward, matching the line of his smile.

Jake winked at her.

"A write-off, that's all we were to investors," Pete said. "Jake!"

She filled with revulsion as Jake's eyes strayed from her face to her crotch and down the legs of her oversized khaki trousers. She was relieved when he shifted his gaze to the jewels. "Look at it," he told Pete. He reached down like a man scooping water to his face from a basin. Coins fell between his fingers and rolled on the deck, behind the file cabinet and into the trapdoor opening.

"You'll stay with us a day, then we'll let you go," Jake had told her, nodding overly sincere, a bad actor or one who didn't care.

Now Pete raised himself on his knees, extending a fat gold medallion to Jake.

"Look at the Greek cross," he breathed. "It could have been minted yesterday."

Jake took it, ran his fingers around the rim, ran the flat of his tongue over it. "Ummmm. What's it worth?"

"The lion is León, the bars from Naples. All the houses are represented on the Hapsburg Shield. Tyrol! Granada! Austria! Brabant!"

"How much?" Jake repeated, more interested in value than lineage. He picked up a plastic spoon on Diane's plate, shoving mashed potatoes into his mouth. "You're not hungry?" he asked her. He made sucking noises when he ate.

Pete said, "In bulk, it's worth four thousand. To a collector? Seventy. But look at the details. The cross! The assayer's mark!"

"Yeah." Jake stuffed coins in his pockets. "I'll study 'em in my bunk. Hey stewardess! You like a bracelet?" He dangled a gold band inlaid with diamonds.

How about a knife instead, Diane thought. What she said was, "It's beautiful." She was thinking, If I could get out of the handcuffs, maybe I could get the knife.

Jake laughed and pocketed the bracelet. She wished the third man was here, the white-haired man in the fisherman's sweater, who reminded her of Ernest Hemingway. Of the three of them, he made her feel the safest. But he also made the least sense. He'd seemed oddly embarrassed when she'd come on board, standing around stiffly, averting his eyes. Then he'd grown so-licitous. "She's cold," he'd told Jake. He'd brought her the oversized trousers, and made sure Jake got out of the cabin when she put them on. She'd hoped he might want to let her go, but then he'd been the one to put on the cuffs. The key lay on the file cabinet, five feet off. Five feet. The distance on an airplane from the galley to the first row of seats. It might as well have been five miles. She burned with frustration.

"I better check on our friend," Pete said, groaning as he forced himself to his feet. "Old bones," he said. "Too bad those Turkish doctors can't change that, never mind my face."

Her chest grew cold. If he left, she'd be alone with Jake. "Professor," she called. "When you run current through the silver, why does that make the tarnished part go away?"

Jake smashed his fist into the bulkhead. "Got the wasp," he said.

Pete paused at the door. "Don't worry about him. He's got rough edges, but he's a good kid." He closed the door behind him.

Jake finished the mashed potatoes, licking the last lumpy bits from the plastic spoon.

He rummaged in the treasure awhile, putting occasional gems in his pockets. She knew even when he wasn't looking at her, he was feeling where she was.

"You don't like grouper?" he said at length. The hearty host to the woman in handcuffs. "I caught it myself."

In stewardess training, the instructor had told them, "Agree with what a hijacker says. Ask him questions without threatening him. Make him feel important. Get on his side."

"You caught it? How big was it? It was delicious," she said.

"It wasn't bad," he said. He dug at food lodged in his teeth with a fingernail. "You want something to drink?"

"Thanks."

Jake leered. "Why the fuck should I give it to you." The suddenness of his mood change terrified her. Don't panic, she thought. In Argentina once, a stewardess had saved a planeload of passengers by pretending to be a hijacker's friend. After the hijacker had let her leave her seat, she'd opened the exit and dozens of people had gotten out.

Jake was sliding along the far wall, dragging his fingers across the tacked-up maps. He flicked the microfilm machine on and off. He was like a dog staking out territory, circling her.

"Where'd you learn to cook like that?" she said. "Every time I cook fish, I burn it."

"If you liked it so much, why didn't you eat it?" he snapped. But he went to the refrigerator, snapped the top off a can of orange juice with a smiling duck logo. He shoved it at her and she sipped it, not tasting it, glad to have something in her hand. Big protection, she told herself. Juice.

Jake fell into the chair opposite, with the stuffing coming out. His heels splayed in gold, with coins sticking to the bottoms of his feet. "Steak, that's what I want from now on. No more fish, not for the rest of my life. Red steak, with juice running out. You like steak, long legs?"

"Sure, I like it."

Jake dug into his pocket and came out with a foil packet he unfolded. He held the powder on top up to his nose. Loudly, he inhaled.

"Oh yeah," he said. His eyes watered. Jake snuggled into the chair. "I heard stewardesses like it, you know, like to get it on in planes." He scratched the inside of his thigh. "In bathrooms with passengers. In cockpits with pilots."

"I've heard those stories, too," Diane said.

She thought, Talk slower. Find something to say to this creep.

She thought, If he gets any closer, I think I'll throw up.

Jake laughed. "Tell me the truth," he said. "You did it, I bet."

Distract him. She said, "There's so much treasure here. You'll be a rich man." No answer. He was just staring at her. She said, "That other man really looks like Ernest Hemingway; I could swear it's him."

Wrong topic. He bolted up. "What do you want to know about him for?" he said. "You like him?" Her trapped feeling grew. "You think he's your friend? He's the one who killed your buddy Wheeze. And tried for Raleigh." Inside, she reeled.

He got a beer from the fridge, more agitated now. Maybe if she kept him talking, someone would come down. Or he'd calm down. "Can I have more juice?" she said. He'd liked it when she wanted juice.

Jake shouted, "What am I, your fucking servant?" He gulped more beer and wiped his mouth with the front of his hand. His changing moods seemed rooted in the same violent pool. "Women," he said. "More. You want more."

Her skin crawled, but he didn't come closer. His eyes followed hers to the claw hammer near the couch. "Answer me," he said. "Say something, you stupid . . ." He'd been near the edge since he forced her on the skiff, and now he seemed about to go over it. "YOU WANT MORE?" he screamed.

She could only move a foot to either side because of the handcuffs. Jake seemed to be growing larger in the cramped hold. "You're right," she said. "Why should you get it for me?" She looked away from him. He said, "Ah, I'll get it." When he did, she said, "Thanks, you're being sweet."

"Sweet. That's a good one. I like that. Sweet."

Diane decided it was time to take a chance. "My wrists are bleeding," she said. "I can't go anywhere, you're twice my size. Could you, could you loosen these?"

Jake froze. She watched the muscles on his face go hard. "I'm rich, huh?" he said softly. "I'm sweet. I'm twice your size, you cunt." His hand drifted toward his groin, but she shifted her gaze to his face so she would not see what he was doing. His hips thrust forward.

"Want to see something?" Jake said. She couldn't keep the revulsion off her face any longer. "More treasure?" she said hopefully.

"Yeh, you want to," he said.

An easiness had come into him. He'd come to a decision. For Diane, the world reduced itself to Jake, advancing side to side with the slow motion of the boat. A smile deepened on the right side of his mouth. His face had gone shiny.

This is it, she thought. Diane drew back, pulled her legs to her and pressed against the back of the couch. The pipe oozed cold condensation on the back of her neck. She had never been so terrified in her life. Don't move too soon, she thought.

He was almost on top of her. "I'll be nice," he said. There was honey in his voice. "Where'd you get such cute feet? They are very cute feet," he said.

Jake reached for her.

"I like them," he said.

He was expecting the right foot when she feinted with it, and, still smiling, moved to block it with the back of his wrist.

Jake was completely surprised when her left heel slammed into his groin.

Jake fell back, eyes bulging. He doubled over. His hands pressed his body where she'd hit him. A gagging noise came from his mouth. "Grnnndddddd."

Diane's self-control broke. She struggled with the handcuffs. "Help!" she screamed. The engine boomed louder. She pulled against the cuffs, trying to reach the claw hammer. Through the two-inch gap between her shaking fingers and the handle, Pete's gold medallion gleamed on the floor. Jake still gasped for air, but his gasps grew shorter, easier.

Jake straightened slowly. His eyes bored into her, copper-colored holes.

Blood dripped on the couch from her wrist. "Oh God," she said. "I'll kill you, you bastard."

Jake's hands dropped from his groin. His forehead dripped sweat and she smelled the grease on him. And then he smiled, waded in again. Diane lashed out, but he was ready this time; he caught her ankle, no problem, whipping it sideways and forcing his body between her kicking legs. She clawed at him. His fist raised high. He'd clenched it sideways like that when he'd crushed the wasp.

Raleigh stood on the prow of Abel Quade's *Avenger* looking out to sea. It was dusk and the rain had stopped. The sky was beautiful. By some trick of light, two suns seemed to be going down, not one. In both east and west, anvil-shaped clouds glowed, purple and pink.

The Key Rey water tower faded with distance. The line separating night from day clearly delineated itself on the horizon, blue draining from the top of the sky, oozing out of the bottom. Waves dropped to swells. The *Avenger* followed the last rolling sheen of light on the water, a beam. Boats they passed fanned out from Key Rey, heading toward the reef and night dives.

Raleigh fought the feeling of helplessness. The notion that they could follow an invisible line on the sea into this vastness and find Diane mocked him. The ocean went from blue to dark green. Then it was warm black, with only scattered red and green port and starboard lights far away in the darkness. He'd been made blind.

The loudspeaker crackled above him, from the bridge. "We can't see anything. It's raining too hard." Quade had patched the coast guard channel through the intercom, so Raleigh could hear. He glanced over his shoulder and up along the sleek, streamlined, white front of the pilothouse. Quade's face was pale and round behind Levolor blinds, slats of flesh divided by shadow. He was a white-faced tropical Buddha in a leather sea chair, blue cigar smoke drifting as he gazed out to sea.

"How much did you invest with Pete over the years?" Raleigh had demanded of Quade an hour earlier, back in his garden. "A hundred thousand, is that what you told me? Maybe even more." Sezar had taken him there instead of to the coast guard. "This is a local problem," Sezar had assured him. When Raleigh had protested, asking to go to the state police, Sezar had said, "You're still in custody. Abel or jail?"

They'd found Quade lying in the cool shadows in his immense patio backyard, in the alcove formed by the crumbling horseshoe-shaped walls inside the old Spanish fort. Bougain-villea perfumed the air. The sea made whispering sounds on the other side of the wall, where Raleigh could see the antennae of the docked *Avenger*.

"The whole island will know he robbed you," Raleigh had said, seeing Quade was his only avenue of redress. "The whole country."

Quade's men had been scattered around the garden, in fold-ing chairs or against walls, far enough away not to hear, close enough to protect him.

Quade had turned to Sezar. An iced pitcher of lemonade sweated on a table at his side. "You believe this?"

"He convinced me."

Quade had poured more to drink, scratched his cheek idly, leaned back with the refilled glass. Raleigh could feel Pete's trawler drawing farther and farther away. He drove at Quade. "You donated space for his presentations. People will think you're involved, too. Remember the IRS after the *Isabella*? That'll be nothing compared to what happens now."

Quade had yawned and stood up. The men around the garden had started drifting toward him. When they'd boarded the boat, men Raleigh had never seen before had gone below. Big men with rough, bland faces and flower-print shirts. Men who carried shotguns. Men with gold chains around their necks. . . .

"The planes aren't finding anything," the loudspeaker said.

They passed *Lucky Jack*, the oil-belching converted hydro-foil, now a gambling boat. Revelers in bright paper hats danced to a samba band on deck while they chugged toward the three-mile limit. Beyond that, blackjack and slots would be legal.

They came up swiftly on a trawler, and Raleigh's heart pounded hard. "They'll probably have disguised the boat," he'd told Quade.

But when the searchlight raked the side of the trawler, two

196

black men came out of the wheelhouse, shouting angrily. And Raleigh saw the boat wasn't Pete's. The bridge sat too far aft on the deck.

The light clicked off. The *Avenger* surged into the night. Glancing up at Quade, Raleigh saw Quade's men disappearing off the bridge, going back below. They'd come topside for the trawler. One of them carried an Uzi.

In the dark, it seemed like hours passed. Again and again, the searchlight stabbed out. It lit up two old men in deck chairs on the poop of a cabin cruiser, their fishing rods on holders. It illuminated four men in sleeping bags, groaning in the brightness on the bottom of a Boston Whaler anchored for the night. Diving equipment lay in the boat.

The half-moon rose and went behind clouds. Bursts of heat lightning came from ahead, huge dull explosions without form, funnels of light that seemed to burst out of the sea. Raleigh fought off another wave of futility. Someone had come out and stood beside him, he realized. It was Sezar.

"Forty knots," the detective said. He held out a Styrofoam cup to Raleigh and Raleigh smelled coffee. The wind whipped the steam from it and mussed Sezar's hair. "That's three times his speed."

The folded map, which Raleigh held, flapped against the railing. It was the Marquis's route. Pete had handed it out after his lecture. But in the dark, Raleigh couldn't even see the dotted lines on the white paper.

"It's the zigzagging loses us time," Sezar said. "Boats all look alike on radar. Liner. Sailboat. Everything's a goddamn green dot."

"We're turning back, low on fuel," the loudspeaker said.

On the bridge, the lights were off now. A thin green line moved behind the slats, crossing Quade's face in an arc. Radar reflection.

Raleigh squinted in the direction they were moving. He saw the tiniest red light ahead.

What if Pete really sank, he thought.

Another boat materialized out of the blackness, ghostly. A man and woman scrambled to pull on clothes in a motorboat. The man shook his fist into the searchlight.

The *Avenger* turned west.

"It's like Times Square out here," Sezar said.

Raleigh looked at him.

"What do you think?" Sezar said. "I never go anywhere?"

They cruised past two low, dark islands, darker humps in the inky sea. The searchlight scanned the mangroves, the skinny stems and tumbleweed-shaped roots, looking for a trawler at anchor. A lone blue heron stepped over mud flats, unreal and two dimensional in the light.

"Where are we anyway?" Raleigh said.

Sezar laughed. "That's Bird Island."

Bird Island faded. It was gone.

"Jake, what are you doing?" the voice from the doorway said.

The blow Diane had been expecting never landed. When she looked toward the voice, the white-haired man stood against the door frame, arms folded over his fisherman's knit sweater. Jake spun away from her, his fist slowly coming down. With the door open, the noise from the engine room seemed thunderous.

"She kicked me," Jake said.

"And you couldn't get away, is that it?" The man strode into the cabin, bulkier than Jake but shorter. "I knew you'd be here," he said. His eyes were very black and they concentrated on Diane. He tried to kill Raleigh, Jake had said. But the man seemed gentle when he bent over her, examined her wrist where she was bleeding. He frowned. "Are you all right?" he asked.

"Is she all right? I'm the one who got kicked," Jake said.

"I've never been better," Diane said. She could feel her wrist throbbing badly where she'd flayed back the skin. "What time is the volleyball game?"

"Jake, get a bandage."

Jake made no move to leave. "This has nothing to do with you," he told the man.

"Peroxide, too."

But Jake had recovered his composure. He was four feet away, by the microfilm machine and against the narrowing part of the opposite wall. "You know what's going to happen to her in the end," he said. "What difference does it make what I do to her first?"

Both mens' heads practically brushed the low ceiling.

Jake moved up behind the bearded man, who still examined Diane's wrist. "I didn't cut up anyone's ears," he said.

"Jake," the white-haired man warned.

The words were no surprise, but the air seemed to have drained from Diane's lungs. To Diane, both men moved in slow motion. The pain started in the hollows of her eyes and spread sideways, digging into her temples. Objects in the room detatched themselves from the whole, her senses breaking them into pieces. The gold. The men.

"You know we can't let her go," Jake said. "She knows we're alive."

Her vision cleared. The white-haired man squeezed his eyes shut and Diane could feel an almost physical torment washing from him. Someone else had emanated this feeling recently, this sadness. She asked herself, Where?

"Why'd you call Raleigh?" the man snapped at Jake. "Why couldn't you leave her alone?"

Jake soothed him. "That reporter, I took care of him." Jake's eyes flickered to Diane. "She isn't worth arguing about," he said.

But he bent and when he straightened, Jake wielded the blackened short sword. The corroded blade extended half toward the floor, half toward the white-haired man. Diane could see gaps in the steel where bits had flaked off the edges.

Both men seemed to have forgotten she was there. The animosity involved much more than her, she saw.

Jake threw out one hand, like Hamlet giving a speech. "I'm a millionaire," he said. "My Mercedes." He meant the boat. "My tux." He touched the dirty cutoffs. Jake laughed. "Twenty years of crap from him and I'm not going to take it from you, too."

Kill each other, Diane thought.

Jake breathed hard. He imitated Pete, higher and academic. "Jake, we can't spend money. Jake, fry the fish instead of broiling it." More bitterly, he said, "And then we found the *Isabella*. He put my share back into the search. He did it when I was high. Made me sign things."

"Don't tell me what to do!" Jake screamed.

Once in a movie, Diane had seen a man use psychic powers. Merely by looking at objects, he could move them across rooms. Couches. Ashtrays. The key glinted on the file cabinet, five feet off.

Diane noticed the white-haired man had knocked the claw hammer closer with his foot.

Jake was saying, "Go away for five minutes. We're going to dump her anyway. You'll agree in the end, you know you will. Who cares if she gets poked first?"

If she could reach the claw hammer, maybe she could hit Jake. She leaned, straining. She grunted in pain.

Hemingway shook his head. "What's the matter, Jake? Can't get a girl unless she's handcuffed?"

Diane fell back, away from the hammer. "You know what your problem is?" Jake said. The white-haired man dropped to one knee and came up with another sword. Jake looked more nervous now, but he continued. "You forgot what it's like to get laid. How long's it been? Six months? Have her after me, hell, before! I don't mind sloppy—"

200

Jake snapped his head sideways; he'd heard something. The white-haired man faltered too, thrown off guard. Not trusting Jake. Or taking his eyes off him.

"He's stopping the boat," Jake said.

Diane heard it too now, the lowering drone of the engine. The rocking motion of the trawler changed, going forward and back instead of side to side. Slowing, the boat was caught in new swells.

"What's the matter with him?" Jake said. "I fixed that pump."

And then, above the other sounds, a new one came to her. A high, familiar wail that she could not believe at first. But it grew clearer. It drove the fear from her.

From over the water, muffled, swelling.

Jake frowned. "Bagpipes?" he said.

Diane wanted to scream her joy at them. The glorious rising tones of "Amazing Grace" grew even louder, staticky, as if they were being broadcast over a loudspeaker. She had no idea how Raleigh had found her. He was magic sometimes.

Jake said, "What th . . ." and lowered the sword.

But the man who looked like Hemingway didn't seem surprised or confused. With a kind of resignation, he nodded at the music. Diane sensed it confirmed something he had expected. He stood sideways to her. One hand came up to grasp his front fringe of hair. She thought he was pulling at it but gasped when a wig slid off. Black hair shone beneath, shiny and full. The black eyes looked familiar. He turned to face her fully, his hand pulling at the beard. And then it was gone, too.

The man was Kazanjian, the marine patrolman. The man who had stopped her and Raleigh at sea a week ago.

For an instant, neither of them spoke.

Then she said, "You. You killed Wheeze."

Kazanjian told Jake, weary, almost relieved, "Raleigh found us."

The engine purred, idling. The trawler had stopped.

Jake bolted from the room.

She remembered Kazanjian, crisp and confident in his shark-gray uniform. "You better carry a gun out here, it's dangerous," he had told Raleigh after asking questions about Salinger. She remembered the sadness she had detected in him then. It seemed to be washing from him now.

When she glanced at the wig in his hand, he said, half-holding it up, "They said they would let you go. I didn't want you to identify me." He should have looked younger without the white hair, but the lines had deepened around his eyes and mouth since she'd seen him last. Every feature was downturned, toward the floor.

"I didn't think it would go this far," he said. She had to strain to hear. He was almost whispering. "She's so sick, my wife," he said. "I didn't have money left, for the right doctors, the experts."

"Wheeze is beyond doctors," she said.

"She's in so much pain," Kazanjian said, folding his arms close, speaking as if he had not heard. "I found a place in Switzerland. She feels better there. I saw a picture of it, in the Alps. She has lots of windows. And there's snow. She loves snow. I told people I'd sent her to Arizona, that she was too sick to answer mail."

"Let me out of these," Diane said, pulling against the cuffs.

Kazanjian shook his head no. "I was always honest before," he said. "I never took anything. I had offers, but I didn't care." He took a step toward her, palms out. "I boarded Pete one day for a regular check, and found the gold. He'd been careless, excited, and he hadn't hidden it well. He said I could have a third. All I had to do was patrol near their boat on the days they dived, warn them if the coast guard was near. Board other boats that came close." Kazanjian nodded. "Do you know how long I can keep her comfortable for a third? I was broke. All mortgaged up, and I kept getting bills from the doctors. They were going to kick her out. I told Pete no at first. But then I was escorting them in, and I kept looking at the gold, looking at it."

202

"You want absolution from me?" Diane said. "Ask Wheeze."

"I liked Wheeze," Kazanjian said miserably. His lips were drawn back. She could see the tips of his white, strong teeth. "Medical breakthroughs happen all the time. Maybe if she stays there, they'll find a way. *Nothing's going to stop me from getting that money to her.*"

"Does she know you killed for it?" Diane said.

Kazanjian shook his head. "I don't care what happens to me. I'm going to turn myself in after she's—if she's gone. There's nothing left for me."

She heard running footsteps on the deck above. Coming down the ladder. Kazanjian was saying, "We told Jake to stay out of it. He does things on his own. Those calls to Raleigh, and bringing you here . . ." He trailed off.

Jake ran into the cabin. He carried two machine pistols, short, ugly mechanisms of blue steel. The ammunition clips were longer than the small barrels.

Jake looked terrified.

"It's Abel Quade," he said.

Kazanjian took one pistol, all business now. He had the confidence of a man whose fate was immaterial to him. Diane heard the gun click when he pressed the safety on the stock. He drew back a bolt, which made a jagged, metallic noise.

The bagpipe music stopped.

"Raleigh," she screamed, not knowing if her voice could penetrate the sides of the ship. "RALEEEEEEEIGH!"

After Kazanjian and Jake ran out, Diane began to weep.

THIRTEEN

As the last strains of Raleigh's "Amazing Grace" cassette died across the water, Raleigh silently swam toward Pete's ship. He could not see the *Avenger* anymore. Quade had brought it to the other side of the trawler, to distract Pete's crew.

Raleigh watched the trawler's gunwale as he swam, ready to dive, to hide. No one looked back.

"Don't go," the builder had advised as the searchlight swept over the brackets that had once held Pete's blowers. The *Avenger* had caught him on an open stretch of sea, no islands or ships visible. "I'll deal with him from here," Quade had said.

His men had been scrambling up from below, positioning themselves along the prow, and at portholes, readying their Uzis.

Raleigh had paused before he'd climbed into the water. "I can help her," he'd said.

Now he felt the steel form of Quade's Mauser, wedged inside a waterproof pouch, in the back of his swimming trunks. The trawler loomed, longer and sturdier than the quicker yacht. It was sixty feet end to end, low at the stern, the flat-roofed pilothouse nestled against the prow. Tire bumpers hung from chains below bilge holes. Lights glowed behind curtains in the pilothouse.

Raleigh heard Pete's voice hailing the *Avenger*. "Abel! We found it! Millions! Oh, Abel!" The professor actually seemed happy the *Avenger* had come.

Ten feet to go. Muffled by distance, Quade's voice came across the water, southern, soft. "Pete," he lamented. "Pete." Jake would be on the trawler. Maybe the man who looked like Hemingway, too.

"Pete's got machine guns on board," Sezar had said, on the *Avenger*. "He bought them years ago, when he was looking for the *Isabella*."

Quade was saying, "Did I offend you in some way, that you would cheat me?" Raleigh heard sadness in the voice, not anger.

The tire bumpers hung low enough so Raleigh might pull himself up on one. He remembered the layout of the trawler. The pilothouse took up a third of the deck, with its galley, bunk room, and captain's quarters inside. Or maybe Diane was in Pete's office, in the hold.

"You're right, Abel," Pete called. Two more feet. "No excuse. I was wrong. A victim of baser impulses. I should have known you would find out. But Abel, the gold! When you see it, you'll understand."

"This is what I want you to do." Quade sounded reluctant, a parent about to administer a spanking. This will hurt me more than you, he seemed to say. Raleigh touched the hull and something in the water slammed into his shoulder, knocking him away from the boat. "Gather up your crew," Abel was saying. Raleigh stifled a cry of panic. Shark, he thought. "Climb into the Zodiac," Abel said. Raleigh spotted the glistening shell of the sea turtle that had hit him. The turtle moved off on the surface of the sea, oblivious they had ever collided. Quade said, "And get over here, right now. We'll finish this discussion on the *Avenger*."

Raleigh caught his breath. He breaststroked back to the trawler.

Pete wasn't giving in so easily. "I'll pay for what I did, I will," he reasoned. "But what was the big injury to you? A few hours inconvenience? I'm not saying I shouldn't be punished. But you're a fair man, everybody knows that. I'm asking for fair punishment. A bigger cut for you! Twenty-five percent!"

Raleigh gripped the tire and swung himself up, careful not to expose himself above the gunwale. He heard men moving around on deck. He envisioned Jake clutching one of the machine guns.

"Besides," Pete said, clearer now, "we have an innocent party on board. I know you don't want to hurt her." Raleigh felt his teeth clench. He reached around for the waterproof pouch.

The trawler bobbed in a swell but he kept his balance. On the other side of the gunwale, he heard the click of a safety unlocked. "My friend Raleigh Fixx must be on board if you played that music," Pete said. "Come out!" To Quade, he reasoned, "A wild shot, she could be hurt. You don't want that." His voice rose. "And who's that? Jules!" he cried, like an uncle spotting a favorite nephew. "Police, too!"

Raleigh had frozen at the mention of his name. Nobody in Key Rey had ever seen him play the bagpipes. It was his private hobby. He played at sea. The only one who knew besides Diane was . . .

The booming in Raleigh's head crescendoed. He remembered the man who looked like Hemingway, rising out of the cypresses at the cemetery. He remembered Kazanjian leaving Cap'n Bob's just before Wheeze was killed.

"I'm sure you could prevail upon your nephew," Pete was saying. "There's plenty here to satisfy his sense of justice. Raleigh's, too. Raleigh! Where are you?" Raleigh pulled the pouch close, but the zipper stuck. He could not get at the Mauser. Pete was saying, "Why jeopardize yourself? And her? I'll have Jake load the Zodiac with treasure, to the brim! Diane will come, too. No risk on your part. No damage. No tricks. I know I can trust your word, Abel. Believe me, I hate giving in to you. I feel your wrath. But you tracked me down."

In his mind, Raleigh screamed, Do it!

The zipper slid a fraction of an inch, then stuck again.

Quade's politeness was used up. From his tone, Raleigh could tell the discussion was over. "I'm out of patience, Pete. I don't think you appreciate the dynamics of the situation. The money you offer is interesting, but it's mine anyway now. And this isn't a question of money. If I give in to you, the next man'll think he can cheat me, too. And then offer money if I catch him." Quade paused. More remotely, he said, "If you would have come to me in the beginning, made this offer then, I might have been intrigued." The zipper moved another quarter inch. "But I have to show my people what happens to thieves," Quade said. "You don't determine the punishment, I do. You have three minutes to get that Zodiac into the water. Talk if you want, but I'm counting. Three minutes. . . . Two minutes and fifty-five seconds . . ."

A voice whispered, on the other side of the gunwale. "I'll take the prow, you take the stern."

Fucking zipper.

Raleigh thought shooting would erupt, but Pete kept talking. "Ah, Abel, you and your principles. What about your boys, then? You boys! How'd you like to split eighty million dollars. No exaggeration! That's what I'm offering. Eighty million . . ."

"Two minutes and a half . . ."

"Eighty million. Of course, it wouldn't be eighty million after you divided it up. It might only be *five* or *ten* million a man. You won't get that much from Mr. Quade."

"You're making things worse for yourself," Quade called.

The zipper opened enough so Raleigh could insert two fingers into the pouch, which he turned upside down, trying to draw the Mauser out by its handle.

But suddenly, the voices started arguing across the water, from the *Avenger*. In the melee, it was hard to make out individual words. He heard Abel shout, "What are you doing?" and another voice, "Why the hell not?"

A shotgun blast came from the *Avenger*.

The sound of glass breaking. A scream.

I don't believe this, Raleigh thought.

"Now!" he heard Pete shout. The trawler jolted into gear, the sudden movement slamming Raleigh against the bumper, the tire smashing his fingers against the hull. The pouch was dropping, falling.

It splashed into the water. Already it was gone, ten feet behind.

Now the spatter of Uzis split the night from the *Avenger*, and more shotgun blasts. A minute ago, the demon of vengeance himself had been about to swoop down on Pete, guns blazing. Now Raleigh clung to a tire, alone.

He poked his head above the gunwale. Moonlight washed the empty afterdeck, the spread nets on the hoists, the back of the pilothouse, the Zodiac lifeboat, the dark open ladderway to the hold.

The port and starboard running lights went out. So did the lights in the pilothouse.

From across the water, a barrage of machine gun fire.

Raleigh climbed over the gunwale and crept to the back of the pilothouse on deck. He reached the half-open window and flicked a curtain of rags aside with one finger. He looked inside. In the faint moonlight, he saw a pornographic magazine on an empty bunk, the blond centerfold leering up at him. Gold coins lay scattered on the pages.

Muffled voices came from the bridge, farther inside. "We can't outrun them." It was Jake. The voice on the phone. Pleading now. Raising Raleigh's fury. "Let's leave now. Take the Zodiac!"

208

They would be standing there, cocked machine guns in their arms. Incredibly, Pete still sounded jovial. "Wait! Wait!" He was having the big adventure of his life. The one he had dreamed about since being a boy. "They're killing each other," he told Jake. "Listen!" A long burst of fire came from across the water. The lights on the *Avenger* were growing smaller. Raleigh could no longer make out the outline of the boat.

"The winners may be in no condition to move," Pete said. "If Abel loses, we hand over some treasure. So what? Even if he wins, our lights are off. They'll have to go to radar. We can lose them if we pass other boats."

Raleigh snuck into the passageway between the pilothouse and gunwale. He tried another window. Diane wasn't in the captain's quarters, either. He saw, dim in the sparse light, a glossy book with huge white letters on the bunk. *TREASURE HUNTING IN THE AEGEAN.*

If only he hadn't dropped the Mauser. But he retreated to the back of the pilothouse, took a long breath, looked down into the hold and started down the ladder. The engine thundered. The diesel smell drove up at him. Quade and the *Avenger* were gone; they might never have existed. In Vietnam, he'd been a pointman a couple of times, the man who detached himself from the squad and went first, through the jungle, alone. The man who had to sense the enemy before the others, who listened better, smelled better. Raleigh sent his senses out, like antennae. He thought, Where's Kazanjian?

As he climbed down, he knew his feet were exposed, his waist. Raleigh peered into the hold.

There wasn't even starlight in the engine room. It had to be thirty degrees hotter down here.

Raleigh's eyes adjusted to the dark. He stood on a steel catwalk flanked by roaring engines. He moved toward a slit of light glowing under a door. Raleigh guessed that Pete had left the light on because there were no portholes down here. He spotted a wrench on the edge of the catwalk and hefted it, felt the warm, oily heaviness of it. He reached for the door, turned the knob slowly, and cursed to himself. The door opened toward him, outward. He would have to back up along the catwalk to get in. An alert guard inside would have extra time to react.

She's not upstairs. She's got to be in here.

In the slowly opening vista, he saw a sitting chair, a desk. Diane!

Raleigh moved inside fast and pulled the door shut. Alive, she was alive! When he reached her, she pulled him down with her free hand, gripping the back of his head as they embraced. "The key's on the file cabinet," she whispered. "Raleigh. Raleigh. I didn't think I'd see you again." There were tears in her eyes. She was so beautiful. She looked like some kind of war-orphan beauty queen, with grease smudges on high cheekbones and that crazy frizzy hair, so wild.

"Don't worry about me. There's three of them," she told him. "That man Kazanjian, he was Hemingway."

Raleigh's jaw tightened at the blood on her wrist. The deck tilted; the trawler was changing direction. Disappearing into the night. Raleigh picked up a knife from the treasure piled on the floor. He had not paid attention to Pete's find before, but he saw it now and it stunned him. He heard himself breathing. "God," he said. "There's so much of it."

"Is it the coast guard up there?" she said. "I heard voices."

"Not exactly." There isn't anybody up there, he thought. Plus, he had no idea where they were. Ten miles from land? Thirty? Swim for it, he wondered. In Vietnam, he'd learned how to use stars for direction. But he wasn't sure which direction would take him to an island.

"The police then," Diane said.

"It's just us," he said. "You know, Diane. This is the sickest place in the world." Coins slid along the deck as the trawler changed course again. Raleigh used to think—as a private mental game when he met her—Would I love you if you lost your legs? Yes. If you got fat? If you cut your hair? Yes. Anything. "Maybe we can take the Zodiac if no one's on deck," he said. But when the trawler changed direction a third time, turning hard to port, hope rose in Raleigh. And then he heard it, a faint pop. He froze, listening. Be a shot, he hoped. Be the *Avenger* coming back.

The sound came again, louder now. A steady stream of gunfire.

"It's Quade," he said. Abel Quade and the inbred idiot cavalry.

"Upstairs and over the stern deck, then over the side," he directed.

The knife felt puny. He was ready to go. "After all," he said, winking at her, reaching for the door. To give her bravado he said, "We have to get you home to call back Rosco in New York."

"Rosco?"

More shots came from up top. And closer, answering machine-gun fire.

"Rosco, yeah, he wants to buy the play."

She pulled him back. "He liked it? Rosco? Oh my God," she said. "What did he say?"

"Can we talk about this later?"

Raleigh envisioned the *Avenger* coming out of the night. He ripped the door open. The firing grew wilder as they ran down the catwalk, reached the ladder, and started to climb. He saw stars up top but no people. But from the sound, he estimated two machine guns were operating on deck. One louder, closer. The other higher-pitched, probably at the prow.

He faltered on the ladder when a voice up top cried, "I got Quade!" But he kept going. In the fraction of a second he looked out, into the open, he saw a man in a fisherman's sweater on deck, firing a machine gun from the hip, spraying it as the

Avenger bore down on him, oblivious to the hail of bullets. One of Quade's men in the crow's nest of the *Avenger* threw up his arms, toppled over the side.

The gunman in the sweater must have sensed Raleigh's presence. Without breaking fire, he spun, bullets stitching the deck, coming toward Raleigh. Raleigh fell back into the hold. Wood splintered overhead, showering him with shavings.

"Back!" he cried. He'd glimpsed Kazanjian's face as he fled. Kazanjian would think he was armed, would come after him. Raleigh ran with Diane back toward Pete's office as bullets whined overhead. A slashed fuel hose reared like a snake, hissing and pumping diesel fuel in a fine prism spray.

Kazanjian scrambled down the ladder, firing.

Raleigh pushed Diane into Pete's office, slammed the door, shoved her out of the way. He hit the floor and rolled right as the door splintered from bullets. He scrambled in the gold, the emeralds, spotted the blackened sword. Raleigh scattered coins lunging for it, rolling back to the door as bullets slammed through wood, over his head.

He'd have less than a second when Kazanjian came in at them. But the door!

Diane was running toward the door, knife in hand.

"Get d—" The knob started to move. Raleigh threw himself at the door, smashing it with his shoulder, feeling it hit Kazanjian on the other side, the firing thunderous, the door splintering above Raleigh's head. He rolled left, thrusting the blade around the door as he bulled forward, onto the catwalk. Bullets cracked past his cheek.

And then the blade was making contact with something, going into the sweater, sinking in. Raleigh kept driving forward, grunting, pushing with both hands, forcing the sword across the stomach.

The shooting had stopped. Raleigh glimpsed the machine pistol hitting the catwalk, toppling over the side, into the engine pit.

He looked up. Kazanjian was staggering back, mouth open. Raleigh saw the protruding blade and only then realized the sword had broken off at the hilt, which he was still holding.

Blood ran from Kazanjian's mouth. He reeled in the half-light from the cabin, the spraying diesel fuel washing down his face. He gripped the blade with both hands, trying to pull it free, but it cut into his fingers.

Kazanjian dropped to his knees. All the muscles on his face had contorted, drawn back into a skull shape. His jaw was jerking. His lids had half-closed over his bulging eyes, giving him an almost Oriental appearance.

Slowly, he tried to smile. It looked like he was saying, "Thank you."

Raleigh's eyes moved to the shower of fuel, sizzling on the engine, running down the sides.

It's going to explode. He was already backing, fast.

Abruptly the gold coins slid two feet to the right.

The couch crashed into the bulkhead.

The file drawers shot out, spewing papers.

Kazanjian was in the air, a human ball of flame flying down the catwalk at Raleigh, more flames behind him. Raleigh pulled the door shut, slammed it, felt the heat blow it against its hinges.

He opened the door after a moment. The engine room was a mess of flame.

As he yelled for Diane to come, the whole trawler heaved, lifted, and he was thrown sideways. There was a screech of tearing metal and something fell against the door from the other side, slamming it shut. He couldn't hear firing anymore. The boat tilted but it did not right itself; it kept tilting. Everything was sliding on the deck. The microfilm machine crashed off the desk, into the trapdoor opening.

There was no other way out of the office except through the engine room, and the engine room was on fire.

Diane cried, "We're going down!"

213

*   *   *

Professor Pete clutched his shoulder, on the deck of the bridge. He lay moaning against the steering cabinet. "Jake, Jake," he said, but nobody was there.

Another burst of bullets swept into the pilothouse, shattering what was left of the windshield, slicing the radio wire, the mahogany wheel, blasting the radar scope to bits.

Pete rolled into a ball, covered his head with his hands. He could see bone sticking out of his shoulder. "Abelllll."

The lights flickered on and off. He could barely turn his head, but behind him, in the galley, he saw Jake scramble out of the bunk room. Bottles and dishes slid across the deck. Jake looked around wildly.

"Son. Help."

Jake stopped, followed the sound of Pete's voice. He seemed to realize his father was there. His pockets bulged with treasure. A coin fell on deck, rolling.

Pete was crying, pushing himself against the cabinet. "Get them to stop!" he said. "Get them to stop!"

The prow began lifting from the water. Above the shattered windshield, stars were going down. Jake ran out the port door, the pilothouse shielding him from the *Avenger*. Even though nobody on the trawler fired back anymore, Quade's men were having a field day, shooting up the pilothouse.

The stern was almost underwater. Seawater poured over the gunwale and lapped at the Zodiac. Jake untied it, got in, and pushed off. He started the engine and headed away, to the north, where they had passed an island. He tried to keep the trawler between himself and the *Avenger*. But weighted down by treasure, the trawler was going fast. It rose up on its stern and seemed to hang a moment. It began a long glide under the sea.

By the time Jake was half a mile away, the trawler was gone.

Jake was shaking. His mouth worked but only occasional whimpering sounds came out. He still heard the shooting, in

214

his head. But no pursuer appeared and at length he smelled the island, the odor of swamp over the salt aroma of the sea. And then it appeared. Ann Island, the map had said. Jake found an inlet, brought the Zodiac near land, and shut the engine. Muddy ground sucked at his feet as he pulled the craft ashore and hid it in brush. Then he lurched to higher ground. A forest. There were no voices, no campfires. He jerked, startled, but saw only a Key deer, two feet tall, bolting out of the brush.

It was warm and quiet. As his fear drained, exhaustion replaced it. Jake leaned against a tree, folded his arms, and closed his eyes.

When he opened them, it was light. He squinted into the sun. It was a clear day and the clouds were gone. For a moment, he didn't remember where he was. Then he dug into his pockets eagerly. Jewelry spilled onto the grass. Emeralds. Silver. The medallion Pete had shown him.

"I did it," Jake said out loud, slowly. Then he shouted, "Mill—ion—aire!"

A voice to his right said, "Morning, Jake."

The sun blocked Sezar's face as he stepped around a tree, and formed a corona around it. But the voice was unmistakable. He wore his oxblood pointy-toed cowboy boots with fancy stitching on the front.

Jake started to rise, but the gun pointed down at his forehead, out of the glare, and he stopped, sank back.

"You looked so peaceful, I didn't want to wake you," Sezar said.

At the shot, pelicans and herons rose from the swamp, squawking.

The detective considered the body awhile, prodded it with his toe. Blood oozed from a hole in Jake's forehead.

Sezar squatted and turned Jake on his side, gathering coins from the ground and inside his pockets. The morning was hot. He hummed as he worked, no particular tune, just a series of flat notes. When he was finished, he dragged Jake back to shore, heavy work. He took the body across the flats to Quade's Boston Whaler, anchored twenty feet away. The windshield had been broken by bullets; the outboard was dented, but it worked fine.

Sezar managed to get the body on board. He went back to shore, poked around in the brush, and, sweating from effort, carried a heavy squarish stone back to the Whaler.

He set off south by southwest, still humming, steering with one hand while he laid Jake's treasure on the steering column. He took out the .22 and wiped every part of it carefully with a handkerchief. The handkerchief he dropped over the side. In a calm area, where the boat would go straight without assistance, he untied the anchor line from the prow and retied the middle of it around Jake's body, crisscrossing the corpse with rope so it wouldn't work loose. Then he did the same thing with the end of the line, wrapping it around the stone until there was just enough slack to let him lift the stone, anchor, or body over the side without having to pick up all three at the same time.

The boat crossed into dark blue water and Sezar went back to the steering column. The depthometer read eighty feet, then a hundred, a hundred and twenty.

Sezar stopped the boat. He dropped Jake over the side.

For awhile he stood breathing heavily, then he found rags in a compartment in the steering column and wiped the blood off the gunwale and deck. The rag went into the sea. There was a Coke in the small icebox and he drank it all quickly. The empty can he neatly put back in the cooler.

As Sezar started up again, the water erupted where he'd thrown in the bloodstained rag. Shark or barracuda, but he had already drifted too far away to see which.

Sezar picked up the first coin, admiring it, as he drove. It was thin, with a roundish irregular rim and an unscratched shield on one side. The lettering—absolutely clear—read,

PHILIPVS. There was also a numeral 8, probably the number of reales the coin had been worth.

Sezar flicked his wrist and sent the coin skimming over the calm flat water.

He got three skips from the next one and saw the silvery glint of a barracuda investigating the sparkle as it sank.

The next coin went one . . . two . . . three. . . .

One . . . two . . .

Quade's yacht rose on the horizon, sparkling white at this distance, the damage invisible so far away.

The llama earrings came last. He almost put them in his shirt pocket, the beauty taking a little breath from him. But then he shook his head, hummed some more, and he dropped them and they sank.

Diane cried, "We're going down!" Raleigh threw himself against the door, shoved it open, heard the screech of metal being pushed aside. But he had to shut it to keep water from pouring into Pete's office, to slow its advance into the room. The brief view he had had of the engine room told him it would be impossible to leave. He'd seen water roaring in through the side, the surface blazing from oil floating on top. Already the catwalk was submerged, the last ten feet to the ladder impassable flame, knee-high.

Cold seawater rose above their ankles. "Maybe we can swim when it gets high enough in there," he said.

He rummaged at Pete's desk, came up with a flashlight. "How much air do you think is in here?" he asked, testing the flashlight.

"Don't ask me. I've never been trapped in a sinking trawler before."

The deck was tilting, water bubbling up at the surface in little streams. There was a crackling, burning sound from the other side of the door. From the door itself, he supposed, as the flames licked at it.

They smelled smoke.

The lights flickered but stayed on. The deck heaved, throwing them against each other. The couch went buoyant, started to float.

Nothing to do until the water rises in the other room, Raleigh thought. To calm them both, he said, "What did you bring me to eat from Europe this time?"

"Forget it." She shook her head. "You have to wait till you get home."

A mouse swam against the current, near the bobbing chair. "One hint," he said. He looked up at a creaking, groaning. Bulkheads were straining as the ship went down.

"They're chocolate. They're round. You eat them with champagne," she said.

"Egh. Malted-milk balls?"

"I love you," she said.

Raleigh felt the air pushing in on his ears. It seemed thicker. The water rose to Diane's waist. The overhead light went off abruptly and Raleigh switched on the flashlight. "I wish I knew where they put my diving tank," Diane said.

"I didn't see a tank on the stern."

"It might be in the pilothouse. Or in the bunks."

Raleigh tried to picture searching for the tank underwater, in the middle of the night. Swimming down the catwalk. Up toward the bridge, air giving out. Through the doors to the bridge, choking now, all this in the dark. Groping. Check the galley. Turn to the bunkroom.

"Who needs air tanks," he said.

They were thrown apart at a crash, into the water. The deck leveled out, settled.

Dripping, in the light of the flashlight, Diane said, "We hit bottom."

Then she said, "What are you doing?"

Raleigh tried to look down into the water, aiming the flashlight above it. The light just bounced back at him. He gave her the flashlight, went under, and felt with his hands. He pulled the gold bowl with the jaguar handles out of the water.

"Oh," she said. "Souvenirs?"

"No, it's something Pete told me. You made me remember when you brought up the tank. It was how they used to salvage boats, the Spaniards."

She nodded waiting to see what he was talking about. He said, "They used slaves. And diving bells. They dragged the bells along the bottom, filled with air." Raleigh held the bowl over his head, upside down. "*Air*," he said.

Diane understood. She bent over into the water, groping. She came up with another bowl, of blackened silver. It was smaller. A punch bowl. People had probably had fun at parties with this bowl.

"Some diving bell," she said. "But she turned it over in her hands. "Two minutes extra," she said.

The kiss was long and he ran his fingers down her face. The water had reached her chest.

At the door, they stood a moment, gulping air, building it up in their lungs. Raleigh let go of the flashlight. It kept shining for a moment after it dropped into the water. It twirled as it sank, creating a kaleidoscope of orange light on gold. Then it went out.

"I hate malted-milk balls," he said.

Together they heaved against the door. Water crashed in on them, driving them back. In the onrush, Raleigh fought to grip the bowl, to keep it from being washed away. He ducked under the rising water, where it was calmer. He began walking, bouncing forward step by step, holding the bowl with its little air pocket above his head. But his body was buoyant from the air he had sucked in. And the bowl was no heavy diving bell but a flimsy lightweight utensil, filled with air, too, dragging him up. It was impossible to walk with the bowl. Underwater, in the dark, he drew the bowl down over his head and breathed deep, deep. Then he let go of it and kicked, swimming through the doorway into the engine room.

It was almost pitch-black but he saw, close, on his left, a jagged shadow hole in the hull, *a way out*, and he turned, passing out of the boat. Diane had said, "You have two, *two and a half minutes maximum.*"

Raleigh kicked for the surface, felt Diane touch his foot to let him know she was back there. He told himself the surface was close. The pressure clogged his ears, pressed his head in a vise. He'd used up a quarter of his air already. He knew if he let himself panic, he'd waste more. The suffocation began with a tugging at his throat. Then pressure mounted in his chest and his skull began throbbing. His ears rang. He kicked, scooped water.

It was black down here, and he was blind. He let air out steadily, but his chest felt like it was exploding. The dizziness grew. His head hammered. He felt himself losing strength. He was wild to breathe. He couldn't stand it.

And then there was light ahead. The sun! *But it can't be the sun, it's night.* He was losing vision. Hallucinating, he thought. But he felt hands grab him under the arms. People! Divers! Something rubbery went into his mouth and Raleigh had to breathe; he knew water would go into his lungs but he didn't care; only, when he drew in, he felt oxygen. Sweet, sweet air. He tried to twist away, to see Diane. To tell them she was here. But he had no strength and they held his arms, swimming with him, upward. He was at the limit of his strength.

They rose slowly. Raleigh hung between two divers.

They broke surface. He spit the respirator from his mouth.

The silver moon was out. Where two ships had floated on the sea, only the *Avenger* remained, fifty yards off. Debris bobbed all around them. A life jacket. A Styrofoam cup.

"We have to go back," he gasped. But more lights rose from

below. Another diver broke surface, sharing his respirator with Diane.

Raleigh felt strong enough to swim a little. With Diane beside him, nearing the *Avenger*, he saw the shattered portholes, the bullet holes running up the front.

He reached for the ladder and Quade peered down at him from the stern. His shirt was ripped open at the chest. A makeshift bandage wound beneath one shoulder and across his rib cage. He was smiling.

Raleigh felt glad to see him alive.

Over Quade's shoulder, Raleigh saw the crow's nest, empty. The dead man had been carried away.

"Got a little repair work to do there," Raleigh said to Quade.

The builder nodded. "There's someone here you'd like to talk to," he said.

FOURTEEN
▼▼▼▼▼▼▼▼▼▼▼▼▼▼▼▼▼

"I'll tell you why we killed Salinger," Professor Pete said. He stood in the center of the *Avenger's* stateroom, a long cool expanse of mahogany and white wicker. His eyes strayed to the porthole, as if he still saw his trawler that had sunk. Or as if he searched for it while he spoke.

Raleigh and Diane sat side by side on the wicker love seat. Sezar, who had just returned to the boat, leaned against the wet bar, a glass of pineapple juice in his hand. Quade, in fresh white linen clothes, occupied a fan-shaped chair with his bare feet on a blue and white Oriental rug. A thin stream of cheroot smoke wafted from an ashtray beyond a guard holding an Uzi.

"He left a message for me at Rey Del Mar," Pete said falteringly. Bandages looped around his forehead, his arm. They were stained red. "When I went to his boat, he told me Jake had bought drugs from him, paid with a gold coin from the *Nuevo*. Told Salinger it was from the *Isabella*, but Salinger checked the markings, figured it out."

Pete looked at Raleigh but did not seem to really see him. He said, "Jake doesn't think like we do. He's not encumbered by . . ." Pete stood straighter, searching for the word. "Obligation." The guard in a T-shirt reading GONZO TOURS stood on Quade's right, the Uzi pointing at the floor. None of the fighting had damaged anything in the room.

Pete smiled with pride. "He's like the men I wanted to be. A survivor. An adventurer. He should have lived in another century. He got away from you," he said to Sezar, the smallest bit of doubt in his voice. "You said he did. He did, didn't he?"

"Couldn't find a trace of him," Sezar said, picking at his teeth.

Two cinder blocks lay on the rug near Pete, ropes wrapped around each, trailing off on the floor. The engines made a chugging sound. There was an old painting hanging above Quade's chair. A South Sea scene. Natives in a long canoe beneath a volcano.

"Salinger wanted money," Pete said. "I'd already paid Kazanjian. But Kazanjian worked for it. He protected us, patrolled when we salvaged, on Thursdays, kept other boats away. Salinger was insatiable. You couldn't satisfy him. I made a deal, but he wanted more."

Through the porthole, Raleigh glimpsed a sailboat far away, the mainsail sparkling in the late morning.

Pete said, "Kazanjian was on the houseboat when I met with him. He'd come in the back way, underwater, diving. Salinger didn't know he was there. I needed to get Jake's coin, but he didn't have it. He was threatening to go to the police if we didn't make him a partner. Then he said he'd tell his drug connections about us. He said they were rich men, with boats, and guns. He was probably lying, trying to scare me. But it worked. We couldn't trust him even if we paid."

"Give the professor a drink," Abel told the guard. The man with the Uzi poured pineapple juice from a gallon can into a sparkling tumbler. Pete's throat worked as he gulped. "Thanks, Abel." His hands had been cut by glass, as had his cheeks and forearms. Blood flakes dotted his body with maroon.

"I looked for that boat for three hundred years," Pete said

dreamily. He returned to the present. "Well, thirty-two. Ka-zanjian was going to kill Salinger, but then Raleigh came." Raleigh flashed back to the houseboat, to the hallway that had led from Salinger's sunken living room to the back of the boat. Neither of them had gone back there during the visit.

"Kazanjian found the coin behind a photograph. Later he followed you and Raleigh to sea," Pete told Diane. "You were going to Bird Island. He asked questions about Salinger. He came back and told me there was probably nothing to worry about. You see, when Raleigh was on the houseboat, Kazanjian heard Salinger talking about a coin and showing it. But he couldn't see *what* coin." He paused, then said, "Jake's not bad. He just felt a responsibility for causing the problem. He made the call, threatened Raleigh and Diane."

"You were right about the voice," Sezar said to Raleigh.

There was a knock and one of Quade's men entered. Raleigh recognized the thin man he had met in Quade's garden. The man winced as he limped now. "Two hundred feet deep," he told Quade.

"Why don't we move to the stern," Quade suggested. The boat was slowing. He rose and the others followed, the guard behind Raleigh and Diane. The stateroom led directly onto the stern deck, which bobbed four feet above the water. The sea was so deep, it looked dark blue, endless blue.

As the thin man tied the ropes connected to the cinder blocks around Pete's ankles, and double-tied the knots, no one spoke.

Then Diane said to Quade, "You're as bad as he is. You're the same."

Quade chuckled, laid a fatherly hand on Pete's shoulder. Aside, he said to Diane, "Who gave you the vote, anyway?" To Pete, he said, "Remember. Jump when he throws the blocks. Otherwise, you'll hit your head."

The edge of Pete's mouth turned upward. He looked down into the sea.

"Maybe I'll meet him," he said.

"Do it," Quade said.

Pete did not cry out. He made a smaller splash than Raleigh would have thought. Raleigh watched the figure sink quickly, distorted by the sea. Pete's arms seemed to undulate, a trick of light. Finally, there was only a flash of white that might have been an illusion.

The water stopped rippling where Pete had gone in.

Raleigh glanced at Quade. He felt sick. Then he realized that the Uzi pointed at him.

There was a clattering noise. Raleigh saw Sezar had dropped a silver-plated automatic on deck.

Quade turned his attention to Raleigh. "One last piece of business." There was no expression on his face. He waved a hand vaguely to indicate the unimportance of what he wanted Raleigh to do. "Jules dropped his gun. Would you give it to him, please?"

"Oh great," Raleigh said. He'd gone cold all over.

Quade stepped closer. Raleigh saw his round white face. "Raleigh, I didn't pull you out of the sea this morning to throw you back again."

Raleigh felt the Uzi press into his side.

"Sure. Get the fingerprints—*then* throw me back," he said.

Quade sighed. "Some days," he said, "everything is difficult."

Raleigh bent, watching the slats of the deck get closer. He felt the sun on the back of his neck, and he waited for the shot. He grasped the gun. He was starting to throw himself right, the impulse not even entirely transmitted yet, when more steel pressed against his forehead. Sezar said, "Hold up, Bubba."

Sezar took the automatic with a handkerchief, holding it at the muzzle with two fingers. He disappeared into the stateroom with it.

"There!" Quade slapped Raleigh's back. "The last unpleasantness!" Opening the glass door, he said, "I'm glad that's over.

Ha!" The odor of bacon and coffee wafted out to them. "I could use a breakfast," Quade said. In the stateroom, Raleigh saw a folding table had been set up with linen tablecloth and silverware. There was a pitcher of orange juice and a sterling-silver pot of coffee. Plates heaped with eggs sunny-side up, bacon, sausage, grits, French toast, potatoes, and sweet pecan rolls. Quade seated himself, spread his napkin on his lap. "You going to let this go to waste?" he asked.

"I'm not hungry."

Quade reached for the eggs and slid four onto this plate. He shrugged. "Can't make a man eat," he said. The sun streamed through the porthole, dancing on the silverware. Quade speared sausages and piled them near the eggs. "That gun you gave Jules killed Jake," he said.

Raleigh felt Diane stiffen. "No," he said in mock surprise.

Quade broke a yolk with a dipped sweet roll. "You're missing a great meal. My cook's from New Orleans, and they know how to make a real breakfast down there. That gun's my insurance, that's all. You don't want to be tried for murder, do you? No. I don't think you do." He chewed, waved a fork to dismiss the topic. Diane was looking at the French toast. Quade said, "I decided this morning that you were right, Raleigh, and I was wrong. I'm not afraid to admit it. There's no reason to build on Bird Island." Raleigh's brows rose. Quade said, "I should be able to rise above petty vendettas, don't you think?" He broke off a crisp bacon strip in his mouth. Raleigh heard it crunching.

"I've decided to make that island a park, um hmmm, keep that natural habitat and make it . . . make it a nature center." Quade was nodding, pleased with himself. "Birds. Fish. Kids ought to have a place like that they can go. Course, I'll change the name of it to Abel Island, but everything else stays the same."

He beamed. "Deee-licious," he said, and sipped steaming coffee.

"What do I have to do for this?" Raleigh said. "What's my side?"

Quade laughed. "Your side? *Your* side? You don't have to do anything. You've done enough. In fact, I'd like to do more for you. I like you. I like the way you figured this whole thing out. These boys who stuck with me," he said, indicating with a gesture the guard and the thin man and any other man on the boat, "they're set for life. Abel doesn't forget. Them and their families, they'll never have to worry. Food. Doctor bills. Vacations."

"You're offering me a job?" Raleigh said, hardly believing what he heard.

"If you want. If you don't, that's fine." Quade spooned fried potatoes on his plate. More gently, he said, "Now, in a few months, someone might find that sunken trawler down there. Someone might salvage it, secretlike, all that treasure, on the bottom there." Quade smiled.

"It answers my question."

"You wanted Bird Island. You got Bird Island. I believe in paying for a service. If it weren't for your noble impulses, my bulldozers would land there within the month. Saves me a fight with the state, anyway, the way things are heating up. I'm just saying you fit in here, Raleigh. The way you think, the way you do things. *You think right.* All that crap you see on the surface of Key Rey, the parties and fags and rock music, that's tourists, that's the wind. The place runs the way it always did. You're an honorary coconut. You ought to stay here, Raleigh. This can be the greatest place in the world."

Sezar came back into the room. Quade said to him, "Jules. Grits?"

Sezar shook his head. "Just coffee."

Abel poured it for him. "Oh, he doesn't work for me," he told Raleigh. "Our interests just coincided last night. Jules doesn't work for anyone." He laughed. "Sometimes I think he doesn't even work for the police."

Sezar raised the coffee cup, in a toast. "Semper Fi."

"A jury would have done what we did," Quade said, putting butter on the grits on his plate. "You know it. I know it. Why waste their time? Mmmmmm. Butter."

Sezar turned to Raleigh. "Listen to him," the detective said. "I'd like you to stay here, too. I know there's no book for you now. You're too smart to write about any of this. But when you cool down, think about it. You'll come up with another subject. Lots of writers live down here. Ernest Hemingway was here once."

"For twenty minutes," Diane said. "In a storm."

"She's very funny," Quade said. "I can see why you like her."

The engines hummed. Raleigh estimated they'd see the water tower of Key Rey in two hours. In the cabin to which the thin man showed them, there was a king-sized bed with a zebra-skin cover, a stereo, a VCR, a bar, a three-inch-thick carpet, and a Day-glo image of Pope John Paul.

They just looked at each other a moment. Raleigh knew they were thinking the same thing. They were seeing the professor dropping into the depths.

"They probably don't even have Jake's body," Raleigh said. "It's probably two hundred feet down, like Pete."

"Probably," Diane said.

"And if they don't have any body," Raleigh said, "they can't link me to any murder."

"Unless they come up with another use for the gun," Diane said. "Or can find the body if they need to."

Raleigh didn't say anything. After a bit, Diane started undressing. "I'll scrub your back, you scrub mine," she said.

Raleigh sat on the bed. "So that's it," he said. "No book. No story."

"There's Bird Island," Diane said. "Would you rather write the book and have Quade wreck the place, or skip the book and save it?"

"You know what?" Raleigh said, leaning back, feeling the

hairs of the zebra hide tickle his neck. "You know what I've been thinking about? The Amazon. *That's* an environmental story. You know how fast they're burning down the Amazon? Maybe it would be interesting to go there, do a book. Huge fires! Thousands of miles burning! It's important, Diane. It's a book."

"Malaria," Diane said.

"Ahh, you're more likely to get mugged in Manhattan."

Diane's clothes were off. She went to the bed. "I flew into Rio once," she said. "There's diving along the coast. Trans Europe flies there. I could transfer, I guess."

"Hacking through the jungle," Raleigh said, revving up. "Up at dawn, with the guide! Anacondas! None of this crap that goes on around here. Money. Me, me, give me money. Or nuns," he said, "in running shoes. And they aren't even nuns. They're guys dressed up."

Diane tugged at his buttons. She sneezed. "I think I'm allergic to this zebra," she said.

"And no more murders," Raleigh said.

"The only problem," he said, "is we're broke. No advance from a book. We could sell the boat. We ought to get a thousand from the car. You can live cheap in Brazil."

She slid off the bed, reached into the pocket of her pants on the floor. She threw something on the bed, beside him. It was green, glistening.

It was an emerald the size of his thumb.

"We'll think of something," she said. "I'll buy you lunch when we get back."

ABOUT THE AUTHOR

▼▼▼▼▼▼▼▼▼▼▼▼▼▼▼▼▼▼▼▼▼▼▼▼▼▼▼▼▼▼▼▼▼

BOB REISS is the author of four previous novels and a frequent contributor to many national magazines. He is married to author Ann Hood and lives in New York City.